BUCKY FOLLOWS A COLD TRAIL

*Also by William MacLeod Raine
in Thorndike Large Print*

The Fighting Edge
The Glory Hole
High Grass Valley
Under Northern Stars
Gunsight Pass

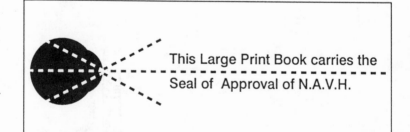

This Large Print Book carries the
Seal of Approval of N.A.V.H.

BUCKY FOLLOWS A COLD TRAIL

WILLIAM MACLEOD RAINE

Thorndike Press • Thorndike, Maine

Library of Congress Cataloging in Publication Data:

Raine, William MacLeod, 1871-1954.
   Bucky follows a cold trail / William MacLeod Raine.
     p. cm.
   ISBN 1-56054-214-4 (alk. paper : lg. print)
   1. Large type books. I. Title.
[PS3535.A385B83   1991]   91-19656
813'.52—dc20   CIP

Thorndike Press Large Print edition published in 1991
by arrangement with Houghton Mifflin Company.

Cover design by James B. Murray.

The tree indicium is a trademark of Thorndike Press.

This book is printed on acid-free, high opacity paper. ∞

BUCKY FOLLOWS A COLD TRAIL

CHAPTER I

The loungers on the station platform saw two men step down from the vestibule of the Pullman. The first, a blond, aged about thirty, received scant attention. All the interest was in the younger passenger descending. Bucky Cameron was the last man in the world except one that Toltec had expected to see. Eyes focused on him with surprised resentment and beat an unvoiced question at his insouciance.

The object of this scowling regard took it without turning a hair. He was a slim neat young man, standing about five feet seven inches in the custom-made shoes he wore. His gray suit was well-tailored, and he carried it with distinction.

White teeth flashed from the darkly tanned face in a derisive smile as his gaze passed deliberately from one to another.

"A committee of welcome?" he asked, dragging the words in a drawl.

One of the men blurted the question in the minds of all. "What in hell you come back here for?"

Bucky's glance raked the man and dismissed

him as negligible. He was a station idler, a slack-mouthed gossip who had small weight or influence in the place. No need to waste words on him.

Before Bucky reached the taxi stand, his eye fell on a Mexican boy he knew. The lad was evidently hanging around in the hope of picking up a dime. Cameron had been cooped up in a sleeper all night and wanted to get a breath of fresh air into his lungs. It would be pleasant to walk to the hotel. He beckoned the boy and passed him his bag.

"*Buenos,* Juan," he said with a smile. "The Toltec House."

A murmur of anger, entirely disregarded, pursued him as he walked away. Ignored but not unnoticed. Tim is right, he thought. All Camerons unpopular just now. The dumbness of popular opinion disgusted him.

Those staring at him found insult even in his cocky walk. He moved as if there were springs in the balls of his feet, so lightly that it seemed without effort. They were chagrined at letting him get away with his effrontery, the more so since they could not quite understand why. His soft brown eyes, shaded by long-lashed lids, just missed effeminacy, an effect enhanced by his small silky mustache. Perhaps the recklessness of spirit dancing in the pupils recalled to them his turbulent re-

8

cord. All his youth he had been a madcap, always in and out of scrapes. Moreover, a point never to be forgotten, he came of a line of fighters. The Camerons were individualists, always had been, men who knew how to stand on their own feet.

"Struts like a goshdinged li'l bantam," one of the men growled.

"He's sure gonna get his comb cut plenty," another contributed.

Bucky swung into Front Street, Juan by his side. It was good to see his home town again, though the circumstances of his return were unhappy. In the untempered sunlight the city looked peaceful as old age. Between the buildings, beyond the town, his imagination could picture the shining desert stretching to the far horizon. The train from which he had alighted was already rushing through it. In his father's time a herd of antelope might have been seen flitting in and out of the silvery sage. Those days were past, but a magic light still flooded the atmosphere. It was strange, he reflected, how civilization had wiped out the wild animal life with one exception. The pigeons and the turkeys were gone. Deer were scarce. Even in the mountains one did not see a bear in five years unless he was hunting big game. But in a certain stretch of rough country — a district of splintered peaks and dark cañons and mountain parks seen rarely by law-abiding citizens — the wild human life of forty years ago was repeating itself with the same wary and vigilant furtiveness.

At sight of Bucky men stiffened with surprise. His arrival was a sensation. That must be because he was his uncle's nephew. The young man grinned, sardonically. He had come on important business, and he meant to see it out. Folks could like it or not as they pleased.

Inside the Crystal Palace, just ahead of him, he heard a burst of laughter, a clamor of voices. Through the swing doors of the saloon burst three or four men. At sight of him they stopped precipitately, the mirth wiped from their faces as a wet sponge obliterates writing on a slate.

The first of them, a large dish-faced man with a thin-lipped evil mouth, cried out, "Well, I'll be damned."

"Quite likely, Mr. West," Bucky agreed.

"If it isn't Dude Cameron," cried a bandy-legged man in Levis.

"In person," admitted the owner of the name lightly.

The third member of the party that had just poured out of the saloon was a tall, broad-shouldered fellow, black-haired and dark. His heavy eyebrows met in a frown.

10

"What brought you back?" he said curtly.

"The Pacific Flyer."

"Don't get funny, Cameron. I'm telling you that this town is fed up with your gang."

"Friendly of you to mention it, Mr. Davis. I suppose you're telling me for my own good."

The bandy-legged man made a contribution, with righteous severity. Several citizens had stopped and were listening.

"Toltec won't stand for you, not after what you did to poor Max Buchmann. I'm surprised you had the nerve to come back from where you was holed up and show yore face here."

"Mr. Pete Quinn of the Red Rock district, who came back himself once," Bucky retorted, lifting his hand to those present in a little gesture of introduction.

Dark anger showed in Quinn's face. The reference needed no explanation. Years ago he had come back from the penitentiary, where he had been sent through the efforts of a Cameron.

"I'll stand just so much from you," he murmured.

"Folks here have made up their mind about the whole Cameron outfit," West carried on vindictively. "From the start they always acted like they were kings of the range. Those days are past. While yore Uncle Cliff stayed up in the hills and did his dirty work under

11

cover he could get away with it, but when he came to town and started his robbing and murdering —"

Bucky's voice rang out in challenge: "That's a lie."

From the gathering crowd someone called out, "Facts don't lie."

"Not when you get your facts straight," Bucky flung back. "You have them all wrong in this business."

"What I aimed to say," West went on, "is that Toltec won't any longer tolerate killers and robbers."

"Tough on the Red Rock scalawags," Bucky drawled. "Have you boys picked the next district you expect to infest?"

"Fellow, you can't talk yoreself out of the jam you're in by throwing mud at decent cowmen," West cried, his gash of a mouth a slit of menace. "You're in this First National business up to yore neck. If Haskell does what he'd ought to do, he'll arrest you soon as he knows you're here."

"And if he doesn't, why Toltec can take care of the matter itself," Davis added.

One of the townsmen murmured assent.

"Take care of it how?" asked Bucky.

"You'll find out how," Quinn said thickly, anger still simmering in him.

It came to Bucky, from the sullen silence

of the waiting circle, that the situation was more serious for him than he understood. They were associating him with his uncle, and on the evidence at hand Cliff Cameron had robbed a thousand depositors of his bank.

The young man spoke to the Toltec men within hearing, quietly, not raising his voice. "I'm not looking for trouble. I came here to clear my uncle's name, to prove false the lies being told about him. From his enemies I ask nothing, but I do expect fair play from his neighbors in town who knew Uncle Cliff for a square shooter who never wronged any man."

"Better clear yore own name first before you start white-washing his," Quinn cried harshly.

"That's right," a listener approved.

The brown eyes of Cameron grew hard as agates. "I'm not talking to scoundrels who robbed my uncle for years and were hammered down by him so that they hated the ground he walked on, but to you decent people who don't belong in the penitentiary. Uncle Cliff is innocent. I'm going to prove it before I'm through."

"You've got a nerve to come back and try to play innocent," West roared, "with Max Buchmann hardly cold in his grave. Cliff Cameron is guilty as hell, and even if you weren't on the ground you were helping him on the dirty job."

Except for Bucky himself the echo of assent was unanimous. He felt the heat of their anger beat upon him.

"What do you mean?" he demanded. "I haven't been in town for a year. How could I be in this bank robbery, if that's what you mean?"

"How do we know you weren't here under cover?" someone asked.

"You came back like a dern fool to try to bluff it out," Davis charged. "And you made a big mistake sticking yore head out for the rope, I'll say."

Bucky began to wonder if he had not made a mistake. There was something back of this he did not understand. It was clear that public opinion assumed he had aided and abetted his uncle and that his return to town was an outrageous challenge of impudent guilt to decency. His enemies would if possible blow the smoldering anger to red-hot fury.

"If Sheriff Haskell wants to see me, I'll be at the Toltec House for an hour and after that at the ranch. I'm here to see this thing through. All I ask is a little time to clear it up."

"All you'll get is a rope or a bullet," Quinn snarled.

"I'm not talking to rustlers and crooks like

14

this fellow and his friends who do business at night in other men's stock," Bucky said quietly. "They are known enemies of us Camerons. I'm appealing to the decent folks of Toltec, those who knew my uncle and respected him."

A little red-faced man flung a question hotly at him. "If Cliff Cameron is innocent where's he at? What has he done with our money? Why did he light out like a scared coyote after the robbery?"

"I don't know where he is, Todd," Bucky replied. "That's one of the things to be cleared up."

"Yeah, you want it clear as mud, don't you?" jeered Quinn. "We're not complete idjits, fellow. Buchmann is found dead. The bank is robbed. Cliff is missing. What more do you want?"

"I want to find out who robbed the bank and killed Buchmann. I want to find out what became of my uncle."

"So you claim you don't know where he is," Quinn said.

Bucky's steady gaze rested on the seamed face of the bow-legged man. "I don't know where he is, Pete, as I mentioned a minute ago. Do you?"

Quinn began to bluster. "If you're claiming —"

"I'm claiming just one thing — yet," Bucky's low clear voice cut in. "That Cliff Cameron is as square a man as ever lived."

The young man turned away abruptly and walked across the street to the Toltec House, the Mexican boy still shuffling at his side.

As Bucky approached the desk the loungers in the lobby chairs straightened to watch him. A group of three sat smoking not far from the cigar stand. One of them was a plump little man with a round moon face and horn spectacles back of which twinkled jolly benevolent eyes. He was telling a funny story, with the exaggerated gestures of an oldtime actor. A flicker of astonished hostility, banished almost instantly, showed behind the glasses.

He rose quickly to meet the young man, waving the lighted cigar in his hand.

"Well — well, here we are back in the old town," he cried heartily. "Welcome home again."

Bucky stopped and smiled blandly. His fingers were in his pocket searching for a half dollar to give the Mexican, so that he was unable to shake the soft fat hand outstretched to him.

"It's a great thing to be sure you can rely on your old friends, Richman," he said, with the faintest accent of irony.

Richman ignored any rebuff that might have been meant. "Just in, I suppose. Did you bring any news from Cliff?" he asked smoothly.

"Not any," Bucky drawled. "What news of him there is can be got here in Toltec. Thought maybe you might have some for me."

The plump man was solicitously regretful. "Sorry, Bucky. I certainly wish I had. You surely must be worried about him."

"Be seeing you later," Bucky said, and moved with his bag to the desk.

Jud Richman watched him go. A frown disturbed the child-like candor of his round face.

"Now what in hell did he come back for?" he asked.

One of the other men said he was wondering that himself.

CHAPTER II

Kathleen heard her father's explosive voice as she stepped out of the French window to the porch. "He's come back to get killed."

"Looks like," the heavy answer came, almost in a growl. "I don't aim to lie awake nights about that."

Garside slammed his fist down on the little

table beside the chair in which he sat. "No. I don't want him rubbed out."

The girl stopped, held up abruptly by the significance of the moment. The man standing with straddled feet in front of her father was Dan West, a ruffian whom she detested. He was chewing tobacco, the quid standing out in his leathery cheek. Slate-colored eyes, expressionless as those of a dead cod, rested on the banker.

"You struck up a friendship with the Camerons, Clem?" he asked.

The president of the Valley Bank brushed the sneer aside abruptly. "Not now or ever. But I expect to do business with him."

"So you don't want him killed — yet?"

"Don't put words in my mouth, Dan," Garside ordered. "What I'm saying is that I don't want this boy killed."

"I heard you," West answered sullenly. "Well, I'm not figuring on bumping him off right away. It was Brad served notice on him."

"Call him off."

"How can I call him off? He gave the kid twenty-four hours. Too late to rue back now."

Kathleen moved forward swiftly. "Who has come back to get killed?" she demanded. The dark eyes of the girl challenged her father. The other man she ignored.

Garside was taken aback, but his poker face did not betray the fact. He and West had not been talking three minutes. How much had she heard?

"Young Cameron," he told her. "Got in on the Flyer this morning. I put my point too strong. He won't be killed, unless the law does it. But he's a fool to come back while the town is still so excited."

"What did he come back for?" she asked, her eyes shining.

"Looking for trouble," West said savagely.

"What reason does he give?"

The girl spoke to her father. For her West was not on the map.

"To clear Cliff's name, he claims," answered Garside.

"How can he do that? If Mr. Cameron isn't guilty, why did he run away? An innocent bank president wouldn't do that, would he?"

Her father smiled, blandly malevolent. "You'll have to ask Bucky Cameron. I haven't learned the answers."

West watched the young woman, resentfully — the slim figure beautifully poised, the lifted head with its clean-cut look of pride. A sultry fire stirred between the man's heavy narrowed lids. Her contempt filled him with a sulky fury.

19

"He never had any sense," Kathleen said, the smooth brown of her cheeks tinged by a wave of underlying pink. "Always a show-off. I suppose that's why he has come back, to make everybody look at him and admire him for a wonder. The best way would be for nobody to pay any attention to him."

"You have to notice a mosquito buzzing around your head," Clem said.

"It would be silly to take him seriously. After all, he has a right to be here."

"In jail," her father added curtly.

"Very well. In jail." She frowned down at Garside, too disturbed to let the matter rest yet. "I can't believe he is in any danger. Toltec is a civilized town now."

Dan West laughed, and the sound of his evil mirth was not assuring.

"But if he is somebody must look after him till the law takes charge," she said.

"Why talk about the law?" West sneered. "It's made to help fellows like him. He'll hire some slick lawyer to get him off. Let the folks he has ruined cook his goose for him, I say."

"What you say isn't important, Dan," the banker said coldly. "Not when you talk like that."

Garside leaned back in the chair and looked up at his daughter. She was in riding breeches and boots. From the edge of the beret copper curls pushed out abundantly. The girl looked completely modern, with the surface hardness of her sophisticated class and generation. Yet she was amazingly vivid. Clem wondered by what trick of heredity he had for daughter this restless young creature so alien to the crude frontier life through which he had shouldered his ruthless way to success. He was a survival of the old days, a cattleman who had become in time a banker. His morals were far from puritanic, but her comments on life frequently startled him.

"You asking *me* to nurse the Cameron brat?" he inquired.

"Someone has to, it seems. Fools have to be protected from their folly." She tapped irritably one of her riding boots with the lash of her crop. "I don't like him any better than you do. I think he's detestable. But if his enemies mean to take advantage of his unpopularity to kill him you'll have to stop it."

"None of my business."

"It is, too, since you're a decent human being." Kathleen added a rider. "Everyone would say, because we're not friendly with the Camerons, that you had stood aside and let the ruffians who hate him do this thing for you. It doesn't matter that it wouldn't be true. You'd be blamed just the same. I don't have to tell you this, though. You know it already. I heard you say you wouldn't let him be murdered."

"There's no danger of that, I've told you. Fools shoot off their mouths. It doesn't mean anything."

"Doesn't it?" West asked, menace in his grin.

Kathleen did not look at the man, but a horror of him crept over her.

"We can't leave it to chance," she urged imperiously. "Just because we don't like him we have to protect him. Don't you see that, Dad? It's up to us."

"Suppose you keep out of this and let me play the hand," Garside told his daughter bluntly. "Run along and roll your hoop. You attend to your golf score and I'll make out to manage my own business."

Kathleen knew when she had said enough. She made a friendly derisive face at him and walked away.

"She's certainly an up-and-coming young lady," West said, his dead eyes following her.

The banker did not intend to discuss his daughter with this man. He picked his wide Stetson from the table, said shortly, "We'll see Haskell."

Clem Garside was a big bulky man, red-faced and white-haired. He had the solid impressive look that befitted Toltec's leading citizen. As he walked down the street there was heavy power in his stride. When he spoke to those he met, as he did constantly, his hearty voice boomed. His direct and curt approach was effective. It left the impression that there could be no guile in this forthright simple soul.

He turned in at the Toltec House. A man was at the hotel desk writing a telegram.

The banker said to the clerk on duty, "Any arrivals this morning?"

"Two on the Flyer," the clerk said. He lowered his voice and tilted his head toward the man with the Western Union blank. "This gentleman and Bucky Cameron."

"Didn't I tell you he was here?" West cut in.

Garside lifted his eyebrows in the direction of the stranger, and the hotel employee understood he was suggesting an introduction.

The clerk indicated the man at the desk filling out the yellow sheet. "This is Mr. Mitchell — Mr. Garside," he said, and by way of explanation: "Mr. Garside is our leading banker."

Mitchell stopped writing, transferred the pencil to his left hand, and offered the right. The banker gripped it firmly.

"Pardon," Garside boomed. "I'm looking for the other man who registered just now, but I'm glad to see any visitors to our town.

A traveling man, may I ask?"

"Not now. I have been. Just now I'm looking for a good location for a specialty men's clothing shop, one that will be up to date and strictly first class."

The president of the Valley Bank observed that the stranger was a light-haired smooth-faced young man in ultramodern city clothes, slender but well built. Garside was a booster for his city. He began to promote the town at once.

"Toltec is the place for you," he said confidently. "I'll talk with you about our advantages, Mr. Mitchell. Call on me at the Valley Bank tomorrow at ten. Ask for Clem Garside, the president."

Mitchell looked pleased at this attention from the local magnate. "I'll certainly look you up at ten, sir," he promised.

"Good. Do." Garside caught sight of Richman and beckoned to him. He walked a few steps to meet him. "Well, there's one born every minute," he said.

"Referring to your friend who got in a little while ago?" asked Richman, beaming at him.

"Did he say he was my friend?" demanded the banker curtly.

"I didn't hear him say so," the plump man replied suavely, "but I wouldn't be surprised if he wouldn't need a few friends soon."

"Tell the Red Rock crowd to keep their hands off him, Jud."

"Why, I can tell them what you say, Clem, if I see any of them," the other said, still smiling pleasantly. "I don't suppose they would pay much attention to me, though."

"See they do. I understand Brad Davis has made threats. Get him out of town."

Garside stepped back to the clerk. "Jim, have a boy take me up to Cameron's room."

"Shall I call him up first, sir?"

"No. I'll announce myself. Wait here, West."

The banker took the elevator to the fifth floor and followed the bell hop along a corridor. He gave the boy a quarter and dismissed him.

At his knock a voice invited him to enter.

Bucky was shaving. He turned, razor poised, and looked at his visitor. His eyes narrowed slightly.

"Honored to have the great man of Toltec come to welcome me," he said with a touch of irony

"Am I welcoming you?"

"*You* tell me."

"If a warning is a welcome. You were a fool to come back here so soon after what Cliff did."

"What did he do?"

Garside brushed the question aside as irrelevant. "Hotheads are liable to jerk you up to a telegraph pole," he said, frowning at the young man.

"If it is put up to them right," Bucky agreed. "I'll say this. In the first place I'm not responsible for my uncle's actions. In the second place he is the last man in the world to kill a bookkeeper of his own bank to rob it. Cliff Cameron is a square shooter. You've been his enemy twenty years and you know him from the ground up. The town has gone crazy because its money has been looted from the bank. But you're not fooled a little bit. You know Uncle Cliff didn't do it. There's something back of this, and I'm here to find out what it is."

The keen gray eyes probed at Bucky from under grizzled brows. "Did he send you back?"

"No, he didn't. I don't know where he is, or what has become of him." The brown eyes meeting the gray ones had become hard as obsidian. "If I could ask a few questions and get true answers I would know more about this."

"Ask questions of Cliff?"

"Of his enemies."

Unwinkingly Garside stared at Bucky. "I see. I'm his enemy, and I planned this to ruin him. Then I fixed it up with Cliff to light out so I could lay the blame on him. It makes a lot of sense."

"Did I name you, Mr. Garside?"

"You'd better not." The arrogance of the older man boiled up. "I won't stand for a whippersnapper like you making such insinuations about me. You haven't sense enough to pound sand in a rat hole. Toltec has figured you are in this crime with your uncle, and you come strutting back here inviting trouble. You'll last about as long as a snowball in hell."

"Why does Toltec think I'm in this?"

"Because your uncle left a letter in his desk — a letter from you, in which you told him to count you in on this deal."

Bucky thought swiftly — remembered the letter. "I mentioned robbing the bank, did I?"

"Practically. You said it was a dangerous business — and that you could see the penitentiary doors opening for you — but to count you in all the way from hell to breakfast."

"I said too much or too little," Bucky answered dryly. "It happens I was talking about another enterprise."

"So *you* say. Young fellow, you're in a tight, as we used to say in the old days. I'm the only one can save you, and soon as I show up you start insulting me. If I walk through that door now you're gone."

"Out of great friendship for me and my family you came to offer help," Bucky said, a faint inflection of sarcasm in his voice.

Garside retorted, callously brutal: "I came because it doesn't suit me to have you strung up. If it did I wouldn't lift a hand — not a hand."

"Interesting," Bucky commented.

He excused himself for a moment, washed the soap from his face, dried it with a towel.

"You have a proposition to make, Mr. Garside," he said casually, while he rolled and lit a cigarette.

"Yes, sir." In the banker's voice was the hectoring note of the bully. "You Camerons are through in this country — bucked out. Cliff knew it. That's why he pulled off this crazy business of robbing his bank."

"He didn't rob the bank," Bucky said. "I thought I told you that."

"Talk sense," snapped Garside. "Don't try to make a fool of me. Of course he did it. You're asking me to believe that some enemy robbed the bank, snuffed out this bookkeeper Buchmann, and carried off Cliff in his pocket, leaving no evidence against himself but plenty against Cliff." The big man barked out an incredulous mirthless laugh. "I could certainly use a fellow with brains like that in my business. Only there's no such man."

"He was smart," Bucky conceded. "Just a little too smart, don't you think?"

"What you mean?"

"Was Uncle Cliff a complete fool? Would he write it all over the place that he had done the job? Would he leave a letter implicating him? Would he throw away his revolver with two empty shells in the cylinder and the bullets from those shells in the body of Buchmann? Not unless he was loco."

"No crimes would be solved if those committing them didn't make mistakes," Garside said decisively. "The point is, they do."

"Why would Uncle Cliff run away? Why not fix it so that it would look like bank robbers had done it? You're throwing away all the knowledge you have of his character. He was a cool, game frontiersman, a cattleman long before he became a banker. You can't tell me he thought out this crime, then went into a panic after he had done it."

"Your claim is that someone is holding him prisoner?"

"I'm not making any claims — until I know more about it. He's either being held somewhere, or else he was taken away and killed."

Abruptly, Garside pushed this theory from him. "Nothing to it. Listen. Cliff played a losing game for years. He lost money in cattle and in the bank. Hadn't the least idea how to run a bank. Too sentimental. Loaned money to old friends who couldn't make good. Wouldn't crowd them to pay. Carried them along instead of closing them out."

From the bed where Bucky had seated himself, he nodded agreement. "Just what I've been telling you. Not the kind of man to throw down the friends who trusted him and loot the bank into which they had put their money because they knew him. He thought straight and lived straight. As a ranger he ran down some of the worst outlaws in this country. All his life he stood up and took what was coming to him. There isn't enough circumstantial evidence in the world to make me think he did this crooked thing and sneaked off afterward."

"You're one of these slick talkers," Garside said contemptuously. "Better hire a hall. Write an article for the *News* about it."

"Maybe I will," Bucky said.

"Since you're tarred with the same stick as Cliff I expect your story won't go a long way," Garside told him tartly. "I'll not argue with you. I stand on the facts. Here's my proposition. Find out where Cliff is holed up — if you don't know. Get him and Miss Julia to sign to me a legal deed for their holdings in the ranch and the bank. Turn over what interest you own in them. When you've done this I'll write a check for twenty-five thousand dollars for you to divide among you."

"Generous," Bucky drawled, a sardonic grin on his brown face. "The ranch isn't worth more than a quarter of a million, let alone the bank."

"*Was* worth that," corrected the banker. "The equity in it today isn't worth a thin dime. The land is mortgaged to the hilt, and a lot of the cattle have been run off. With Cliff out of the picture rustlers are going to get even busier. The bank is busted. I can salvage something out of the smash, and I'm the only man alive that can. My offer is too liberal, but I'll stand by it."

"We wouldn't want you to rob yoreself," Bucky said dryly.

"I'll take care of that, young man," Garside snapped. "Don't get funny with me. Keep in mind that you are in a bad jam. Right now I'm standing between you and the rope."

Bucky stroked his little mustache. He did not deny to himself that there was something in what Garside said. It had not taken five minutes after his arrival to discover how inflamed public opinion was. With the enemies of the Camerons to stir this up a mob might be induced to move against him. He did not underestimate the power of the banker. Better sing small and conciliate the man, regardless of his personal feeling.

"I'm going out to the ranch today and I'll see Julia there, but I don't know when I'll get in touch with my uncle. I'll see what she thinks about it. I agree with you that things don't look any too rosy for us."

"You're right they don't," Garside said sharply. "You're sunk."

"I wouldn't go that far," Bucky remonstrated mildly. "Now about this deal, Mr. Garside — I can see plenty of difficulties. First, we'll have to get in touch with my uncle. I don't know how long that will take."

"Make it snappy." The voice of Garside was hard, his manner arrogant. "Don't make a mistake, boy. Cliff is whipped. It took me twenty years to do it, but he is down at last. If he doesn't accept my proposition he doesn't get a cent. Put that clear to the pig-headed old fool."

Bucky nodded. "If and when I see him. Since I'm sure Uncle Cliff didn't rob the First National, I can go into this with a clear conscience, but if you feel he did it, maybe you'd rather drag him back to justice."

"I'm not the sheriff of this county."

"But as a law-abiding citizen —"

"Forget it." A threat rode roughly in the banker's words. "No shenanigan. I'm holding the whip, and by God I'll use it. You'll dance to my music. I intend to take over the C C ranch. Neither you nor Cliff can stop me. All you can do is put ropes around your necks."

"Which would be unpleasant," Bucky admitted.

Garside strode out of the room.

The lax look of surrender went out of the face of Bucky instantly. He rose from the bed, his eyes shining. Almost in a murmur, he spoke his thoughts aloud.

"When a crime is committed for money," he said to himself, "find the man who profits most from it." He padded up and down the room, his thoughts racing. "The fellow who robbed the bank got away with a big haul, but Mr. Garside gets both the bank and the C C ranch, a right good pickup. Would you call that coincidence, Bucky? Maybe, and maybe not. Wouldn't it be possible for Mr. Garside to have helped coincidence along — by having the bank robbed? If he did, he would get the loot, the bank, the ranch, and at the same time be rid of the Camerons. What a swell break that would be!"

Bucky smiled grimly. He had found one likely suspect.

CHAPTER III

Bucky telephoned to the C C ranch and asked Tim Murphy, the manager, to send a car to town for him.

Even over the wire Bucky caught Tim's excitement. "Toltec is no place for you, son, not now. You lie low until the car gets to town."

Young Cameron laughed. "I'm not on the dodge, Tim. All right. Shoot the car along. And Tim — put Julia on the wire."

The voice of Julia came breathless. "Is it you, Bucky — really? Oh, I need you so much. Father — father —" She broke down for a moment. "Come as soon as you can, please."

"I'll be there in time for lunch," he promised.

"It's been so dreadful — alone."

"You won't be alone now," he said cheerfully. "I'm here to stay."

After he had hung up he walked down stairs to the lobby. A big-bodied man of middle age, bald and gray, walked into the hotel.

"I've been trying to get into touch with you for some time, Bucky," he said.

"I'm here, Sheriff," Bucky said briefly.

"About this bank robbery." Haskell came forward, smiled, shook hands. He had the specious urbanity of the professional politician. "Thought maybe you could give me some information. If we could find Cliff now, so as to get his story."

"I don't know where he is."

"Too bad. Seems to me if I was Cliff I would come back and straighten this out. No use beating about the bush, Bucky. This business doesn't look any too good for him. Mind, I'm not giving my own opinion. I was always friendly to Cliff. If you want to do him a service you'll tell me where he's at."

"Hard of hearing, Haskell? I said I didn't know."

"Maybe you can explain that letter you wrote him."

Bucky looked at the plump politician coolly. "Maybe I can. Is it necessary?"

"The boys think it is, Bucky. You'll have to admit yourself it drags you into this affair."

"Nothing to do with it. The letter referred to our fight against the Red Rock rustlers to protect our stock against their raids."

"You said in it maybe you'd have to go to the penitentiary."

"Yes. I meant that our enemies own too much of the law around this man's town and that if we had to shoot a few ruffians in defense of our property the incident might be twisted against us." On Bucky's face, as he looked at the sheriff, was a slight satiric smile.

This cool young man disconcerted Haskell. He had a wholesome respect for the Camerons, down and out though they seemed to be at last.

"You hadn't ought to talk that way, Bucky," the officer reproved. "You know loose talk like that about the law not being straight is bad medicine."

"It's worse medicine not to have it straight, Haskell. There are officers in this town who fit right in the vest pocket of Clem Garside."

The sheriff raised a fat protesting hand. "Now — now — now."

"Did you come here to arrest me?" Bucky asked.

"Yes, sir. Only a formality, as you might say. You'll be released on bond."

"I see," Bucky said dryly. "And who is going on my bond?"

"Clem Garside."

"Good of Clem. Nothing like a tried and true friend to stick closer than a brother in time of need."

"Clem's all right. If you'll come to the courthouse with me we'll fix it."

Together they walked down the street. Haskell fairly oozed good will to his constituents on the street. He had a cheerful word for everybody.

They met Pete Quinn and Brad Davis. Richman was with them.

The black-haired cattleman frowned at Bucky, his eyes hungrily hostile. Quinn asked a question.

"You locking him up, Haskell?"

"Clem has gone bail for him."

"Clem?" In blank surprise Quinn stared at him. "Has he thrown in with this scalawag?"

"You'd better ask him, Pete," the sheriff said amiably. "He didn't tell me about that."

Within a half an hour Bucky was back at the Toltec House. He stood at the door a minute, then strolled up First. At the Crystal Palace he caught another glimpse of Quinn and Davis.

Those he met stared at him. Some turned to watch his jaunty progress down the street. He could feel in the air their sullen anger. One woman let her resentment escape in bitter words.

"Where's the money you and your uncle stole from me and my fatherless children?" she cried.

Bucky stopped, said gently: "You're wrong, Mrs. Breed. My uncle never stole a dollar in his life. I've come here to find out who did steal it — and to get the money back if I can."

Gradually the anger died out of her face. "I never would have believed it of him," she cried, a sob in her voice. "Money I had earned a dime and a quarter at a time taking in washing."

"*Don't* believe it of him, because it isn't true," he urged. "Cliff Cameron would never have done that in the world."

"But he did. He's gone — with the money."

"He's gone, but not with the money. Listen, Mrs. Breed. I'll make you a promise. If the robber and his loot aren't found — and if I live — I'll make good your loss out of my own pocket."

Strangely, she was convinced he told the truth. "God bless you if you do, Bucky Cameron," she prayed.

He left the main business street and walked into the residence section of the town. Presently he came to a new fashionable addition laid with winding roads and triangle for grass and shrubbery. The houses here were expensive, attractive both in themselves and by reason of skillful landscape gardening. As he strolled past one of these, a rambling red brick built in the English style, he looked at it with more than ordinary interest. He knew the people who lived in it.

The crack of a gun sounded. Instantly

Bucky knew that somebody had fired at him from the sumac bushes across the road. Since he was unarmed, this was no time to investigate. He ran up the winding roadway leading to the house. Again, twice, a revolver roared. Bucky took the porch steps three at a time, saw an open French window, went through it into a small conservatory opening into the living-room.

In front of a large alcove window of leaded panes a young woman was standing beside a desk reading a letter. To Bucky, as he moved into the room, it seemed that the setting had been designed to harmonize in color scheme with the slender figure of its mistress. The rays of the sun streamed through the glass and put her in a spotlight. The Bokhara rugs, the upholstery of the comfortable chairs, the whole tone of the warm cheerful room, lent accent to the vividness of the girl.

She glanced at Bucky. Instantly her figure stiffened.

"What are you doing here, sir?" she asked.

"I've been hearing that question all morning," he answered. "One might almost think I wasn't welcome."

She was still in riding clothes, but she had flung the beret on the desk and from the short copper curls crowning her head, light gleamed.

"I ask you what you are doing in my father's house," she said, her chin lifted.

"Finding sanctuary, lady." A flicker of sardonic humor sparked in his eyes.

"What do you mean?"

"From the town's enthusiastic welcome to the prodigy. Toltec is getting ready to kill the fatted calf."

"I suppose you can't help being a fool," she said coldly. "You had to come back and get into trouble."

"Am I in trouble? Here in dear old Toltec, where everybody loves me?" He felt beating in his throat the pulse of excitement danger always started. Flippantly he offered a tag of verse.

"For burn and breeze and billow,
Their sangs are a' the same,
And every weeping willow
Soughs Cameron's welcome hame."

She looked at him scornfully, and in her voice was the singing sting of a whiplash. "Not an hour ago I heard a man say you ought to be killed."

"Doesn't approve of me," he said with cheerful surprise. "Of course you set him right and explained what an estimable character I am."

"I said what I thought of you." She turned

40

to pick up the beret and crop from the desk. Evidently she meant to waste no more time on him.

"Don't move," he begged. "You've no idea how effective you are in that spotlight. A sort of golden girl *tableau vivant.* Goddess of the morning. That sort of thing."

The angry color stormed into her cheeks. They were old enemies, had carried on the family feud in childhood and through their school days. He always knew how to get under her hide.

"I don't care to listen to your effrontery," she said. "I asked you what you are doing in this house. Will you please answer — or leave?"

"Thought I did answer. Well, let that go. Mind if I leave by the back door?"

"I don't care how you go, just so you do," she retorted sharply.

He bowed with debonair mockery, turned, and walked to the door.

Kathleen's frowning gaze followed him. A doubt disturbed her. He had mentioned sanctuary. Did he mean from immediate danger? She was given to swift impulse. Now she weakened her curt dismissal of him by adding a warning.

"He meant what he said — that man. You're not safe here."

"Awf'ly nice of you to take so much interest in me, Miss Garside," he said. "Unless you're trying to get me away before I rob the Valley Bank."

She answered, her lissome body straight: "I don't take any interest in you whatever. All I'm afraid of is that if anything happens to you evil-minded people might think we had something to do with it."

"They might," he agreed. "Especially if it happened in front of your house. Tell your friend I expect to be around quite a while and he'll have plenty of chances to shoot me in the back. No use messing up your lawn."

"What are you hinting at?" she cried.

He was looking at his hat, with a sardonic smile. There was a small hole in the brim. She remembered the sharp explosions heard a few minutes since. Perhaps they had not been caused by the backfire of an automobile. Her eyes dilated.

"Has someone been shooting at you?" she demanded.

"I got that impression," he admitted.

"You're not — hurt?"

"Only my feelings."

"Was it just now — here in front of the house?"

"Yes. You're a good guesser. It seems your friend did mean what he said."

42

"He's not my friend," Kathleen protested indignantly. "It was that man Dan West. You know now how dangerous he is. He said another of his crowd was going to make trouble for you. Brad somebody or other."

"I talked with the gent," Bucky drawled. "Yes, they're both more dangerous than rattlesnakes. They don't give warning before they strike."

"Leave these parts at once," she said peremptorily. "Next time they won't miss."

"I was thinking of taking part in the fireworks myself next time," he suggested with deceptive mildness.

"No. Get out. If you don't you'll be arrested anyhow."

"I've already been arrested — and turned loose. A good friend went bail for me."

"He didn't do you any service," she snapped.

"I'm sure he meant to help me. It was your father."

"Father?"

"Yes. I'm returning the friendly call he made on me a little while ago."

"He doesn't want your blood on his head," the girl said coldly in explanation. "If you have any sense you'll leave."

"You know I can't help being a fool," he reminded her. "I'm going to stick it."

His grin annoyed her. It was so character-istically impudent. Resentment blazed in her eyes.

"You strut around playing you're some kind of god who can't be hurt. All right. You've had your warning. We're not to blame if you get killed."

"I'm sure the coroner's jury will exonerate you," he said. "Have to go now. Be seeing you again."

"How do you know the men who shot at you are gone?" she asked swiftly.

"The kind that fire from ambush get out in a hurry."

"Wait until we make sure."

"I'm sure enough."

Kathleen thought a moment. "I'll get father's gun for you."

A little smile was on his lips as he watched her walk out of the room with the easy rhythm that distinguished her. He resented her as much as she did him, but she entertained him more than any girl he knew. She had a fine animal vigor. There was a swift untamed fire in her always ready to blaze up whenever they met. Usually he could get under her skin because he controlled his temper better.

She brought back a .38 army Colt and handed it to him. He examined the weapon to make sure it was loaded.

"I'll always be grateful to you for saving my life," he said, an imp of ironic mirth dancing in his eye.

She said, barely controlling her anger, "You can return it to the bank."

Bucky departed by the same window through which he had entered. He was thinking that the little devil had not got any change out of him this time.

From the window Kathleen saw him sauntering down the sidewalk, a picture of a young man of leisure very much at his ease.

CHAPTER IV

Tim Murphy was waiting restlessly in front of the Toltec House. At sight of Bucky he came striding toward him.

"Goddlemighty, boy, where you been?" he scolded. "Didn't I tell you this town has got Cameron-phobia? You ought to have stayed indoors. Some of the Red Rock bunch are in town too. For four bits Mex one of them would bump you off."

Bucky laughed as he shook hands with the big weather-beaten foreman. "I've been calling on a lady, Tim."

45

"Of all the doggoned idiots," Murphy fumed. "What lady?"

"Miss Kathleen Garside. I was returning a call her father made on me."

Tim stared at him in surprise. "If you figure you can fix up a deal with Clem Garside and not come out the little end of the horn you're 'way off, boy. He's got you where he wants you and he'll turn the screws on."

"Do you know, I suspected that, Tim? My call on Miss Kathleen was not exactly a business one." Bucky took off his hat and looked at the bullet hole in it. "Someone took two-three cracks at me and I jumped for the nearest house like a scared rabbit. It happened to be the Garside place."

"Someone shot at you?" Tim cried. "Who was it?"

"I'm not sure." Bucky's eyes had drifted across the street and were resting on some men standing in front of the post-office. "I reckon I'll go ask."

He strolled across the road. The foreman called after him, "You damn fool!" and followed at heel.

Bucky touched a black-haired, broad-shouldered man on the arm. The man turned and gave a sudden start. He was Brad Davis. One of the others with him was Pete Quinn. Richman also was in the party, not quite happy about it in spite of his fixed smile.

"Don't you owe me a hat, Brad?" said Bucky mildly.

"What d'you mean owe you a hat?" retorted Davis, bristling.

Once more Bucky took off his hat and examined the round hole in the brim. "If you are expecting to be a modern Wild Bill Hickok, you've got to do better than that, Brad."

"You're a liar if you claim I shot at you," Davis cried.

"I don't say you shot at me," Bucky answered, his cool eye resting on the man. "All I say is you nearly hit me. Maybe you were aiming at the man in the moon."

Quinn offered an alibi. "I've been with Brad all morning. Never left him a minute. So he couldn't have done it."

Bucky transferred his gaze to the cowpuncher. "Oh, you've been with him all morning. Interesting."

"We haven't been off Front Street."

Murphy cut in. "I saw the pair of you sneaking back along Monument Avenue not ten minutes ago."

"One C C man supporting another," Davis jeered, and added belligerently: "Say, what is this? You birds looking for a fight?"

"I'm looking for a new hat, but I don't suppose I get it," Bucky replied. "Tough luck, boys. You're not likely to catch me unarmed again."

He and Murphy walked back to the Toltec.

"They did it all right," the foreman said. "When they turned and saw you they gave themselves away."

"Yes. You ready to take off for the ranch, Tim?"

The manager of the C C said he was. Ten minutes later Toltec lay miles behind them.

"Glad you came back, Bucky," Tim said. "We're in for a lot of trouble, but I'd hate to lie down and let these scoundrels wipe us off the map without a fight. This bank robbery has given them the chance they have been waiting for a good many years."

"Tell me about that," Bucky replied. "All I know is what I've seen in the papers. Of course I know Uncle Cliff didn't do it. But where is he? What's become of him?"

"I wish I knew. He's never been seen since that night."

"He was trapped and made to bear the blame of the murder. No doubt about that."

"The way I figure it," agreed the foreman. "Trapped and killed."

"What we want to do first is examine all the available facts and sift them. When did you see Uncle Cliff last?"

48

"I saw him in the bank the day of the robbery."

"Did he act normal?"

"Same as he always did. Kinda easygoing and slow. We were talking about selling some beef stock. By the way, he said he wished you would come home."

"I wish to God I had come sooner," Bucky said fervently. "Maybe I might somehow have prevented this . . . You didn't notice anything different at the bank. Nothing that you thought about afterward?"

"No. The monthly payroll for the Malpais dam construction gang came in while I was there. I watched him and Buchmann and young Ferrill store it away."

"Could outsiders have known the payroll for the dam was there?"

"They could if they had watched. It comes in about the same time every month. That was no secret."

"A lot of money?"

"I don't know how much. Quite a lot, though. More than eight hundred men are working on the dam."

"Notice any of our enemies hanging around? Or any tough-looking strangers?"

"No. Might have been some. I couldn't say." The foreman leaned back and relaxed. A long strip of gun-barrel road, with no traffic in sight, stretched before them. "I left town about dark and drove out to the ranch. Cliff called up Miss Julia and told her he wouldn't be home but would stay that night at the club. He did that a couple of nights a week when business crowded him. About half-past two in the morning I was wakened by my telephone ringing. It was Sheriff Haskell calling me up to tell me the bank had been robbed and Max Buchmann killed. Of course I got right up and went to town. Thought maybe Cliff would need me."

"What position did Buchmann hold in the bank? I don't remember him very well. He hadn't been here long when I left."

"He was a bookkeeper, the head of the office. They say he was a swell hand at figures. Sometimes he helped at a teller's window at luncheon time . . . Well, I couldn't find Cliff. It seems he got a call at the club over the phone about half-past eleven or a little later. He was playing poker. He excused himself — said he was going to the bank. After he left the club nobody has ever seen him since, except those mixed up in the robbery. He absolutely and completely vanished."

"Didn't give any clew as to who wanted him when he left the club?"

"No. Just said he was needed."

"When was the robbery discovered?"

"About half-past one. That real estate fellow Jud Richman noticed the bank was on fire. Haskell was with him. They called out the fire department. When the firemen broke in, the whole back part of the building was ablaze and pretty well gutted. They found Max Buchmann's body just outside the vault. It was badly burned, but they could tell he had been shot in the back of the head. Cliff's gun was found beside him, and the bullet that killed him had been fired from that gun."

"No doubt about its being Uncle Cliff's gun?"

"None," Murphy replied. "I identified it myself. You've seen it a hundred times. So have I. It was the same one he used when he was a ranger captain."

"Any fingerprints on the gun?"

"No. It had been wiped clean. But there were prints on the gasoline can."

"What gasoline can?"

"The murderer had drenched the furniture and Max's clothes with gasoline. Poor Buchmann was burned so badly the public wasn't allowed to see the body. The fellow who killed him must have been some kind of a fiend. He had crushed the poor fellow's face in with some kind of blunt instrument."

"You didn't see Buchmann then?"

"Sure I saw him. On the slab. You know

he was completely bald. His wig had fallen off and was partly burned. So had some of his clothes. They buried him as he was, without even removing the high-built shoe he used for that crippled leg of his. He was a forlorn old guy. Nobody but Cliff would have given him a job, but you know how Cliff was about lame ducks."

"Yes. Whose fingerprints on the gasoline can?"

"Cliff's." The foreman added, fiercely, "Little as Cliff was, I'll betcha it took three men to hold him while they made those prints."

"Unless he had been knocked unconscious first," Bucky said. "Someone was thorough — too thorough. He wanted to be sure suspicion would point to Uncle Cliff. Tell me this, Tim. Would Uncle Cliff have had himself and the whole bank staff fingerprinted as a protection to depositors if he had intended to rob the First National himself?"

"His enemies claim he didn't mean to do it then. Their point is he got so damned hard up he didn't know which way to turn. Of course it's true he had to mortgage the ranch two years ago and we have had some bad cattle years. He was so doggoned good-hearted he hadn't the heart to foreclose on his friends when they got into trouble. Naturally they made him the goat all they could."

"All right. Getting back to the fingerprints, wouldn't he have destroyed them after the crime? And one more point that sticks out like a sore thumb: would an old cattleman who knew he was in danger from that hour leave his gun instead of taking it with him? Why, he wouldn't feel dressed without it."

"If you're trying to tell me Cliff didn't do it, boy, you're wasting yore breath," Murphy said. "I know damn well he didn't."

"I'm not. What I'm trying to do is to put myself in the place of the criminal. Maybe we can tell from the things he did what kind of a fellow he is."

"I know that already. He's a devil."

"I mean, know how his mind works. He and his friends — if there were others in this with him — took Uncle Cliff away with them after they had killed Buchmann and robbed the bank. Is he still a prisoner? Or is he dead?"

"Dead," exploded the foreman. "The rats would have to kill and bury him to protect themselves."

"That's likely," Bucky admitted. "But not certain. It depends on who did this. Uncle Cliff was stubborn as a mule. Maybe they are holding him while they try to force him to sign a paper."

Tim slanted a curious look at him. "Yore

mind is running a different way from mine. I'm thinking of the Red Rock crowd. Cliff didn't live two hours after they took him from the bank."

"They may have done it under orders from someone else," Bucky said. "Or they may not have done it at all."

"Orders from who?" Tim asked bluntly.

"Clem Garside has served notice on me he means to take over both the bank and the ranch. Don't you think this business has been a lucky break for him?"

"I'll say so."

"It makes him top man in this county, with nobody left to dispute it."

"That's right." Tim stared at his friend so long that the car almost ran off a bank. "You think —"

"I think it's possible. If so, Uncle Cliff may still be alive."

Tim shook his head. "No use in foolin' ourselves, Bucky," he said gently. "Cliff has passed over the divide. Look at it sensibly. Clem is a smooth proposition. He has been inching forward for thirty years, all the time with his eye on the C C ranch, knowing you Camerons were a careless lot and that yore foot was likely to slip financially some time. But Clem doesn't step outside the law, not when anybody is looking. This was a brutal business, not the kind Clem would have pulled off. On the other hand it's right up the alley of the Red Rock gang. They hate the ground Cliff walked on. He has ridden them rough for a long time, even if they got away with a good many of his cows now and again. Personally he shot down 'Gene Sturtevant in a fight when he caught him branding a C C calf. These nesters are the killer type. This is earmarked as their job. Look at what they did to faithful Max Buchmann. Hadn't a thing against him, but he got in their way or else was a witness of their deviltry. Why did they bushwhack you today? Because they are scared you will learn the truth. Mark my words, boy. If yore uncle's body is ever found it will be under a pile of rocks up a gulch in the Red Rock country."

"I'm not saying you are wrong, Tim," Bucky replied. "We've been fighting these thieves ever since I was a kid. If they could get either Uncle Cliff or me they wouldn't hesitate a second. What I do say is that this isn't quite their kind of a job after all. They would have drygulched my uncle, but Dan West would never have thought of getting rid of him and at the same time throwing the burden of this crime on him and me. That took brains. Some fine Italian hand was in it. Whose?"

"You don't hate Clem half as much as I do,

55

but there's no sense in letting some half-cocked idea lead us on the wrong trail. Guess somebody else."

"All right. What about that little grinning, gum-shoeing scoundrel Richman? He has hated Uncle Cliff ever since he was slapped by him in the post-office before a dozen people. The Red Rock crowd always have come to him to front for them. You can't tell me he isn't in on some of their dirty deals."

"Nor me, but you'll have a hell of a time proving it on him. And I don't think he has the guts for anything as big as this. His size is getting rid of rustled stock, I'd say."

"What were he and Haskell doing around the First National at half-past one in the morning, just after it had been robbed?" Bucky wanted to know.

Murphy squinted his sun-bleached eyes at the younger man. "For that matter what were Cliff and Buchmann doing down at the bank in the middle of the night? Must have been a reason. Something got them there. Something they had heard — or knew."

"If we knew that we'd probably have the answer to the whole mystery," Bucky said. "One thing is reasonably sure. They were there because they thought the bank was in danger. But I'll admit that doesn't tie up with what we know of Uncle Cliff. It would not be like him to be caught napping after he had been warned. Buchmann was different. I hardly knew him, since Uncle Cliff took him on just before I left, but he seemed an absent-minded sort of an old coot. Not much good in a fight, I would guess."

"No. A gentle fellow — sort of a hermit — not really old, though. Maybe forty."

"This young fellow Ferrill, who helped put the payroll money away — What about him?"

"He's a bit of a highroller, I've heard. Spends a good deal for a hundred fifty dollar a month teller. But I don't know anything against him."

"I'll look him up . . . It's good to be back at the ranch."

When the car stopped at the porch of the big house Julia came flying out to meet her cousin. She flung her arms around his neck.

"Oh, Neil, I'm so glad you've come," she cried, a sob in her throat. "It's been terrible — alone."

Bucky knew what she meant. He held her soft body close for a moment after he had kissed her, then stroked her fair hair gently. But he did not tell her it would be all right about her father. There was no use feeding false hope.

The girl was rather small, like her father, and her tired blue eyes held the weariness of exhaustion after long fear. She was a pretty young thing, very feminine and clinging, as graceful as a butterfly.

"I'm going to stay here and look after you," her cousin promised.

They walked into the house, Julia still clinging to his arm. Over her shoulder she called to the foreman. "Lunch is ready, Tim. I had a place set for you."

A few minutes later Murphy joined them at table, his face washed and scrubbed till it shone.

"I'm not very hungry," Julia said wearily, declining a lamb chop.

Bucky gave orders cheerfully, with mock severity. "Temporarily I'm the head of the house, young fellow, and you're going to eat."

"Whether I want to or not?" she asked, smiling a little, with troubled gravity.

"Yes, lady. Take that chop on your plate, and don't just play with it. These peas are delicious. I'll help you to some. You look as if you hadn't eaten a bite in a week. It will be different now. We have work to do, and we won't mope."

To her own surprise Julia discovered she was hungry. Already she felt better. The masculine shoulders of Bucky had taken on the load. She noticed that it did not interfere with his appetite.

CHAPTER V

Bucky was busy trying to analyze the fore-man's elementary balance sheet for the C C when Bud Keller came to him with a message.

"Tim wants you should come down to the barns and meet a guy," the cowboy said. Bud was a lean lanky man whose overalls did not come down much more than half way on the legs of his high-heeled boots. He was freckle-faced and brindle-thatched, and his unfinished face wore perpetually an amiable smile.

"Has the guy got a name?" Bucky asked.

Keller rubbed his unshaven chin. "I reckon he has, but I didn't catch it. He's a kind of scrummy-lookin' fellow."

Bucky walked down to the barns with Bud.

The foreman drew Cameron aside. "I didn't bring this bird up to the house because I thought Miss Julia might be around and I didn't want to arouse any false hopes. This Dutch Dieter here claims the Red Rock gang have a man cached in the hills and are holding him prisoner."

"Great news, if it's true," Bucky said.

"If it's true. I thought we could go to my

59

cabin and you could talk with him."

"Good idea," assented Bucky.

The three men walked to the quarters of the foreman. Murphy closed the door behind him and invited Cameron and the stranger to take chairs. Bucky sat down opposite a heavy-set man of Teutonic appearance. He was rough and unkempt, and he had shifty shallow eyes. Young Cameron had seen him before. His small mountain ranch was in the hills back of the C C.

The ranchman told his story. He had been up with a sick cow one night and had seen four men riding the ridge road above his place. Three of the men had been armed, the fourth had not. His hands were tied behind him, and one of the others was leading his horse.

"Recognize any of them?" Bucky asked.

Dieter hesitated. "I thought one of 'em looked like Brad Davis," he said at last. "Couldn't swear to him."

"Clear night?"

"Pretty clear. There was a moon."

"But they weren't very close. How far would you say?"

"Maybe seventy-five yards — or a hundred."

"What night was it?"

The answer came pat. "Night of July seventeenth."

"How do you happen to remember the date so well?"

"Next day I heard about the bank robbery."

"And you associated these men with the robbery?" Bucky asked.

"I wouldn't say that." The man's shallow eyes shifted to the foreman and back again. "I thought it kinda funny. So late in the night you might almost call it morning."

"Were you in town today, Dieter?" Bucky asked casually.

"No. What you getting at? Why would I be in town?" the rancher demanded. "And if I was, what then?"

"Not important," admitted Bucky. "Took you quite a while to get down to us with the news, didn't it, Dieter? Seven days to cover fourteen miles."

"I didn't decide to come till I heard you were here," the hillman said resentfully. "I don't have to mix myself up in other folks' business unless I want to. And I'll say right damn now I don't care whether you believe me or not."

"Who told you I was back?"

Bucky's careless question almost threw the ranchman off guard. He opened his mouth to answer, then closed it abruptly and glared at the young man.

"I dunno who told me," he said at last. "Yes,

I do, too. It was Cad Fuller, on his way back from town."

Bucky knew that however Dieter had learned the news it had not been from Cad Fuller. Groping for a name, the man had seized on that of one of his neighbors.

Apparently Bucky brushed aside suspicion. "I expect you're after that thousand-dollar reward my cousin posted for information leading to the finding of her father. I certainly hope you get it. If this man they're holding prisoner turns out to be my uncle and we rescue him alive we shall always be grateful to you. We'll start soon as we can get a bunch of the boys together." To Murphy he suggested: "Dieter must be hungry after his ride. How about asking Jim Wong to fix him up some supper? A bottle of beer might go well."

While horses were being run up and saddled, Bucky and the foreman examined available weapons. It was on the cards that there might be a battle in the hills.

"Do you swallow Dutch's story?" Tim asked.

"It's full of holes you could throw a cat through, yet it may be true in the main," Bucky said. "He couldn't recognize for sure any of the men he saw on the ridge because it was too dark, but there was light enough for him to tell that one rider had his hands tied behind him and his horse was being led. He wasn't in town today, but he knew I was back and lied about who told him. Maybe he is a decoy, or maybe he is just frightened because he is betraying the Red Rock outfit for the reward. We'll know which later."

"Hmp!" grunted Tim. "We may not know it if he leads us into an ambush and we're wiped out."

"Dutch is going to ride between you and me. We'll watch him every foot of the way. If and when we get close to a trap he'll show it by his nervousness. He'll have to arrange his own getaway before the band begins to play. Probably he'll want to drop back for a minute or two. That will be a signal for us to look out."

"He's a lousy son of a gun," the foreman said sourly. "Betraying either us or his neighbor thieves. If he isn't a rustler, preying on C C stuff, I'm a Mexican. We've known it for years, but we can't prove it."

Bucky broke a .45 and examined it. "Because he's that kind of a treacherous scoundrel his story may be true. The thousand dollars would tempt him, even though he knows the risk of giving away Brad Davis and his crowd. On the other hand —"

"On the other hand," Murphy finished for him dryly, "we won't be sitting on any horseshoes, since likely enough we're the lambs being led to the slaughter."

"Maybe we'll turn out wolves in sheep's clothing," Bucky amended. "Dieter's story may be bait to draw us into an ambush. I grant you that. These Red Rock scoundrels know that I think Uncle Cliff has been either killed or kidnaped. So they feed us a little come-on stuff. That's a possibility. We'll have to take a chance, as slight a one as we can."

"One thing is sure," the foreman said harshly. "They're guilty as hell of the First National crime, whichever way the cat jumps. If Dieter's story is true, they took Cliff. If it isn't, they are trying to wipe you and me out because they're afraid we will hang the goods on them if they don't."

"You go too fast for me, Tim," his friend demurred. "Couldn't it be this way? Cliff has gone. His name is under a cloud. So is mine. Some people may even suspect you, because you have been so close to us. Now would be the time to rub us out. Without a leader left on the C C, they could raid our range and run off thousands of cattle; and in addition to that by destroying us pay all debts in full."

"Hmp!" snorted Murphy. "It might. None the less I'm of the same opinion still."

Eight of them took the road, not counting Dieter. They rode across the north pasture for five miles, then wound up into the hills. Most of the men moved in single file, not too close together. Dieter was flanked by Bucky and the foreman, except when the path was too narrow. Then one of them went in front of him, the other just behind.

"We're going all round Robin Hood's barn," complained the hillman. "We'd ought to cut up past Gillespie's."

"More scenery this way," Bucky told him briefly.

Dutch slid a suspicious look at him but dropped the subject.

In the darkness it was rough going. At times the brush was thick. The horses clambered through greasewood, flung aside scrub oak. Boulders filled the beds of dry streams as they plowed up gorges. Great hills loomed close. After the moon came out fantastic shadows leaped at them. In the silence of the night the immensity of space pressed upon them. Riders looked around uneasily, searching the vague outline of vegetation for signs of danger. It was possible that at any moment the blast of gunfire would shatter the stillness.

Possible, but not probable. Bucky took pains to mention that they were working into the Red Rock country by a flank movement. If the hillmen were looking for them, it would not be by this approach.

"What you mean, looking for you?" Dieter blustered.

Murphy explained, eyeing him coldly. "Some of them may be mind-readers and may know you're giving them away, Dutch."

"You've acted all along like I'm lying to you," the ranchman protested sulkily.

"We know you wouldn't do that, Dutch, not one with a heart of gold like yours," the foreman jeered. "Especially since you know we'd get excited right away if there was trouble and pour a pint of lead into you."

The man was shaken. His gray face twitched. "I wish I'd never come down to tell you what I know. I'm quitting you here. You can go on, or you can go back. I don't care which."

"You're staying with us," Bucky told him curtly.

"Looky here," the man whined, "I'm not looking for trouble. I came down to do you a service and you treat me like I'm a hydrophobia skunk."

"You've got a just complaint, if you're really trying to do us a service," Bucky admitted. "Put it in the bill, Dieter. One hundred dollars extra for hurting your feelings . . . All right, boys. The horses have quit blowing. We'll be on our way again."

They clambered up a gully-filled trail down which water had poured in torrents during the rainy season. It brought them to a hill ledge, along which the horses crept in the semi-darkness, their hoofs slithering on a downgrade in outcrops of quartz and disintegrated granite. To their right, so close that a bad slip might have plunged mount and rider into it, yawned the shadowy chasm of the gulch, so deep that the eye could not pierce the lake of blackness at the bottom. A great boulder field of immense rocks stretched over the mountain face above the trail. They were in the Red Rock country now.

Tim Murphy had gone forward to lead the party, and a young fellow named Curly Teeters was on guard behind the hillman.

Bitterly Dieter complained to him: "I'm not going to stand for it. This little squirt Cameron has got no right to hold me here. I'm a free man, and I don't have to let him drag me around."

"That's right," Curly agreed cheerfully. "You can jump into the gulch any time you've a mind to."

Bucky turned in his saddle. "No talking back there. We're getting close."

They dropped down to a stream, crossed it, followed the bank. Bucky gave instructions for his men to keep well apart. Just ahead of them was Dolores Cañon, a likely point of attack.

Dieter swung down from the saddle.

" 's matter, Dutch?" inquired Curly.

"Saddle's loose. Got to tighten the cinch. You go ahead, and I'll catch up."

Bucky rode back. "What's up?"

Curly was dismounting. "Going to help Dutch fix his saddle," he explained.

"I don't want no help," Dieter exploded. "You lemme alone. I ain't so crippled I can't tighten a cinch, you doggoned fool."

To the man ahead of him Bucky called a message: "Tell Tim to wait. We're held up a minute. I'm going to take the lead from here. Ask him to come back."

Dieter's horse had turned, so that it was facing in the direction from which they had come. He was standing back of it fumbling with something. Bucky had a sudden suspicion that it might not be the cinch.

He brushed past Curly's horse, which had begun to move up the creek after the others.

"Keep back, both of you," Dieter cried.

In the moonlight there was the flash of steel. A gun roared. The bullet whistled past Curly's shoulder. That young man stopped in his tracks, completely taken by surprise. Dieter fired again, just before Bucky crowded forward into him. The weight of the horse hurled the hillman against the trunk of a pine. He clung to it heavily, gun still in hand, jarred by the shock of the impact.

68

Bucky covered him. "Shove up your hands," he ordered.

The hillman jerked his revolver up, toward Bucky this time. He never had a chance to fire it. Two weapons barked, so close together in time that the sound of them merged into one. Dieter's body sagged, slid down the trunk of the tree. He turned as he fell, striking the ground face first.

Curly moved cautiously toward him. A thin trickle of smoke came from the barrel of his Colt. His face was drawn and startled.

"He shot first, Bucky. I had to do it," young Teeters said.

"I know," Bucky agreed. "My bullet is in his body too."

He got down from the saddle and examined the prone figure.

The other members of the party crowded round. They asked questions, offered opinions.

"Examine his gun," Bucky said quietly to the foreman.

Murphy did so. "Two shells empty — just fired," he reported.

"He tried to slip away," Bucky told the men. "Pretended his cinch was loose. When we came close he drew his gun and fired twice at Curly. Even then I gave him a chance to throw up his hands. But he wouldn't have it that way. Raised his revolver to fire at me.

Then we let him have it."

"Explanation satisfactory to me," Murphy said. "All right with you boys?"

The chorus of assent was unanimous.

"Why did he do such a crazy thing?" Bud Keller asked.

"He knew the Red Rock gang is waiting for us in Dolores Cañon, and he didn't want to be blasted down when they poured a volley into us," Bucky answered coolly. "His first idea was to light out. When we spiked that he had to shoot his way clear."

"They're waiting for us — right in there?" Keller said, fumbling his words in surprise. "Gosh all hemlock, how d'you know?"

"It doesn't make sense any other way. Why else would he be in such a hurry to get away? He had to escape now. A little later wouldn't do. So he tried to smoke a way for himself."

"My God, they almost trapped us," a young rider cried.

"Not quite that close, Jim," Bucky said. "Tim and I had our eyes open."

"We going in after these birds?" Teeters asked.

"No. But we're going to make sure they are waiting for us."

A rifle cracked, and a bullet whined over their heads.

"We know that already," the foreman said

grimly. "Get yore horses, boys, and find cover in the rocks. We're bunched too close."

Bucky gave sharp orders. "We're not looking for a fight. They'll do the crowding, if any is done. But if they attack, shoot to kill."

The riders scattered, each finding his own cover. Occasionally a rifle cracked. Once someone, two hundred yards away, lifted his voice in a yell of derision. But the Red Rock men came no closer.

Bucky passed the word for a slow withdrawal. The C C riders had to get out while the darkness still held, or run the chance of a pitched battle in the morning. This Cameron did not want. He knew a garbled story would be given out to the public, one in which all the blame would be laid on him. Since any lie circulated would be believed, he could not afford even a victory with casualties.

The C C men drew back, as quietly as possible, most of them leading their horses until they were out of range. They headed toward home by the most direct route. There was no longer any need for secrecy. Four or five miles below Dolores Cañon they turned up a small creek, following it until they came to an open meadow.

"We'll camp here," Bucky said.

There was not a chance in a thousand that their enemies would find them in the darkness

— not one in a hundred that the Red Rock men would be looking for them now the trap had failed — but Bucky set guards to protect the party in the event of a surprise. He and Teeters took the first turn.

The little mountain park, far up in the high hills, with countless pinpricks of light gleaming from the vault above, gave the young men a sense of their insignificance. They were tiny atoms in a vast universe of space. The silence of the night, its immensity, pressed upon them.

Curly shivered. "This wind is sure enough cold," he said.

"Nice if we could light a fire, but we'd better stick it out without one," Bucky said. "We don't want that wolf pack howling down on us."

The foreman and Bud Keller relieved them. Bucky rolled up in a blanket and fell asleep instantly. When he awoke the sun was coming up over a crotch in the hills.

"Come and get it," someone shouted.

To Bucky there came the odor of bacon and coffee mingled with the acrid smell of pitch pine. He washed in the creek and joined the others. All of them ate ravenously, appetites sharpened by long hours in the crisp rare air of eight thousand feet altitude.

They caught and saddled. Bucky and Tim

rode in the van as they moved down the creek toward the junction. The stream meandered round a pineclad hill, and the C C men followed its course.

Just before they reached the point where the brook emptied into the larger creek Murphy dragged his horse to a stop abruptly.

"Look who's here."

Six men were riding down the Dolores Cañon trail. Bucky recognized them as the leading spirits of the Red Rock outlaw tribe. Among the group were West and Quinn and Davis. Another was Big Bill Savage, an immense hairy man all brawn and bone. Beside him rode a twisted, wizen-faced old chap known as Tuffy Arnold. Usually Tuffy was credited with being the brains of the outfit, a sly slippery customer not to be trusted out of sight.

In another twenty-five yards the two parties would have come together.

Brad Davis ripped out a sudden oath and pulled up his mount. "Here are the dirty killers," he cried.

Bucky had not stopped his sorrel gelding. He rode to the edge of the creek separating the two parties.

Tim called back to his men in a low voice: "Don't jam too close. Kinda scatter along the bank."

"You came a long way to kill poor Dutch,

Cameron," West cried.

Bucky looked the Red Rock contingent over coolly. "Dieter asked for what he got, West. He tried to lead us into the trap you had set. When he saw he would have to go in too, he tried to shoot his way out. You ought to do better than that when you fix up an ambush. Tuffy must be getting old and rusty if that is his best."

"You're a damned liar," West snarled. "You murdered Dutch."

"He fired twice at Curly before we lifted a hand," Murphy cut in. "He was aiming at Bucky when two of the boys cracked down on him."

"Which two?" demanded Quinn.

"Never mind which two, Pete. It was self-defense."

"Charge it to me," drawled Bucky, stroking his little mustache.

"And me," Curly added. "I was in it."

"Grass will grow over yore grave for that, Curly," West told him.

Bucky watched closely Quinn and Davis. Tuffy Arnold would be for peace, at least until he was out of the danger zone. The giant, Big Bill, would take his cue from West, who despite his reputation as a dangerous gunman preferred the odds to be in his favor. The sixth man was a nonentity. It was Bucky's opinion that there would be no battle now unless Quinn or Davis started it in impulsive anger.

"You came up here lookin' for a fight, did you?" challenged Davis.

Cold-eyed, Bucky met his angry glare. "You know why we came — because you set a trap you expected us to walk into like fools. Don't tell your lies to us, you scoundrel. Keep them for Toltec. You brought us here to be murdered." He stopped for a moment, and moved the sorrel into the shallow water at the edge of the creek, as if he were afraid they could not all hear what he said unless he was near enough for his voice to drown the rippling of the water. When he spoke again it was in an even monotone that made the scabrous epithets with which he blasted them more telling. He searched his vocabulary for long-drawn blistering words, and not once did he repeat himself. His mouth hardly moved. The muscles of his face did not alter a line. Both hands rested on the horn of the saddle, but there was a catlike litheness in his body that might awake instantly to violent eruption.

They listened to him, held by some dominant force in him that compelled attention. They felt the urge of a spirit full of fire and passion but controlled by a masterful will. His audacity was amazing. It brought back memories of other Camerons, his father and his uncle, men who had walked with bleak faces into deadly peril.

"You can't talk that way to me," cried Davis, face black with rage. "I won't stand it from any man alive, let alone a little girl-faced dude like you."

"I am talking that way," corrected Bucky. "I'm telling you that you're a thief, a liar, a coward, and a murderer. The only reason you don't draw now is that you're afraid I'll kill you in your tracks."

Tuffy Arnold pushed forward his horse. He laid a restraining hand on Davis's knee. "Hard words don't break any bones, Cameron," he said, shaking his head reprovingly. "You've got us all wrong. I don't know what you've got in yore nut, but there's nothing to it. If Dutch was alive he would tell you so. And this talk about shooting folks in their tracks isn't going to do you any good. We've got past those days."

Davis brushed the old man's hand aside impatiently, but West's heavy voice bore his down when he started to talk.

"We're not looking for war, Cameron," West boomed. "And we're not ducking it either. All of us have got yore number. You're one of these bully-puss fellows who go around with a chip on their shoulder. Only reason your bluff hasn't been called is because he-men like to pick someone of their size."

"Come on, boys," Tuffy advised. "We're peaceable citizens going about our own business. No use getting upset over what this fellow says. This country has done made up its mind about him. He'll have to do some more fast talking to explain away this Dutch Dieter business."

He turned his horse and started down the trail. West followed, Big Bill at his heel. The other members of the party hesitated, but after a moment took the trail after them.

Tim Murphy looked at his dapper little chief oddly, reappraising him in his mind. He had thought he knew the young man pretty well. In the public mind Neil Cameron had been accepted until recently as a wild youngster born with a silver spoon in his mouth, one with a flair for clothes and for gay comradeship. He had a reputation as a gambler, and because of it had won even as a boy the nickname of Bucky. Tim could have told anyone who wanted to know that he was a chip off the old block, fearless, trustworthy, and sound at bottom. Now the foreman began to think the lad had the same capacity for leadership that had marked his father and uncle. His intrepid challenge to the Red Rock gang had been a stroke of genius. It had enhanced him tremendously with his own men and it had correspondingly diminished the bad men who had bullied the riders of the C C ranch.

"You sure read them their pedigrees, Bucky," Tim said with a laugh. "I don't reckon you left much unsaid. Didn't know you had such a flow of language. We'll have to elect you to Congress."

"Have to talk turkey to ruffians like them," Bucky answered carelessly. He swung his horse into the trail. "All aboard for the C C, boys."

Murphy rode beside him. "Those scoundrels killed Cliff," he said bluntly. "No doubt about it."

"Not proven," Bucky excepted. "But one thing is sure. He is not a prisoner in the hills. If he were, they wouldn't have invited us to this party. They wouldn't have dared make a play that they had him cached. That is one idea they wouldn't have promoted." He added, gloomily: "I'm about ready to give up, Tim. Uncle Cliff is dead. If he isn't hidden up here, where could he be?"

"I knew all the time he was dead," Murphy said harshly, to hide his feeling. "They took him up into the hills and killed him in some gulch that first night."

Bucky reserved an opinion. He still had Clem Garside in the back of his mind.

They reached the ranch house about the

middle of the morning. Julia came out to the porch to meet Bucky as he dismounted stiffly.

"Where have you been?" she cried, her eyes shadowed with worry.

"Up in the hills," he told her evasively.

"Mike Andrews has been calling on the wire for you or Tim. At last I made him tell me what he wanted. He says that Sheriff Haskell is getting together a posse to arrest you for killing a man." The girl looked at him piteously. "Is it true, Bucky? Has there been more trouble?"

Bucky nodded. "Yes. We had to kill a man — after he tried to shoot down Curly Teeters and me. There was no other way."

Already his mind was busy with the problem before him. Tuffy Arnold and his companions had lost no time in telephoning their side of the story to town. They were on their way to reinforce it by word of mouth, but they had not run any risk of not getting in with the first version. Haskell of course was a dummy and would do as he was told. Bucky wondered what position Garside would take.

"Where was it? How did it happen?" Julia asked.

"At the mouth of Dolores Cañon. A man named Dieter came to us last night with the story that he had seen men taking a prisoner into the hills the night of the bank robbery.

We had to find out if it was true. It was only a trap to lead us into an ambush."

"Are you sure?" she begged.

"Quite sure," he answered gently. "They were waiting for us at Dolores. This man Dieter gave it away. He tried to leave us and when we prevented him he began shooting."

"You didn't find out anything about Father?"

"No." Bucky looked at his cousin gravely, pity in his eyes. "He isn't a prisoner in the hills. If he had been, they wouldn't have told us he was there."

Tears filled the eyes of Julia. "I've known in my heart all the time that he is dead," she said.

Bucky did not attempt to deny that she was right.

"I'll have to go to town," he told her.

"What for?" she asked, in quick alarm.

"To face this charge. We don't want to wait till they come and get us. Better give ourselves up."

"They'll kill you too, as they did Father," she wailed.

He shook his head, smiling at her confidently. "I don't think so."

CHAPTER VI

Bucky stopped the car in front of the office of the *News*. "Like to see Henning a minute, Tim," he said. "You and Bud better come up with me. I wouldn't want someone to pick you off while you're sitting in the car."

"I don't reckon anybody wants us that bad," Bud Keller said, looking round uneasily. None the less he unlimbered his long legs and stepped to the sidewalk.

A sign informed them that the editorial offices were upstairs. Through a swing door Bucky pushed into the city room and asked the girl at the switchboard where the office of Mr. Henning was.

She brushed a lock of flaxen hair back into place and chewed gum indifferently. "Name, please."

"Tell him Bucky Cameron wants to see him."

She shot a slightly startled look at this mild youth with the little mustache. His appearance did not fit the stories she had been hearing about him. But she plugged in promptly, and a moment later a nasal voice was saying into the mouthpiece, "Mr. Bucky Cameron to see you, Mr. Henning."

The plug was pulled out. "Mr. Henning will see you. Room 17. Second to the left."

"Wait here, boys," Bucky said, and passed through the gate.

The telephone operator had no interest in the weather-beaten foreman or the lanky puncher. Her gaze followed the young man strolling toward the publisher's office. The eyes of women often turned his way.

Bucky walked into the office upon the glass door of which was lettered the legend, ED-WARD HENNING, PUBLISHER.

The editor was a rotund, highly colored little man with cold blue protuberant eyes. He had known Bucky since the young man was a youngster in grade school. But his greeting was coldly formal.

"You wish to see me, Mr. Cameron?" he said.

"I want to tell you the true story of what happened last night."

Henning buzzed a bell at the side of his desk. "I'll call a reporter."

"How about my telling it first to Ned Henning?" asked Bucky with his engaging smile.

"I'm a busy man, Mr. Cameron."

"Any busier than you were when you used to trot up to see Uncle Cliff about extending your account in the days when the First National saved you from going under?" Bucky inquired with gentle irony.

The publisher flushed angrily. "Young man, I thought you said you had brought a news story."

"I have," Bucky replied. "But that wasn't the only reason I came." His steady eyes rested on Henning, a touch of scorn in them. "I wanted to find out something."

"What is it?" snapped the editor.

"No le hace," the young man drawled, coolly disdainful. "I know the answer now."

A young man walked briskly into the room. "You sent for me, Mr. Henning?" he said.

"Get this story from Mr. Cameron," his chief ordered. "Bring it to me after it is written, Smith. You can take the story here."

Smith was a slender weary-eyed man. He shook hands with Bucky. "Glad to see you back, old-timer," he said. "Missed you in the poker games. But if you stick around here you want to carry a rabbit's foot and a big gun."

"Perhaps you'd better get the story, Smith, if you're quite ready," Henning suggested tartly.

Bucky told what had occurred from the time Dutch Dieter came to the C C until the return of the party.

"Wish you'd bumped off four-five more of

that gang, not mentioning any names," Smith said cynically, gathering his notes to depart. "But right now that's not the popular view. This town has been cussing those fellows for years. Now it has turned round and started cussing you. Boy, I wouldn't be here at all if I was you, but since you're here you had better have eyes in the back of your head."

Henning said curtly, "I'll wait here for the story, Smith."

Bucky walked out of the room with the reporter, not giving the editor another look.

"The old son-of-a-gun going to crash through for you?" Smith murmured out of the corner of his mouth.

"No. Haven't you read the editorial in your own paper? Not a word in defense of Uncle Cliff. A lot of crocodile tears about a good man gone wrong and heap much indignation because he betrayed his trust."

"Hell, I wrote a couple of them," Smith said. "Think of the old devil throwing down on your uncle after all Cliff Cameron did for him . . . Well, so long. Hope you'll be luckier than I think you will."

Henning stood in the doorway of his office. "Like to see you a moment, Smith."

Bucky explained, his sardonic gaze on the editor: "Mr Henning wants to be sure you do me justice, Bill."

"Get anywhere with him?" Tim asked Cameron as the young man rejoined his companions.

"No. He's gone over to Garside. And once he used to call me Neil and make talk about how I was a fine boy worthy of my father and my uncle, with his fat hand on my shoulder."

"Hmp! He's got it figured out the Camerons are through." Tim added, growling: "Never did like him, even when he wouldn't hardly buy him a new pair of pants without coming to ask Cliff about it."

They returned to the car and drove to the courthouse. As Bucky drew up Kathleen Garside passed in her sport coupe. She gave no sign of recognition.

The sheriff was not in his office. Bucky asked the young woman at the typewriter to tell Haskell he would be back again in an hour.

"I'll tell him if he comes in," she promised.

It was on the tip of her tongue to urge this cool and debonair young man to get out of the country as quickly as gasoline would take him. He looked too gentle to cope with the hard men opposed to him. To think of that warm smile and the gay friendliness of the long-lashed eyes wiped out forever filled her with sharp compunction. Miss Webb was a part of the political machine and knew a good deal of what was going on secretly. It was her opinion, now that the Camerons had made themselves vulnerable, that they would be destroyed by their enemies.

"I think the sheriff is looking for you," she added, and hoped he would understand it as a warning.

"I've heard so. Tell him to wait here for me."

Miss Webb's gaze followed his light-footed retreat until he vanished in the corridor. She was angular, had a muddy complexion, and wore thick-lensed glasses. Never in her life had she had a beau. But in two minutes Bucky had set her heart aflutter. There was something in him that stirred the dormant romantic impulse in her.

They left the car in front of the courthouse and walked to the office of a law firm that bore the name "Lewis & Lewis" on the door.

A middle-aged man with a well-shaped bald head was giving some directions to a stenographer. He looked up, saw Bucky, and came forward with outstretched hand.

"Heard you were in town," he said. "I've been wondering when you would come around, boy."

"Mostly so far I've been calling on my enemies," Bucky told him with a grin. "Just getting round to my friends."

"I heard about a call you made on some enemies last night," the lawyer said. "Come in and tell me about it, Bucky."

Cameron and the foreman followed Lewis into the inner office. Keller stayed in the reception room.

At their entrance a young woman looked up.

Blandly Bucky asked, "Am I disturbing a conference, Miss Garside?"

Kathleen's scornful gaze rested on him. "I thought you would be in jail by this time."

"Not yet. I'm on my way."

"It's all over town that a band of ruffians went up into the Red Rock country, attacked some ranchers, and killed one of them."

"That the story your friend West brought to Toltec?" he drawled.

"I told you once I have no such friend," she answered, her eyes bright and hard.

"My error," Bucky said.

"That wasn't the way of it, Miss Garside," blurted Murphy. "We went into the Red Rock country because a scoundrel came to us with a story that Cliff Cameron had been seen there. It was a trap to wipe us out. We got wise to it in time and then this fellow Dieter went to shooting. In self-defense we had to kill him."

"Very interesting, I'm sure." Kathleen rose from her chair. "I'll be going, Judge. I expect

87

your clients are very anxious to have a private talk with you."

"The criminals conferred with their attorney before being locked up," Bucky said blithely, quoting from an imaginary newspaper. "A lovely young woman was present to cheer them in their hour of need."

Kathleen looked at him with hot anger. Small white teeth, strong and even, gleamed between red lips.

"I'll do my cheering when you're convicted," she said.

"Come, come, young people," the lawyer protested, smiling at them. "A lawyer's office is no place to bring a quarrel."

Ignoring this, the girl said, "Then I'll expect you to do the best you can about that business, Judge," and walked out of the room, chin in air.

Lewis smiled ruefully. "Wasn't it Mahomet who said we must accept women as they are with all their curvatures?"

"I suppose your way of accepting them is by remaining a bachelor," Bucky said dryly.

"I was a hot and turbulent young man, and I had my dreams like others," the lawyer said placidly. "I had too much temper for my own good — too much silly pride — until it was too late. When I learned better it no longer mattered. Well, well, time cures all ills, one way or another . . . What can I do for you?"

Murphy said bluntly: "Nothing much. All we ask of you is to see we're not sent to the penitentiary or hanged."

"Perhaps you had better tell me first the story of your trouble up in the Red Rocks," Lewis suggested.

They gave him an account of their expedition. He asked questions, gave, rather doubtfully, an opinion.

"We ought to be able to clear you of any legal difficulty in connection with that. I presume your men will all testify they were attacked, and that you can get evidence showing Dieter fired at you twice and was about to fire again."

"Four of our men can swear to the last point, all of us to the first," the foreman said.

"Good. Of course I know you weren't in any way to blame. The point is to get others to see this. The bank robbery is the great stumbling block. If we could clear that up, so as to remove prejudice from the minds of people . . . I think Cliff was killed and his body hidden somewhere in a shallow grave. If we could prove he is dead, that he didn't rob the bank, and that you didn't help him, the rest would be plain sailing."

"We haven't a thing to start from," Murphy said despondently.

"I don't agree with you," Lewis differed. "To begin with, we feel absolutely sure Cliff could not have committed such a crime. It was not in his character. Moreover, if he had been doing it, a cool old-timer like Cliff would never have written all over the place that he had done it."

"Fine," agreed Murphy. "We all know that, but it isn't evidence you can take into court. I'm looking for facts to set my teeth in. The only way to clear Cliff's name is to find the guys who did it and pin their ears back."

"I've read that there never has been a perfect crime," Bucky said. "The men who did this have left plenty of clews if we have brains enough to pick them up. It's like cutting a trail in the hills. Tim here can read sign a tenderfoot would never know existed, but compared to a dog or a wolf he is a rank amateur. If we're not too dumb we can run down the real criminals."

"We saw them this morning up in the Red Rock country," Murphy replied grimly. "I'm not too dumb to know that. Say the word and I'll join you in blasting them off the map."

"Would that prove them guilty, Tim?" asked Lewis, with a dry smile.

"No, that's out," Bucky said. "I'm not running a private war. I came back to see justice done. This is a matter for brains and not blazing guns. It is just as if we had before us a sheet of blank paper with the whole story of the crime written on it in invisible ink. Stamped all over this job are the tracks of the scoundrels who did it. Only trouble is that our eyes and our brains aren't trained fine enough to see them."

"Hmp!" grunted the foreman. "What you aim to do about it, Bucky? Get you some high-powered glasses and order a new set of brains?"

"Do the best with what I've got," Bucky shrugged. "One sure thing is that I can't do much if I'm tied up in a cell at Sheriff Haskell's hotel."

"I doubt if I can get you out, at least for the present," Lewis said. "Maybe in a week or two, when the excitement has died down."

"All the boys who were with us last night can come in to tell their story," suggested Bucky. "Only reason I didn't bring them all along was that I was afraid the town would think so many of us was a threat."

"Well, we'll see what we can do," Lewis said, rising from his chair. "Might as well be moving to the courthouse."

The four men walked down the street toward the office of the sheriff. On the steps of the Valley Bank, just coming out, was the man who had come to Toltec on the same train as Bucky. They had sat opposite each other in the diner.

Bucky spoke to the stranger. "How is it going, Mr. Mitchell?" he asked. "Does Toltec look good to you as a location for your store?"

The expression in the eyes Van Dyke Mitchell turned toward Bucky startled him. In them dark fury raged. For a fraction of a second only. Then a mask dropped over the face, wiped out the boiling hatred, and left the countenance as smooth and placid as a mountain lake beneath a summer sun.

"Oh, it's you, Mr. Cameron," Mitchell said, after a moment during which he had plainly struggled to get his voice under control. "I don't know yet. With my limited capital such an investment is a serious move for me, so I want to take my time in deciding. I like the town. I'll say that."

Bucky introduced Mitchell, with an explanatory word, to his friends.

"I've been having a talk with Mr. Garside," explained the stranger. "Naturally he is interested in building up Toltec and takes an optimistic view of the opportunities here. He feels there is room for a first-class specialty men's clothing store in the city."

"You can't go wrong if you take Clem Garside's advice," Murphy said with heavy sarcasm. "It will be absolutely disinterested."

"He seems a broad-gauge man," Mitchell replied, answering the letter of the foreman's words. Hesitantly he added, "I hope this Red Rock matter people are talking about this morning is an exaggeration, Mr. Cameron — that it won't turn out — dangerous."

Garside had come out of the bank and was standing on the top step. He took in the group with one swift glance, looked at Mitchell, looked longer at Bucky.

"I hear you've been raising hell again," he said bluntly.

Bucky answered Mitchell with Hotspur's impatient words. His eyes were on the blond haberdasher, but the challenge was for the banker:

" 'Tis dangerous to take a cold, to sleep, to drink; — but I tell you, my lord fool, out of this nettle, danger, we pluck this flower, safety.' "

"By God, you'd better pluck it soon," Garside advised with brutal brusqueness, his cold protuberant gaze on Bucky.

"Didn't I tell you he was loaded to the hocks with the milk of human kindness?" Murphy murmured.

"If you're thinking of starting a store in Toltec and want it to be popular, Mr. Mitchell, you'd as well be careful of your associates," Garside warned.

Mitchell lifted his eyes to the white-haired banker. "I'll remember that," he said thickly.

The C C men and their lawyer walked on.

"What's the matter with that fellow Mitchell?" the foreman asked. "He looked at you like he wanted to see you dead, Bucky. He was crazy with hate."

"Something funny about that," Bucky said thoughtfully. "He was looking through me, not at me. That look didn't come into his eyes when he saw me. It was already there. I've got another guess about who he was hating."

"Meaning?"

"Did you notice him when he told Garside he'd remember his advice?"

Murphy said he had not.

"The blazing hate was there again. He'd just come out from talking with Garside when we met him. He was still thinking about the man he had just left."

The lawyer glanced at Bucky. "Garside and this man are practically strangers. Isn't your imagination running away with you, young fellow?"

"I expect so," Bucky admitted. "Doesn't look reasonable, does it? Maybe Mitchell's lunch didn't agree with him and he's sour at the world."

None the less Bucky did not for an instant believe his own explanation. Absurd though it might seem, he could not help feeling that Mitchell and Garside had come into conflict and the former had been bested. The banker was an expert at draining his countenance of meaning when he wanted it to be blank, but unless Bucky was mistaken there had been a flicker of derisive triumph in the fixed stare he had turned on the other man. It occurred to Cameron it might be a good idea to have a talk with Mitchell. If the stranger was at odds with Garside it would be worth while finding out why.

The deft fingers of Miss Webb were still busy with a typewriter when Lewis and his clients walked into the office.

"The sheriff back yet?" asked the lawyer.

She glanced at the closed door of the inner room. "He's in conference." Through her thick-lensed glasses she looked at Bucky. "I'll tell him you're here."

The sound of an irritable voice raised querulously reached Bucky. He had a hunch.

"We'll introduce ourselves," he said, and walked toward the private room.

Miss Webb rose to prevent him, but not in time. Bucky whipped open the door. Three heads were in a huddle at the desk.

The sheriff was saying: "Be reasonable, Dan. No use hunting trouble. I'm with you all the way about this fellow. You know that.

But if they're coming here to surrender that suits me fine."

"Scared to go out and arrest him?"

"What's the sense of making a grandstand play and maybe getting two-three men killed when —"

Haskell stopped, aware that somebody had come into the room.

"Urging the sheriff to do his duty, West?" Bucky drawled.

A pair of dead slate-colored eyes met those of the young man. The thin-lipped gash of a mouth in West's large dish face set in an ugly crooked line. "Someone invite you into this private talk?" he asked sourly.

"When I told you this morning what a low-down, contemptible, murdering scoundrel you are I didn't expect to get a chance to tell it to you again so soon," Bucky said evenly, and to make the record complete added some blistering epithets not intended to placate the big man from the hills.

Richman rose with his conciliatory smile. "Now — now, Bucky, I wouldn't talk that way. There's been enough trouble, heaven knows. Why can't everybody show a more friendly spirit? If you would forget and forgive —"

"I'll forget and forgive West the day he is buried," Cameron cut in curtly.

Haskell lifted a fat hand. "None of that talk,

Bucky. It doesn't buy you a thing. I understand you and your boys are here to surrender. That will be fine."

Lewis phrased differently the purpose of their visit. "We have heard you want to see my clients and have come to find out why."

"You know damn well why," West cut in harshly. "For murdering Dutch Dieter."

The sheriff, annoyed, remonstrated. "Will you let me manage my own business, Dan? I can talk. I'm not dumb."

"Better go slow, Haskell," the lawyer advised. "I'll mention facts we can prove by many witnesses. Dieter came down to the C C last night with a story that during the night of July seventeenth he saw four riders pass his place. Three of them were armed. The fourth was bound. He thought the prisoner was Cliff Cameron. My clients didn't wholly believe the story, but they realized it might be true. They had to find out. A bunch of C C men rode up to the Red Rock country, Dieter along with them. At the entrance to Dolores Cañon Dieter tried to slip away. My clients insisted he stay to prove good faith. He drew a gun and fired twice. Even then Bucky gave him a chance to throw up his hands. He tried to shoot again. In self-defense he had to be killed. The C C boys were attacked from the cañon mouth. They drew back under fire. Nothing can be

97

surer than that this was a deliberate attempt to ambush them."

"That's their story, is it?" sneered West. "If you ask me I'll say it's too thin a one to get by."

"We're not asking you," Murphy retorted. "No decent citizen cares what you think."

"My clients intend to swear out warrants for the arrest of six men charged with assault with deadly weapons." Lewis went on evenly, as if he had not been interrupted. "The names of the men are Daniel West, William Savage, Peter Quinn, Bradley Davis, and two known as Tuffy Arnold and Nevada Jim."

"They can't prove it," West cried, slamming his fist on the table.

Lewis said quietly, "We're not trying the case here."

The sheriff threw out his fat hands in a gesture disclaiming responsibility. "I'm an officer of the law, Judge. Nothing for me to do but serve the papers arresting your clients."

"Can you guarantee their safety after you have taken them into custody?" the lawyer asked.

"What you mean, Judge? This is a law-abiding town." Haskell registered injured surprise.

"Yes, but certain enemies of my clients have been going about stirring up the worst elements. Are you prepared for any trouble that may arise, Sheriff?"

"There's not going to be any trouble," Haskell said. "If there should be, I'll take care of it."

"I should make very sure of that," Lewis advised, steady gaze fixed on the politician. "If you failed to meet the situation it would ruin you."

The sheriff brushed that aside resentfully. "What about the other C C men I want — Curly Teeters especially?" he asked.

"Give me a list and I'll see they come in to you."

West rose. His ugly mouth set to a sneer. "Always slick as a greased pig, Judge," he snarled, and went straddling out of the office. To Miss Webb he said, loud enough for the others to hear, "Betcha five bucks against a 'dobe dollar the shyster has them out of stir before night."

Miss Webb made no comment.

CHAPTER VII

The sheriff and Bucky walked up Front Street, the other two prisoners just behind them. There was nothing to show that the men from the C C ranch were under arrest. Haskell conversed amiably with Cameron. He had the politician's instinct for avoiding enmities. As yet he had not examined the men to see if they were armed. It would be time enough to do that when they reached the jail.

A good deal of attention was focused on the party. News of the Red Rock trouble had spread and Toltec was excitedly waiting developments. West and his crowd were in town. There might at any moment be another clash.

Someone shouted a greeting to Bucky and walked across the street to him. The man was a rancher, big, bronzed, middle-aged.

"Want to tell you, boy, that we're with you against these scoundrels till the cows come home," he said, shaking hands with all three prisoners.

"Good news, Mr. Munson," Bucky answered cheerfully. "I counted on you."

"I saw Lewis five minutes ago, and I'm out

now hustling bond among your friends."

"Thanks a lot. We wouldn't want to out-wear our welcome at Sheriff Haskell's hotel."

"You'll be hearing from us soon," Munson told the C C men, and waved a hand by way of temporary farewell.

At the Crystal Palace they turned down a side street. Back of the saloon was a new business block not yet tenanted.

"Toltec is growing right fast," the sheriff mentioned. "We're coming out of the depression fine. I notice —"

Bucky felt a blow against his shoulder. At the same instant the blast of a gun sounded. The echoes of the shot reverberated between the two brick walls of the buildings.

Swiftly Bucky moved forward, gun already in hand. He heard the thud of running feet. Someone was in a hurry to get away. The footsteps stopped for a moment, were followed by the clip-clop of a horse's hoofs. When Bucky reached the back of the unoccupied stores, horse and man had vanished round the next corner.

Cameron pulled up. A man cannot outrun a bronco, especially a man who has just received a slug in the shoulder. Tim Murphy joined him.

"See who he was?" the foreman asked.

"No. He had a horse tied to that two by four."

"Knew we were coming this way."

"Or guessed it. I don't think Haskell was in this. Wouldn't be like him."

"Someone must have seen him make his getaway."

"Maybe. But he's gone now. Inquiries can wait. You have a casualty on your hands."

Murphy's head slewed round. His eyes jabbed into those of his friend. "You hit?"

"In the shoulder — or the lung. Not sure which."

Bud Keller, his usual grin wiped out, cried, "The damned killer!"

Cautiously Haskell peered round the edge of the building into the alley. He did not want to stop any bullets.

"I heard the scoundrel lighting out," he said. "Find out who he was?"

"Where's the nearest doctor's office?" Murphy flung at him.

"A block away. Doctor Raymond. Someone hurt?"

The foreman put an arm around the shoulders of Bucky. "Can you walk?" he asked.

Bucky grinned. "Outran you to the alley, didn't I? I'll make it under my own motor power."

"I'm sorry for this, boys," the sheriff said nervously, his gaze shifting to and fro to make sure no other sharpshooter was within range.

They were moving back toward the street.

"You'd better be," Murphy told him bitterly. "Likely you mentioned to some of yore friends we'd be coming along this street."

Haskell looked at him, aghast. "You don't believe that, do you?" he said.

"No, he doesn't," Bucky answered.

"Lemme help you," Haskell proposed. "My God, I wouldn't have had this happen for anything."

Bucky declined his offer of assistance. "Keep your eyes peeled, boys," he said. "Not likely there are any more of them sticking around, but you never can tell."

The wound was bleeding. Bucky felt the moisture spreading over his chest. He could see the shirt was soggy. Murphy suffered more than he did, for as yet pain had been deadened by the shock. The foreman knew that a bullet through the lung might prove fatal.

Doctor Raymond was in his office. He cut away the shirt, examined the wound, and dressed it.

"How bad?" Bucky asked.

"The bullet tore into the muscles. It missed the lung. I'm sending you to the hospital, young man." The doctor was a young man, well trained, efficient, and sure of himself.

"Have to take that up with Sheriff Haskell," Bucky said.

Haskell agreed at once, almost eagerly. "Sure. Just as you say, Doctor. This is a bad business."

"I'm going with him," Murphy mentioned, grim eyes on the sheriff.

"Fine. That's all right." Haskell tried to brush with his hand a worried look from his face. "I'll go with you. I'm going to see he's protected. Haven't ever had anything like this happen before. If I knew who had done it I'd have him under lock and key before night."

"We'll go in my car," Doctor Raymond decided. "Better than waiting for an ambulance. We can all ride in it."

The sheriff sat beside Raymond in the front seat, the C C men in the rear.

"Get a two-bed room," Murphy told the doctor. "I'm sick enough to spend a few days in the hospital myself. No objections, Haskell?"

He reckoned not, the officer said, if Murphy would promise to give himself up whenever wanted.

"Okay," the foreman agreed, "but you're not to want me until Bucky is safe out of the hospital."

A nurse in training took possession of Bucky and prepared him for bed. Presently he was wheeled into the operating room and Doctor Raymond probed for the bullet and dressed the wound.

"I want you to have a special," the physician said. "It's a matter of nursing mostly from now on."

"Now look here, doctor," Bucky remonstrated. "Just because I have a little pill in my shoulder — or had before you took it out — is no reason for having a nurse spend all her time with me. Tim here will look after me fine."

Raymond paid no attention to the protest. "Do you know whether Miss Graham is working, Sister?" he inquired of the nun in attendance.

"I don't think so," Sister Mary told him. "She went off a case yesterday."

"Get her if you can."

Miss Nancy Graham arrived an hour later. She was a long-limbed young sylph, light and swift, and the fluent grace of the slender body in motion was like music. At sight of her Tim Murphy went into a small panic. She was only a kid. What did the doctor mean by sending a girl so devastatingly pretty on a job like this? How could he be expected to lounge on the bed in comfortable ease with this soft-eyed youngster in the room?

Nancy Graham found nothing disturbing in the situation. She went about her business without any self-consciousness. Neil Cameron was her patient and she was his nurse. He needed skillful impersonal care, and that was what she gave him. Since she did not know what the big cattleman was doing here she took an early occasion to find out from Sister Mary. To learn that Tim Murphy was here on guard to prevent his friend from being murdered lent excitement to what had become an old story. Nancy had been a graduate nurse for two years, but she had not ever before taken care of a handsome young man, just shot down by his enemies, who was for the moment the most talked-of and romantic figure in the city.

Tim did not know that back of her cool poised aloofness the girl was chuckling at his embarrassment. It was late in the afternoon when she asked him abruptly whether he too had been wounded or was he suffering from shell shock. She slanted her inquiry saucily with a piquant laughing scrutiny under her long lashes.

That the little baggage was making fun of him Tim understood.

He explained laboriously that he was not sticking around because of ill health but from a sense of duty.

Out of a long silence the patient murmured an explanation.

"Tim's afraid of girls, Miss Graham. He's one of these misogynists. Thinks the Lord made a mistake when he operated on Adam's rib."

The foreman blushed. He did not know what a misogynist is, but he suspected it was something improper.

"You got no call to give me names like that, Bucky," he objected. "It probably ain't so, Miss Graham."

"I hope it isn't," she said demurely. And to Bucky, severely, "You're not to talk."

He smiled. "Can I look?"

Nancy offered him a drink, lifting the pillow under his head a trifle so that he could use the glass tube with less effort. "Now you'd better try to go to sleep," she reproved gently.

"You're the boss," he said.

Bucky dozed. Tim fidgeted. This was sure a hell of a way to spend an afternoon. He ought to be out at the C C. Maybe he had better call up on the phone and give orders to shift that bunch of yearlings to the south pasture.

"Why don't you sit by the window and smoke?" the nurse suggested, speaking in a low voice in order not to disturb the sick man.

"Can I smoke?" he asked eagerly.

"Why not? If you do maybe it will make you forget how sore you are because I'm here."

"How do you know — ?"

He stopped abruptly, to amend his sentence.

107

"What I hate is being here myself. This is no place for a healthy man. Course I'm not kicking. Long as Bucky needs me why —"

"But you think he doesn't need me," she flashed.

"Looky here, Miss. I never said any such thing. Does seem they're kinda robbing the cradle for nurses, but —"

"I'm twenty-four," she interrupted with dignity.

"I wouldn't have took you for more than nineteen, but seeing I've been drug in to the subject I'd say it was more proper to have a — a mature person on cases like this."

"Meaning that I don't know my business?" she asked.

"Meaning that a young lady like you ought to be protected —"

"It's nice to have met you," she cut in. "I didn't know there was anybody left like that." Nancy sat erect, her eyes bright. It was in her mind to pour out on him a few remarks about what nurses had to know concerning the seamy side of life. But she thought better of it. Why disillusion this six-foot infant? "Protected, my eye! Lovely for us nurses, but a screwy way to treat poor patients."

Tim did not know how to explain without offense what he meant. If he had been younger, this was the sort of girl to dream about.

Her fine-textured skin, soft as satin, was colorless as milk, except for a touch of rose bloom in the cheeks. Perhaps the color had been bought in a drugstore, and a lipstick might have added vividness to the mouth. None the less he read into her tempered beauty a pristine innocence. She did not waste a motion. Instinctively she seemed to know exactly what to do for Bucky to make him comfortable. The touch of her firm fingers looked soothing. No doubt she was a good nurse. The point was that so fragrant a young thing, quivering with life (he could guess that in spite of her poised coolness), had no business here at all, according to the old-fashioned viewpoint of Tim Murphy.

"The trouble is you're thinking of me as a girl," explained Miss Graham. "I'm not, while on duty. I'm a nurse. And my patient is just a case, regardless of sex, age, or pulchritude. Off duty, I'm a girl again. I have fun with the other nurses, and various young men who drive me up into the hills or take me to movies. I have been known to neck, but I can take very good care of myself, thank you."

Whereupon she departed for the nurses' rest room to refresh herself with a surreptitious smoke.

Tim sat by the window and lit another cigarette. He looked out upon a scene of sunny somnolence. The house opposite was untenanted. Two women gossiped over a back-yard fence while they watered their gardens. Occasionally the high voices of children at play lifted to him. Cars rolled down the quiet street. Behind the hills the sun was setting in brilliant splashes of color. Maybe it was foolish for him to stay here as a guard for Bucky. After all, the Red Rock outfit was not composed of city gangsters. They would not put the blast on a man in a hospital, but would wait until he got out.

The nurse was not away more than a few minutes.

"If you're gonna be here for a while I'll run out and get me some supper," Tim said. "I don't want Bucky left alone. You understand that?"

Nancy nodded. "You don't think anyone would attack him here, do you?"

"Not if you're with him."

"I won't leave the room."

It was surprising what confidence Tim gathered from the promise of this slim girl with the boyish figure. He had a feeling that when an emergency rose the flag of courage would be flying in the blue eyes.

"I'll not be long," he said.

"Take your time. There's no hurry." She

added, by way of information: "Of course you can have dinner in the room. Hospitals do serve food to the patients."

"I'm not rightly a patient," he explained. "Anyhow, I want to take a stroll through the town and find out what's doing."

"Shall I get a mature nurse for you, so as to have her ready when they bring you back?" she asked.

"I don't aim to be brought back," he said, grinning at her demure impudence. "I'm a tough old-timer, and I don't throw down on myself."

"You'll find Mr. Cameron's night nurse here when you get back. She's more mature than I am. I think you'll approve of her."

"Now — now!" he protested. "Don't you run on me because I'm old and feeble."

Tim fell in with Munson and another cattleman at the Toltec House and stayed with them as long as he was downtown. He thought it was improbable that he would be attacked while he was in their company. West and his allies did not want to array against themselves all the stockmen of the neighborhood.

It seemed to Tim that the sentiment of the town, as he found it expressed at the Pioneers' Club, was more friendly to the Camerons than he had known it to be of late. Perhaps the conversation of those at the Pioneers' was not a fair cross-cut section of Toltec's view. Many of the members were old-timers who had known well Cliff Cameron and his brother. Some of the younger ones were friends of Bucky, and even those who were not satisfied of their innocence in the bank robbery did not believe in assassination.

But even so it was comforting not to feel himself pushing against a cold wall of hostility as he had done in the days immediately following the holdup of the bank. There had been a shift in public opinion. Into the minds of many citizens had crept doubts. They felt that back of this tragedy was some unexplained mystery. After the first cry of rage at the murder and robbery had spent itself men remembered how Cliff Cameron had always stood in the life of the town like a Gibraltar rock of integrity. If there was anything in character it was not possible for him to have done this thing. The return of Bucky had lent weight to the feeling. His enemies had not helped their cause by trying to kill him from ambush.

"We've got to serve notice on these Red Rock rustlers to lay off Bucky," a wrinkled little old cattleman cried, slamming a fist down on the arm of his chair. "I've known his folks ever since I came into this country forty-five years ago, and there never was one of them that wouldn't do to ride the river with."

Garside had walked into the room. He agreed and disagreed. "You all know my opinion of the Camerons," he said. "I won't walk a foot of the road with any one of them. But I stand for law. I'm against bushwhacking. Maybe young Cameron brought it on himself by raiding the Red Rock country last night. I'm reserving an opinion on that. But whatever he has done the law can settle with him. We're past the days when Judge Colt had to settle arguments."

"Then you'd better call off yore friends from the hills, Clem," Murphy told him bluntly.

The hard eyes of Garside rested on the foreman. "Some day you'll go too far, Tim," he said.

"Mention it to me when I do," the foreman of the C C retorted, meeting his gaze with insolent scorn.

"Come, come, gentlemen," Munson interfered. "You can't help this business by any such talk. Clem is right. The law will take care of this. But Dad Crittenden is just as right. We've got to stamp out that nest of wolves in the hills. They don't belong to this day and age."

"How you going to do it — hit 'em over the head with a law book?" Tim asked cynically.

113

Others were drawn into the discussion. Meanwhile Garside, having found the man he had come to meet, took him upstairs to the library for a private talk.

Mitchell drifted into the club. He had been given a guest card by the secretary of the Chamber of Commerce. To the foreman of the C C ranch he expressed regret at the attack on Cameron.

"A dastardly outrage," he said, with feeling. "I like that young man. If the truth ever comes out I feel he will be cleared of the charges made against him."

"You can bet yore last dollar on that," Murphy responded promptly.

They had moved a little way from the group with whom Tim had been sitting. The cattleman suggested that they sit down and have a drink.

Mitchell smiled pleasantly. "I've had my drink quota for the day, Mr. Murphy, but I'll substitute a cigar if you don't mind."

They chatted casually. Tim found him an affable young man, eager to build up friendly contacts in the little city where he was thinking of establishing himself. His manner was frank. He was not at all cocksure. In fact he deferred a little to the views of Murphy, perhaps because the latter was an older man, perhaps because he had lived a long time in the neighborhood and had opinions worth hearing.

Tim was moved to give him a word of advice. "Don't put too much stock in what I say about Garside. Check it up with others. But if you're doing business with him don't trust the fellow any farther than you can fling a bull by the tail. Have everything down in black and white, and drawn up by a good lawyer. If you don't, he'll skin the eyeteeth out of you."

Guardedly, Mitchell admitted that Mr. Garside struck him as a business man not likely to let sentiment interfere with his interests.

"Keep that in mind while you're dealing with him and it may save you money," Murphy warned. "Well, I've got to be getting back to the hospital."

He picked up his Stetson and rose.

"Tell Mr. Cameron, if you please, that I'm among the many who will be hoping for a quick recovery," Mitchell said.

"Wish you'd drop in and see him after he gets better," the foreman answered. "He'll be lonesome after he picks up a bit."

"I'd like to, if you think I wouldn't be intruding."

"I'm sure you wouldn't. I'll let you know when he can see visitors."

Despite Tim's protests Munson and another cowman walked back as far as the hospital door with him.

"You've been noticed around town to-night," Munson explained. "Maybe some low-down scoundrel is laying in wait for you."

Tim found the night nurse, a stubby, round-faced woman of thirty-five, sponging the face of her patient. Her name, it appeared, was Tingley.

"How's everything?" Bucky asked.

"Folks are a lot more friendly. I was at the Pioneers' Club. Everybody was for you."

Bucky smiled whimsically. "I judge Mr. Garside was not among those present."

"He came in while I was there," Tim said. "No, I wouldn't say he was exactly one hundred per cent with you. But he deplores law-lessness. He said so. By the way, Mitchell was at the Club. The stranger who came in with you on the train, you know. Sent his best wishes to you. I had quite a talk with him. Sensible young fellow. I like him."

"I think I wouldn't talk any more," Miss Tingley suggested.

Nancy Graham came out of the bathroom, where she had been repairing her makeup pre-paratory to departure.

Tim had an attack of conscience. "Have I kept you here?" he asked. "You didn't wait for me to get back?" He had followed her out into the hall.

"Didn't I tell you I wouldn't leave the room

till you came back?" she asked.

"I certainly owe you an apology. It must be close to nine."

"Nine-fifteen," she corrected. "But don't be disturbed about it. I told you not to hurry — and you didn't." A smile flickered in her eyes and took the sting out of the reproach.

"I'm sure sorry. If you'll let me I'll take you to the best restaurant in town right now."

She shook her head. "Nice of you, but dinner's waiting for me at home. My car is outside, and I'll be there in five minutes."

With which she turned and walked down the hall toward the elevator. He noticed with what perfect rhythm her slender body moved.

CHAPTER VIII

Bucky was up for the first time and seated in an armchair by the window. Miss Graham had clothed him in slippers, trousers, and dressing-gown. The trip across to the window, even when supported by her arm, had been a wobbly one, but he felt well repaid for the effort. Never before had the world looked so beautiful to him. He had stared at blank walls for a week. The sight of a rose hedge, of the green foliage of trees washed clean by a recent rain, filled him with delight. He was surprised at the keenness with which they stabbed his emotions.

He said something of the sort to the nurse, who was arranging a footstool and wrapping a blanket around his legs to keep him from catching cold.

Nancy looked up and nodded. "I get you. Our eyes are so used to beauty that we don't see it. You remember Stevenson's 'A Poet's Prayer'?"

She read in Bucky's eyes a quick surprise and blushed, afraid he would think she was showing off.

"Do I?" he said. "I can tell better when you've repeated it."

The girl hesitated, a little annoyed at herself. She considered herself a modern young woman who knew her way around, and she was not given to showing sentiment. Though she wished she had not mentioned the verses, she did not want to make too much a point of not quoting them.

"I'm not sure I know just how it goes," she demurred.

"Have a try at it," he suggested.

She frowned, as if attempting to find a starting place, then began, her voice low and melodious.

"If I have faltered more or less
In my great task of happiness;
If I have moved among my race
And shown no glorious morning face;
If beams from happy human eyes
Have moved me not; if morning skies —"

Nancy broke off. "For Pete's sake, I'd forgotten it was a Scotch sermon — and so long."

Bucky clapped his hands. "Go on! Go on!"

She lifted her shoulders in a little shrug. "He asks for more," she murmured, and went on:

"— if morning skies,
Books, and my food, and summer rain
Knocked at my sullen heart in vain —
Lord, Thy most pointed pleasure take,
And stab my spirit broad awake;
Or, Lord, if too obdurate I,
Choose Thou, before that spirit die,
A piercing pain, a killing sin,
And to my dead heart run them in!"

Bucky knew a lot more about the 1935 model in girls than Tim Murphy did, and during the past few days he had done some exploring into the mind of this particular example. Nancy had never volunteered any

119

information of a personal nature, but under the stimulus of questions she had given him a general idea of her father, mother, brothers, and sisters. The Grahams were, he guessed, a closely knit family of middle-class Americans. Before taking up the training course Nancy had been through high school. She was bright as a newly minted dollar. Gay laughter bubbled frequently in her face, took such complete possession of it that the blue eyes almost vanished in mirth. But this was a new side of her. He had not suspected any love of poetry. That it plagued her to have been caught in sentiment he was sure.

"I thought Stevenson was dated — didn't know you young people read him," he said.

"Only graybeards like you," she retorted. "But I don't read him. This stuck in my mind when I saw it years ago."

There came a knock on the door. Bucky slid a hand under the dressing-gown. Under persuasion Murphy had long ago decided his friend was safe in the hospital and had returned to the ranch, but he had stressed the need of being careful.

Nancy walked to the door and admitted Van Dyke Mitchell. He came in, a little hesitantly.

"Mr. Murphy asked me to come and see you, but perhaps you're not ready for visitors," he said.

"You're more than welcome, Mr. Mitchell," Bucky answered, offering his hand. "I'm celebrating my first day up."

It was Nancy's custom to walk out of the room when her patients received callers, but she left Bucky with them only when they were from the C C ranch or when he gave her a nod of reassurance. Now Bucky did not give her the signal. Mitchell was as safe as Sister Mary, but it occurred to the invalid that it would do no harm to find out what impression the nurse got from the talk. Her keen young brain might pick up something he had missed. Very likely there was nothing to be learned from Mitchell, but any lead was worth trying. Bucky introduced his visitor to the girl.

"Have you decided to settle in Toltec?" Cameron asked.

"I've almost decided so, but I'm not absolutely sure yet. It's a growing town — up to date in a way. Yet there's a strong element of old-timers here, substantial citizens who would not be interested in the newest thing in men's clothes."

"What does Garside think about the prospects? By the way, would you like a drink? I have Scotch and bourbon."

"No, thanks. A little early in the day for me." Mitchell's jaw hardened. "I don't know what Mr. Garside thinks. I have come to feel that your foreman is right about Garside's advice. It wouldn't be disinterested."

"You didn't know him very well before you came here?"

Bucky put his statement with the rising inflection of a question, an offhand one tossed out carelessly.

His visitor went on guard, visibly. Even Nancy, who didn't know what it was all about, saw that the man stiffened.

"I didn't know him at all," Mitchell said.

"Only by correspondence?"

"What do you mean? The only letter I wrote here was to the secretary of the Chamber of Commerce."

"My mistake." On Bucky's face beamed his candid smile. "I'll put my cards on the table, Mr. Mitchell. I think you're a detective."

The other man took his time to answer that. When he did it was in Yankee fashion. "What makes you think so?"

"I can't make up my mind whom you represent," Bucky went on. "At first I thought Garside was employing you. If so, he picked someone with whom he can't get along. You don't like him any better than I do."

"That's absurd," Mitchell said promptly, almost explosively. "He doesn't mean anything to me one way or another."

"You say it right heartily," Bucky intimated.

"My only objection to him is that he's hard to deal with," Mitchell explained. "I've been trying to rent the empty store next to the bank from him, but he wants an outrageous price for a lease."

"Still sticking to your story? So am I to mine. My idea now is that you're a government man sent in to investigate the bank robbery. I'm not sure about that, but it looks like a good guess."

"If I were, would I admit it to you, before this young lady?"

Nancy had been watching the blond young stranger. Now she turned to go, her eyes on Bucky for the signal.

He shook his head. "Not necessary, Miss Graham. He's going to stay mysterious. No, he wouldn't admit it to me. I'm one of the suspects." Bucky smiled blandly on his visitor. "When Tim asked you to call on me it suited you fine, since you had been trying to figure out a way to have a talk with me that wouldn't stir misgivings in me. Now the boards are clear. You can ask me anything you like, and I'll tell you anything that won't incriminate me."

"I asked you why you think I'm a detective."

"When we had breakfast on the train you were pleasantly casual, but I saw at once you knew who I was. Probably some of the train-men told you. I felt sure you asked the waiter to put you at my table. It was amusing to see you working round so carefully to the robbery. Just to make conversation, you having read the story in the papers."

"You're quite wrong, Mr. Cameron."

"Prompt to your cue."

"I'll admit the story interested me, just as it did most other people. It's not often a bank president kills the cashier and robs his own bank. The conductor did tell me you were Neil Cameron, and I did ask the waiter to put me opposite you. I have a normal human curiosity, and I wanted to find out what you are like."

"Did you find out?"

"I think maybe you take a good deal of knowing. You are not a very obvious person."

"Let's both be obvious then," Bucky suggested. "I mean to get to the bottom of this thing. I'll not rest till I have the villain who killed Buchmann convicted. If you're here on the same job — and I think you are — why not share what information we have? You don't have to believe all I tell you, since naturally I would direct suspicion away from my uncle and myself. But you can take facts and sort them out for yourself. They may lead you one way and me another. One of us might be right."

"I'm willing to share what I know," Mitchell said, after a moment of thought. "But I'm afraid I haven't found out much yet — except what is public property. Suppose you put your case to me. Tell me what evidence you have that points away from your uncle."

"I'll do that. It's probably stronger to me than it is to you, because I knew my uncle."

Mitchell looked at the nurse and spoke to Bucky. "Don't you think we'd better be alone?"

Bucky gave Nancy the nod to retire. She left the room.

Briefly, clearly, Cameron marshaled and interpreted such of the facts as he knew. The other man listened intently. He asked a question when Bucky had finished.

"Do you think it is possible that your uncle came on Buchmann robbing the bank, was forced to kill him, and then decided to decamp with the money?"

"No. I've just got through explaining to you why he couldn't have killed Buchmann. Leaving out the question of character, he could not have done so bungling a job. The man or men who killed Buchmann took my uncle along and murdered him later."

"Maybe the cashier was in cahoots with the

robbers. Maybe they doublecrossed him — shot him to get a witness out of the way. What was Buchmann like?"

"He was a German — the sort of man who didn't look as if he had ever been young. I'd say he was around forty. Spoke with a slight accent. Wore a toupee and thick-lensed glasses. He was a little lame. I understand he was wounded in the war. Had a gold tooth. Red mustache. Rather careless about his clothes. I don't mean they were not neat, but that they were rather old and threadbare. But he was a crackerjack at figures and auditing books. It was just like Uncle Cliff to give a man of that kind a job, a man who was competent but not prepossessing."

"I meant, what was he like mentally?"

"I don't know. I left about the time he came. Rather a recluse, I'm told. A very honest man, and anxious to please. He often worked on the books at night — checking up, making sure everything was all right."

"A sort of an old maid?"

"Yes. Fussed around in a little apartment and did his own cooking."

"Any friends?" Mitchell asked.

"No, so far as I know. My guess is that he was friendly enough but shy. Very likely had a defeatist complex. Life had probably been a little too much for him. I see what you're getting at. You're checking up on him to see if his associates might have been in this with him."

"Yes. Was he tied up in any way with the men who live in the Red Rock country? Could you find out about that?"

"Don't suppose he even knew them, except maybe by sight. A quiet retiring fellow like Buchmann wouldn't be likely to meet a crowd of riproaring hellions like them. We might make inquiries."

"If you've come back to solve this mystery you must have some suspicions as to who the guilty parties are," Mitchell said, his gaze fixed on Bucky.

"One would think so," Cameron drawled, and his eyes met those of the other.

"With some evidence to back your opinion," Mitchell continued.

"Presumptive evidence, let us say."

"Against the Red Rock gang?"

"I've a notion it would be a good idea to forget them for a while," Bucky said, and lit a cigarette.

"Forget them!" Mitchell repeated, surprised. "Why, a week ago you had a battle with them. They wanted you and all your men arrested for murder. They shot you down in the street."

"Somebody did," Cameron corrected.

"Who did, if they didn't? West and his men were in stirring up the town against you. They said openly they meant to get you one way or another."

"Give them the benefit of the doubt. Likely you're right. Drygulching a man would be their style. Besides, the fellow who shot me got away on a horse. He wasn't a Toltec man. We think it was Brad Davis."

"All right. Why was he so anxious to kill you? Because he was afraid you would find out about the bank robbery."

"You're jumping at that. He might have shot me because he and his friends want me out of the way so that they can make a whole-sale steal of C C cattle. Or he might have been hired to do it."

"Hired? Who by?"

"By the man who *is* afraid I will find out he engineered the bank robbery," Bucky said quietly.

"You — you mean someone in particular?"

"Yes."

Mitchell's eyes searched his face. "Someone I know?"

"Someone you know."

"Not West or any of his bunch?"

"No."

Bucky's visitor continued to stare at him. Plainly his interest was keen-edged. "I can't think who it could be," he said, after a pause.

"The bank was robbed for profit, wasn't it?"

"Of course."

"Who profits most by the robbery?"

"Why, the fellows who got the loot."

Bucky's smile was cryptic. "What loot do you mean — the money taken from the bank, or that to be made as a result of the holdup?"

"I don't get your point, Mr. Cameron."

"With my uncle wiped out, with me under a cloud and perhaps destroyed, what becomes of the C C ranch?"

"You mentioned a wholesale steal of its cattle by the Red Rock rustlers."

"So I did. But even if a lot of the cattle are taken the ranch remains. Who gets it after the mortgage is satisfied? Who takes over the bank and inherits its assets?"

Mitchell shook his head. "I don't know." But if he did not know he could guess. The startled look on his face told that.

"A certain prominent citizen told me, before I had been back in town an hour, that he had been waiting twenty years to ruin my uncle and take over the ranch and the bank," Cameron said quietly. "I heard a rumor today that he is to be appointed receiver of the First National. One of his dummies of course will be the official receiver, but he will be only a rubber stamp."

"You mean Garside?"

The brown eyes of Bucky were steel-hard. "I mean Garside."

"But that's not reasonable, Mr. Cameron," the visitor objected. "He's the biggest man in town, important, rich, respected. It doesn't make sense that he should jeopardize everything on such a harebrained, lawless scheme. Why, he's being talked of locally for United States senator."

"Clem Garside has always been a gambler," Bucky replied. "He started on a shoestring, and he has run it up to a million six times over. Always he has been unscrupulous. Ever since I can remember he has hated us Camerons, especially my Uncle Cliff. He knew we would always stand in the way of his ambition. As long as Cliff Cameron was alive and powerful he could never be senator, could never rule the roost here. The two things Garside loves, outside of his daughter, are power and money. They are the very breath of his nostrils. With us out of the way he takes over a fortune and clears the path for the political honor he wants. All his life he has played for big stakes, but never bigger ones than these. If he has had nothing to do with this damned villainy of wrecking the First National and putting Uncle Cliff out of the way, if a bunch of outlaws played his hand for him without being asked, then I'll say he is the luckiest man alive."

Mitchell considered, rejected the conclusions of Cameron.

"I can't believe it," he said. "Mr. Garside isn't my kind of man. He's too — too self-centered and dominant. But he's in big business — a banker — has a standing in the community. He wouldn't go in for crime, not that kind. The idea is ridiculous."

"The idea doesn't seem ridiculous that my uncle — a banker, in big business also, with a standing in the community — should kill his own employee and rob his own bank," Bucky answered. "All Toltec fell for that view."

"You don't think he actually robbed the bank himself, do you? I mean Garside." Mitchell flung the question at the younger man abruptly.

"Not likely."

"Then who helped him — the Red Rock outfit?"

"Maybe. Maybe someone else. I don't know yet." Bucky's jaw set. His eyes grew hard as jade. "But I'm going to find out — and when I do —"

"I shouldn't like to be one of the criminals, if and when you find out," Mitchell said, with a smile. "I'm glad I've had this talk with you. My judgment tells me you are on the wrong track completely. But I'll say this: I think you are convinced of your uncle's innocence, and you have more than half persuaded me of it."

"Anything to accommodate," Bucky responded. "If you don't like the lead I've given you I'll offer another. I'm quite ready to believe the Red Rock nesters are in this business, but if they are, as I have said, somebody in town is supplying the brains. You object to Garside. I offer the name of Jud Richman, real estate dealer, crook, and all-round scoundrel. He was with Davis and Quinn just before and just after they shot at me the day I reached town. He was consulting with West and our precious sheriff an hour before I was wounded. He loves money, and he hated my uncle with all his rotten heart. It was Richman — and the sheriff was with him, by the way — who discovered the fire in the bank at half-past one in the morning. Give him the once-over while you are considering candidates for the hangman."

"There might be something to that," Mitchell said gravely. "I'll follow up the suggestion."

"Also, follow up a young man named Philip Ferrill, who was a teller of the First National. He has been playing the market in too big a way for one with his salary. He's a long shot, but if this was an inside job he might have had a hand in it."

"Anybody else?"

Bucky thought of mentioning Haskell again, then thought better of it. The sheriff would not be in anything as bold and reckless as this.

"So far I've done all the talking," Bucky apologized. "I'll listen to you now."

"Give me a day or two to work out one or two things that are in my mind," Mitchell said. "I want to think over what you've told me and verify some facts before I do any talking. But I'll say this, Mr. Cameron. Between us I believe we can clear this thing up. You've given me a lead or two I mean to follow."

"Hope you have more luck than I've had so far," Bucky told him.

"Experience tells me that in crimes of this kind you do a lot of underground work before the case is solved," Mitchell said, rising to go. "A lot of it is unnecessary and leads to nothing, but you can't tell that in advance. . . . Take care of yourself and keep out of the way of bullets. Much safer for me to do the investigating."

Nancy came into the room shortly after Mitchell left.

"What do you think of him?" Bucky asked.

"I rather liked him. Does a detective look like that?"

"Like what?"

"Why, just like anyone else — like a prosperous business man."

Bucky laughed. "You've been reading fiction. All detectives haven't pounded a beat. If you knew a man was a sleuth as soon as you saw him he wouldn't be much use, would he?"

"I suppose not. But he looks so — so harmless. You'd never give him a second glance. His kind come by the dozen, if you know what I mean. So much so that I had a feeling I'd met him before. Of course I haven't. After I left did he admit that he is a detective?"

"Practically." Bucky grinned. "He's detective enough to have got out of me all I know without telling me anything he has found out."

"Does he feel that — you and Mr. Cliff Cameron aren't in this?"

"He didn't tell me," Bucky answered dryly.

"Maybe I shouldn't have said that," Nancy rushed on, the color deepening in her clear skin. "But I want you to know — if it matters to you, though perhaps it doesn't — I mean, to have people tell you they believe in you — that there's one run-of-the-mill nurse is sure you had nothing to do with the robbery."

He said, gently: "It is good to hear that from you. Why are you sure?"

Airily she gave a woman's reason. "Be-

134

cause." She added in explanation, "You're a swell fellow."

"That's a considered verdict, is it?" he asked.

"Besides, I nursed your cousin Julia when she had her tonsils out while you were away. I saw a lot of your uncle. Of course I'd seen him in the bank before, but not really to know him. He is a fine man. Anybody but a fool could see he wouldn't do anything dishonorable. I would trust him all the way."

Bucky shook hands with her. "You're a gentleman, Nancy."

CHAPTER IX

Bucky walked along the corridor of the hospital, Nancy's arm tucked under his for support, and took the elevator for the roof. She found a comfortable chair, moved it into the sunshine where he would be sheltered from the wind, and wrapped a blanket round his legs. He read a magazine story, stopping occasionally to luxuriate in the pleasant warmth of the drowsy day. A faint breeze stirred the leaves of the trees. He could see two squirrels playing in the branches of one opposite.

After a time Nancy took him back to his room.

"Tired?" she asked.

He told her no, that he would sit by the window.

"And I'd like a lemonade," he mentioned.

She left to make him one, but returned almost at once, a queer look on her face.

"Visitors to see you," she said. "Your cousin and Miss Garside."

Bucky's eyes danced. This was exciting, though surprising. Kathleen and Julia were not on cordial terms. When they met they bowed stiffly. That was as far as their intimacy went.

"Please show them in," he said.

Julia kissed him. Kathleen did not offer to shake hands. She stood tall and erect, her dark disdainful eyes looking down at him.

"Nice of you to come," he told the daughter of his enemy, his smile derisively grateful. "Miss Graham, would it be too much trouble to ask you to clear the newspapers from that chair?"

Kathleen did not sit down. The long lithe body, with its fine animal vigor beneath the satiny skin, was uncompromisingly hostile. He knew that the mind controlling the smooth muscles was as steel-hard as they. Yet she was feminine from well-shod feet to the crisp copper curls peeping out from the modish hat.

"I asked Miss Cameron to let me come with her," she said stiffly.

"An unexpected pleasure," he assured her.

"No pleasure for me," she differed. "I'm a fool for coming."

"But couldn't resist the desire to say, 'I told you so,' " he suggested.

"I had to see you." Her voice was cold, but beneath its chill they could feel anger racing, as a swift current does beneath the ice of a river. "To warn you. I picked up the telephone extension in my room and listened in on a talk. No names were mentioned, but I knew you were meant."

"Who was talking?" Bucky asked.

"I don't know for sure who was at the other end. Sheriff Haskell was in the house. I suppose he had come to see Father about something. He did the talking from our end of the connection."

"About me?"

"Yes. I got in at the fag end, just in time to hear the other man say they had waited long enough for Haskell to act. He said they would move themselves and do your business *muy pronto*. I don't know what the sheriff had refused to do, but he got excited and asked them for God's sake to wait. The other man laughed, a cruel laugh, and hung up."

"You don't know, but you can guess, who was talking with Haskell," Bucky said, his eyes in hers.

"I can guess, but no better than you."

"West, maybe."

"Maybe. The sheriff called him Dan." She broke out, imperiously, "I suppose you'll still sit around and play at being a stuffed Buddha, just to show off how brave you are."

"You don't put it the way I do," he answered. "But that's all right. I'm much obliged to you for coming. We're keeping tabs on Mr. West and his friends. They can't hurt me while Miss Graham rides herd on me."

"If you won't leave this part of the country why don't you go out to the ranch and stay there?" Kathleen urged.

"Just what I mean to do in a few days. Thank you for coming, Miss Garside."

"You needn't thank me," she said, flinging back his gratitude almost violently. "It's just that I won't have murder done and be a party to it. Now it's off my mind. Do as you please."

She turned to go.

There was a small crash of breaking glass. For an instant none of them moved. They stood, surprised, not sure what it was. Then Nancy darted forward, pulled the blind down swiftly, and dragged from in front of the window the chair in which Bucky was sitting.

"What was it?" Julia asked, shaken and frightened.

Bucky shook off the blanket that wrapped his legs. He put an arm around Nancy's shoulder, gave her a little hug, and said, "Good girl!"

"The bullet must have passed close to your head," Nancy cried. She was white to the lips but quite composed. "It broke the picture glass on the wall almost directly behind you."

"A bullet!" Julia stared, big-eyed, at her. "You mean —"

"Must have been fired from the empty house opposite," Bucky explained. "The fellow had a Maxim silencer on his gun."

Nancy picked up the telephone. "I'll get the police."

"Do no harm — and no good," Bucky said. "He's beating it down the alley by this time. Wait a minute, Miss Graham. Give me the phone. I'll talk with the chief."

He sat on the bed, telephone in hand, waiting for the connection. "Police Department?" he said presently. "Gimme the chief. Bucky Cameron talking. This is important. . . . Chief, this is Bucky Cameron. I was fired at a moment ago through the window of my room at Mercy Hospital. Yes . . . Yes . . . Room 321, facing south, toward Steele Street . . .

Listen, Chief. There's an empty house opposite my room. The fellow must have fired from the second-story window. Probably from a gun with a silencer. . . . Sure I know it's against the law to have a silencer. It's against the law to have sub-machine guns, but gangsters have them. This is what I want you to do. Get into that house and see if the bird has left any evidence behind him. Look for fingerprints — on the window sill and the doorknobs especially. And if you find anything, please let me know. Better come up and see where the bullet struck a wall picture in my room. Fine. . . . That's good. See you later, Chief."

"Someone may have seen the man escaping," Kathleen said, after Bucky had hung up.

"Maybe," Cameron replied. "The police will cover that angle."

"Miss Garside is right," the nurse said decisively. "You'd better get out to your ranch as soon as you can, Mr. Cameron. . . . He didn't lose any time, did he — that man West, whoever he is?"

Bucky walked up to the picture and examined the bullet hole. He could not tell until the lead had been dug out of the wall whether it had been fired from a rifle or a revolver.

"West and his friends — or somebody else — seem anxious to get rid of me," he said. "They are in a hurry. Why the rush — unless they are afraid?"

"Afraid you or your men will shoot them first?" Kathleen asked. "But while you are in the hospital —"

"While I'm here I can't very well shoot them, can I?" Bucky finished for her, with a sardonic smile. "But we're such notorious killers, the Cameron outfit, that they can't sleep nights for fear we'll slaughter them wholesale."

Kathleen flushed. "'Some of you killed that man Dieter."

"Just in time," Bucky added. "No, Miss Garside, that's not what they're afraid of. What's worrying them is that they think I'm on the edge of a discovery — or at any rate getting close to it. They fear I know too much."

"About what?" Julia asked breathlessly.

"About the First National Bank robbery."

"What do you know?" asked Kathleen, her glance darting at him.

Bucky ignored her question. When he spoke, his mind seemed to be on another matter. "Tuffy Arnold was in town yesterday and the day before," he said thoughtfully.

"Who is he?" Kathleen wanted to know impatiently.

"He is a friend of a friend — I mean of an acquaintance of Miss Garside," the young man explained. "Referring to Mr. Dan West. Tuffy and a man named Jud Richman are the brains of the Red Rock outfit. Tuffy advises them at home. Jud fronts for them here, disposes of their rustled stock, sees the law does not annoy them too much. If those two good citizens got together they might decide to take direct action against a common enemy — with the help perhaps of Mr. West. Jud must have got the silencer. It's against the law to sell them, and they are not too easy to obtain. But Jud is an efficient scoundrel in his own furtive sly way. We'll have to make a roundup of the local stores that sell firearms, but that won't do any good. The silencer wasn't bought in town. Jud wouldn't be that dumb."

"The fingerprints in the house," Nancy suggested. "Maybe they will tell who fired the shot."

Bucky shook his head. "There won't be any fingerprints, not if Jud and Tuffy are running the show. None that will help. The fellow who fired at me was warned again and again to wipe out any prints he might make."

"Then why did you tell the chief of police to look for them?" Julia asked.

"They are a wild, careless bunch, the Red Rock outfit," her cousin explained. "Light on brains. It would be like one of them to forget instructions and write his identity on the dusty window sill or on a wall, especially if he chanced to have been drinking. But it's only a long shot."

"It doesn't matter who did it — at least that's not what matters most just now," Kathleen interposed impatiently. She looked at Bucky, and a heat ran through her lithe brown body. "You're not going to be fool enough to stay around here any longer, are you?"

"It matters to me who did it," Bucky returned, his dancing eyes on her. "That bullet didn't miss you much farther than it did me. I resent being shot at while I'm entertaining ladies. It isn't gallant. No right-minded assassin would choose a time like that to earn his pay for an honest day's work. There's a time for everything. Even where there is an open season on husbands a wife ought not to put a period to hers while he is presenting her with gardenias on their anniversary. It isn't good sportsmanship."

"Why don't you talk sense?" Kathleen demanded scornfully. "The point is that you are going to be killed — if you go strutting around the way you have been doing. Anybody but a fool can see it. You've already had two warnings —"

"Three," amended Bucky. "Don't forget they ruined my hat in front of your house." He added regretfully: "A good hat too. Cost me eight bucks."

With a gesture of annoyance Kathleen brushed

this levity aside. "I'm interested only because I won't have people thinking that father is mixed up in any harm that comes to you when he is really trying to protect you," she went on, her color high, eyes sparkling angrily. "If you want to be killed you don't have to choose our yard."

"And all Toltec is your yard now, isn't it?" he said with suave irony. "Since your father has taken it over lock, stock, and barrel. He ought to deport as undesirable citizens those of us he doesn't like."

Kathleen Garside was furious. She looked hot to the touch as she turned to Julia. "If he has any friends they had better have him put in an insane asylum," she said, and walked quickly out of the room.

After the explosive exit Julia was the first to speak. "She's right, Bucky. I don't mean about the asylum, of course. But you can't go on like this. It's terrible."

"He isn't going on like this," Nancy said in her cool matter-of-fact tone. "He's my patient, and I'm responsible for his safety. Right away I'm moving him into another wing of the hospital. Tomorrow we're going out to the ranch to stay."

Bucky said, smiling at her, "I hear my master's voice."

★ ★ ★

The chief of police dropped in to see Bucky after his nurse had moved him to another room.

"You certainly keep things stirred up, young man," he growled, easing himself into a chair.

"Don't blame me," Bucky remonstrated. "I'm not offering a reward for someone to rub me out."

The chief was a hard-boiled officer who had fought his way up from the ranks. His poker face was expressionless as a rock wall.

"What the hell are you doing here anyhow?" he demanded bluntly. "Nobody invited you back to Toltec."

"I came to find out what had become of my uncle and who robbed the First National," Bucky replied.

"You know all about it now, I expect," the chief said, with harsh sarcasm.

"I've wondered a good deal how much *you* know, Chief, that you didn't give to the papers," Cameron mentioned, brown eyes fixed on the officer.

"If I knew anything, why would I tell you?"

"That would depend on whether you think Uncle Cliff was guilty."

"He was there that night. His gun killed Buchmann. The safe was robbed. Cliff disappeared. What do you figure I would think?"

"I would look for a good sleuth like you to dig in after the inside story. You were on the ground early. It's not reasonable to suppose you haven't something up your sleeve — something that puzzled you, maybe, that didn't fit in with the rest of the pattern."

The chief chewed the end of a tattered cigar. He had always felt friendly to Cliff Cameron and he had never liked Garside, but he did not intend to let this interfere with his career. Cliff was through. His enemy was in the saddle. Still, Chief O'Sullivan was not a rubber stamp.

"There's always something in a mystery case that doesn't fit into a theory," he said abruptly. "It may be important, or it may not. One thing I don't quite get. Cliff called me up the afternoon of the robbery and mentioned that the payroll of the Malpais had come in and that he had seen some suspicious characters hanging around. He asked me to have the officer on the beat that night keep a special eye on the First National."

Bucky sat erect. "Did he say who the suspicious characters were?"

"No, he didn't. I kinda guessed he had some of the wild bunch from the Red Rocks in mind. Three or four of them were in town that day. What stumped me was that if Cliff was fixing to rob the bank that night he wouldn't have asked me to check up specially on the First National."

Bucky nodded agreement. "Not if he was intending to light out. He might have done it for a bluff, if he had meant to stick it here and play innocent."

"There was one other circumstance I don't quite get. We found the elk tooth Cliff wore on his watch chain. It was lying near the front door and had been torn off, probably in a struggle. Now Buchmann couldn't have put up any fight. He was shot from behind, in the back of the head."

"But if Uncle Cliff was being taken away forcibly by the assassins, the tooth might easily have been ripped from the chain near the door," Bucky said.

O'Sullivan slanted a hard, suspicious eye at the young man. "Or if Cliff had wanted it to look like he was being dragged away."

"Only it wasn't that way . . . Did you find any evidence in the empty house opposite my room?"

"No. The shot was fired from a bedroom window on the second floor. No fingerprints on the sill or on the doorknobs. The guy wore gloves or wiped them clean."

"What I expected. Did he have a rifle or a revolver?"

"A revolver. Colt's army .38, say. That is

likely why he missed. We dug the bullet out of the wall of your room."

"He had to use a revolver," Bucky argued. "He would have been too conspicuous carrying a rifle into the house."

"Yes. How did the fellow get in? Did he have a key?"

"You might find out who owns the house — and what agent has the renting of it."

"I've found that out already. Garside owns the house. The rental agency is the Richman Realty Company. The key has been turned over to a dozen people looking at the house. Anyhow, a skeleton key will open the back door. Which leaves us where we started from."

"Was anybody seen going to or from the house?"

"A woman hanging up washing two houses away thinks she saw someone going into the yard, but she didn't even notice whether it was a man or a boy. The real estate company has had someone there every day or two looking after the lawn, so she was used to seeing someone around the place."

"People don't notice what they are expecting to see," Bucky observed. "So the psychologists tell us. Their eyes look at a thing without registering it. For instance, if some sisters in their black dresses walked into the police station you would do more than notice them because you wouldn't expect to have them drop in, but I'll bet a dollar you can't tell me how many sisters you have seen here today." He added, with a grin: "I'm carrying coals to Newcastle, Chief. This is old stuff to you."

"I don't suppose *you* saw anyone going into the house," O'Sullivan said.

"No. By the way, Chief, did anyone hear a shot in the bank the night of the robbery?"

"If anyone did he has been holding out on me. You trying to locate the time?"

Bucky drew a cigarette from a package, lit it, looked at the chief. "I was wondering if the killer used a silencer," he said indifferently.

O'Sullivan stared at him a moment, silently, his prognathous jaw tight. "Meaning he was the same man took a crack at you?" he asked at last.

"Meaning he might be."

"Who's in your mind?" the chief demanded bluntly.

"I haven't got that far."

"But you have a suspicion."

"A very private one."

"Shoot the works."

"I said private."

"Hell, come clean," the officer snarled. "You're just like the others. They either want to tell more than they know, or else they want to hide half of what they know. Then everybody yaps at me because we don't run down the criminals."

"You're in a tough spot, Chief," sympathized Cameron. "The public expects you to get results or be fired, but if you put pressure on suspects the dear people are horrified at third degree methods. You're damned if you do and damned if you don't."

"You telling *me?*" O'Sullivan growled.

"We're going to clear this thing up before we get through with it," promised Bucky.

"Fine," scoffed the older man, his hard eyes on Cameron. "I'm all set up you're working with me."

"I'm working with you, Chief," Bucky said equably. "But there wouldn't be any sense in telling you a suspicion until it's backed up with facts."

"I don't give a curse about your suspicions. But you know something — or think you do. Probably doesn't amount to a thing. But that's for me to judge, not you."

"Wait till I know a little more about it. But I'll say this. Get to the motive of the bank robbery, Chief. I mean the fundamental motive." Bucky lifted a protesting hand. "Yes, I know what you're going to say, that any idiot would know they did it to get the dough.

True enough. But look back of that. Dig deeper. Who gained most by the robbery? Figure that out, and when you have the answer you'll tell me I'm crazy."

The chief watched him, his eyes narrowed in thought. "That all you got to say, Bucky?"

"Not quite all. The shot fired at me today came from a house owned by one enemy of mine and on the rental list of another enemy. Doesn't that suggest anything?"

"Is Jud Richman your enemy?"

"An enemy of my uncle and of me. You know we almost sent him to the pen for shipping and selling our cattle to the Denver stock buyers two years ago. He just managed to wiggle out by perjured testimony."

"You don't think either Clem or Jud did this personally? I mean shot at you today."

"No, not while killers can be hired for fifty dollars a head."

"That all you've got to tell me?"

"All today, Chief. More later, maybe."

O'Sullivan rose. He looked down at Cameron grimly, still chewing on the mistreated cigar. "This suggestion of yours. No prejudice in it?"

"There might be," Bucky admitted. "Make allowance for that."

"Now listen to me, young fellow. If you don't get out of town and stay out, you'll tell me nothing more. You'll be lying on a slab at the morgue. See?"

Bucky grinned. "I've heard that so often I'm coming to believe it," he answered.

"You'd better believe it," O'Sullivan warned harshly.

While the chief was still in the corridor Nancy announced Mitchell.

The face of the blond, fair-haired visitor showed concern. "I've just heard of the attempt on your life," he said. "My God, Mr. Cameron, be careful! These scoundrels have marked you for death. Get out to your ranch and stay there. Don't give them a chance."

"News spreads fast in this town," Bucky replied. "Where did you hear it?"

"On a police broadcast. Not ten minutes ago. Suspects are being checked up."

"That's hooey to save face. The man who passed you as you came in was the chief of police. He didn't know of any suspects, except my friends from the Red Rock country."

"Why not check up on them?" Mitchell asked. He pulled himself up, cutting off his next words, a sudden excitement in his pink face. "Good Lord! I believe I met the man — slipping back to town — right after he had done it."

"Met him where — and when?" Bucky wanted to know.

"At the corner of Wilson and Fifth, about — let me see — close to four, a little earlier."

Bucky consulted Nancy. "That would be about the right time, wouldn't it?"

"Yes," she said, after a moment's reflection. "It was twenty minutes to four when I started out to make the lemonade. I looked at my watch."

"Can you describe the man?" On the heel of that question Bucky asked a second. "What makes you think he might be the one?"

"There was something furtive about him. I can't describe it exactly. He looked as if he didn't want to be noticed."

"What did he look like?"

"A big, dark man, black-haired. I caught only a glimpse of his face. He wore high-heeled cowboy boots."

"Might be Brad Davis from your description."

"About how old?" Nancy asked.

Mitchell frowned, trying to place the man's years. "Thirty-five, maybe — or older."

"That would fit Brad," Bucky said.

"By the way, if this young lady doesn't talk —"

Mitchell stopped and looked at Nancy, who at once rose to go. Her employer detained her with a lift of the hand.

"You may say anything you like before Miss

Graham," he assured his visitor.

"Good. I've satisfied myself on those points I spoke about the other day." Mitchell ticked them off with the forefinger of one hand on the little finger of the other. "First, Davis, West, and Quinn were in town at the time of the bank robbery. They spent the evening at the Crystal Palace drinking. They were restless. More than once one of them went out for a time and came back. About half-past eleven they left the saloon. Nobody saw them again, as far as I can find out, until about a quarter to one. Then two of them — Quinn and Davis — went to the livery stable and got their three horses. West was not with them."

"You think he was in some dark spot guarding my uncle until the others could bring the horses." Back of Bucky's quiet manner and soft-spoken words raced a keen excitement.

"What would you think? Why wouldn't he be with the others, unless he had to be somewhere else — say, guarding a prisoner, who was either dead or alive?"

Mitchell too spoke evenly, but Nancy felt that his calm was a fraud. He was under a disciplined high pressure. A light triumphant blazed in his eyes.

"You think they killed Uncle Cliff before they left town — or after?" Bucky asked.

"I don't know. After, I would say, if they could get him out of town quietly and without any fuss."

"I think so too. A live man is easier to transport than a dead one. Mr. Mitchell, you have done good work. If you can prove all you say the Red Rock gents will have quite some explaining to do."

"I can prove it, if my witnesses will stand by what they let out to me."

"Some of them won't, if they think it's not safe. I don't suppose they knew what you were getting at when you talked with them."

"No. I was careful about that. We'll have to spring it on them suddenly before the District Attorney, not giving them time to change their stories."

"Our most important citizen — I won't mention his name — is friendly with West and his crowd. You still think he isn't in this?"

"Doesn't look reasonable to me. As I said before, I don't like him. He is selfish and a good deal of a bully. But he's sitting on the top of the world. It has taken him thirty years to get there. He couldn't afford to risk losing everything in one crazy deal."

"No," Bucky conceded, reluctance in voice and manner. "It would be dumb of him. But I hate to give up the idea . . . Is it your intention to arrest the Red Rock men now?"

Mitchell shook his head. "Not yet. We haven't tied them up with the robbery. But we'll get the evidence one of these days and wind a net around them. One of them will get drunk and talk. Or they'll begin spending money. Or somebody will come forward who saw them around the First National Building the night of the robbery."

"It's time for Mr. Cameron to lie down and rest," Nancy announced. "He's had a pretty strenuous afternoon."

The visitor rose. "That's so. Well, I'll be going."

Nancy closed the door after him. "We'll get your clothes off so that you can relax," she said briskly.

Her patient was looking at the girl's beautiful slim legs, with no appreciation of them. His mind was elsewhere.

He looked up, smiling grimly. "Mitchell is right. The inside story is going to break soon. By the way, I want you to send some wires for me."

156

CHAPTER X

At the end of the second day, while Nancy was giving Bucky an alcohol rub, she announced that she was not going to stay any longer at the C C ranch under pay.

"Except for half an hour in the morning and evening I don't have anything to do but play," she said. "I go riding with your cousin and I play cards with you or sit and talk. That's no way to earn seven dollars a day."

"Have you heard me complain?" he drawled, twisting his head round to take a slanting look at her.

"You don't need a nurse any longer."

"I need someone to keep me from worrying."

"You worry a lot, don't you?" she mocked.

"How about staying a few days as Julia's guest?"

"I might do that — if she asked me . . . You may turn over now."

He rolled over and lay with his fingers laced behind his head. "You're a swell girl, Nancy," he said.

Nancy said, "Thank you, kind sir," with

no visible discomposure. "It's more important for me to be a good nurse, isn't it?" she added.

"No, but you're that too." He watched her moving about the room, making things ready for the night. "Seems to me the misogynist has been hanging around a good deal today. You don't reckon he's going to get sick and need a nurse, do you?"

"He says he has never been ill a day in his life."

"Maybe he could get someone to plug him in the shoulder. I've had a fine time since some kind enemy handed me a pill."

"So have I," she acknowledged. "It's been — exciting."

"I hope you get a grumpy old man for your next patient."

"Nice of you. Why?"

"So that you will remember by contrast your favorite patient and think about him."

"I couldn't say off-hand who is my favorite one," she told him, opening a window. "I've had some lovely women under my care. Your cousin is one . . . Is there anything else you want?"

"You mean anything I can have?" he asked.

"If not, I'll say good night," she said, ignoring his question. "I'll leave the door open. In case you need me be sure and knock on the wall."

"Will you come back and tell me a good-night story if I can't sleep?" he wanted to know.

"I've left an amytol tablet and a glass of water on the table. You'll find that more soporific."

"I'm still paying you seven dollars a day, young lady," he reminded her.

"But I work only union hours." She turned at the door to tell him a piece of personal news: "I'm going riding in the moonlight with the misogynist. I'll be back in an hour or two."

"Is that wise?" he asked, instantly serious. "War has been declared on the range. There might be sharpshooters around. Of course it's the dark of the moon. But that works both ways. If you met enemies they might not know you were a woman . . . Send Tim to me before you start."

"You wouldn't spoil my fun, would you?" she asked. "There isn't a chance in a thousand that in a hundred miles of hill country we should meet anybody."

"It's that thousandth chance I want to forestall. Night riders have been known to infest our range to drive away C C cows."

When Murphy came in he grinned sheepishly. "Miss Nancy got you tucked up all right for the night?" he asked.

"Which way are you riding, Tim?"

"Thought I'd take the trail ridge."

"As good as any, if you have to go. Be careful of the girl, Tim. If you meet any of West's scoundrels they might blaze away in the darkness."

"That's why I'm going up the trail ridge. No chance any of them will be there. But I'll sure be careful, Bucky."

"Do that. I'll be worried till you get back."

Bucky did not sleep until he heard Nancy's cheerful voice calling a good night to Murphy from the porch two hours later.

The foreman drove to town next day and came back with a piece of gossip he had picked up at the Pioneers' Club. He interrupted a game of Russian bank to impart it.

"Some of the boys are saying that Clem Garside has been mighty short of cash lately," he said, sitting on the rail of the porch with one foot on the floor. "They claim he's spread out darned thin and if anything cracked he would have to scratch gravel considerable."

Nancy played the queen of hearts on the king of spades and suspended play, looking up into the tanned sun-and-wind wrinkled face of Murphy.

"Who says this?" Bucky asked.

"Well, Munson was one of them — and Luke Mennig. They say he has sunk pretty close to a quarter of a million on that molybdenum mine of his. I understand it's rich as all getout, but what with machinery, building roads, and one thing and another there has been nothing but outlay so far."

"A quarter of a million is a lot of money," Bucky reflected aloud. "If he has backed the mine that heavy I would expect him to feel the pinch. Munson usually knows what he is talking about. But after all, a lot of loose gossip floats around. I could check up on it through Warren Young. He has his finger on every mining proposition in this part of the country."

"I wouldn't know how true it is," Tim said. "I'm just repeating what I heard. Clem left yesterday for the mine. He spends two-three days a month up at Fairview."

Bucky rose. "I'll get on the phone."

Before he could reach it the bell rang. He took down the receiver. Judge Lewis was on the wire. Bucky listened, asked questions.

The others suspended their conversation. They could tell from Cameron's manner that something important had taken place. His cool, indifferent voice had become crisp and incisive.

"Know who they are?" he demanded. Then, after listening to an answer: "Anybody hurt? . . . Did they get away with much?"

161

The man at the other end of the line talked. Presently Bucky said: "Yes, I'll do that. It's just two forty-five now. Tim Murphy is here with me — and my cousin Julia, and my nurse, Miss Graham . . . Call me up again if you find out anything more."

Bucky hung up. To the others he explained what had occurred.

"The Valley Bank has been held up by bandits. One of the tellers was wounded. They got away with a good deal of money. Judge Lewis doesn't know how much yet. He called me up so that we can establish our alibis. The bank was robbed not five minutes ago. Ring the big bell, Tim, and gather all the men who are on the ranch now. I want to make a roster of them against any possible charges that may develop later."

All of the C C riders on the place were checked up. Murphy sent them out on to the range to find and bring in at once those out on duty. They were told to jot down with a pencil the exact time they caught sight of those already in the saddle.

"It's going to be claimed we robbed the Valley Bank," Bucky explained. "That's a lie I intend to knock on the head before it gets a good start. Get going, boys. Round up every C C man as soon as you can."

The men roped, saddled, and departed.

CHAPTER XI

A small sedan was parked by the curb in front of the side door of the Valley Bank. In the driver's seat a heavy-set man lounged. Beside him a newspaper had been spread. Occasionally a nervous hand felt the paper, as if for reassurance of what lay beneath it.

The eyes of the man were alert and restless in the gross, beefy face. They searched the street anxiously and found a figure coming down the sidewalk. It was that of a medium-sized man whose hat was drawn low over the face. The cold, shallow eyes lifted to meet those of the driver. A message flashed between them.

The pedestrian walked into the bank. Simultaneously two others were entering by the front door, the man in the car felt sure. He started the engine and let it run quietly. One hand slid under the newspaper and found the sub-machine gun lying there.

He was a stolid man, unimaginative, but the wait seemed to him unending. The population of Toltec flowed along the busy street. Men stopped for a word of greeting with each other.

Two giggling girls passed, absorbed in their talk. A Western Union messenger boy vanished into the side door of the bank. He was taking a telegram out of his hat. A young woman with a large deposit-book followed him. The engine continued to hum.

There was the crash of an explosion. It might have been a shot, or it might have been a car back-firing. The man in the sedan knew which it was. He raised the sub-machine gun a few inches from the seat, and his lips became a thin cruel line.

Out of the bank flew the messenger boy, as if he had been flung from a catapult. He dived across the street regardless of traffic and disappeared into the entrance of an office building opposite. At his heels came three men, all armed, all in a hurry. Two of them carried sacks. They tumbled into the sedan pellmell, flinging the sacks on the floor. Already the car was in motion.

He swept the sedan round a double parked mail truck, almost crashed an approaching coupe, swerved, dashed down the crowded thoroughfare. The red light at the next crossing did not stop him. He honked across it wildly at risk of life and limb. Bystanders watching the car, as it circled recklessly in and out among traffic, thought that the man at the wheel was drunk.

The sedan raced past a stop sign into a wide avenue, taking the curve at a mad pace. There was a long stretch ahead. After two or three blocks one of the men in the back seat announced that no police car was following. The driver decreased the speed till the speedometer showed forty miles. This was fast enough. The immediate getaway had been made, and it was wise not to attract attention.

"Bump off anyone?" the beefy-faced man asked, from a corner of his slitted lips.

"One," the man beside him said. "Grabbed at a gun . . . Next street's where we turn."

They swung to the left. The driver's foot jammed down on the brake and the squealing tires slid to a halt. Out poured the men. They scrambled into an open car parked just in front of them. The engine roared. The bandits were on their way to the safety of the hills.

The chauffeur of the chief of police went through the streets with siren screaming. At the Valley Bank O'Sullivan flung himself out of the still-moving car and ran up the steps. The crowd, already reaching from sidewalk to sidewalk, made way for him. A policeman opened the door for the chief.

"Tell Brower to detour traffic," the latter ordered, and passed into the building.

He took charge of the investigation, and

from excited witnesses gleaned the facts. Three men had held up the bank. They had known that the money to pay the Malpais dam construction gang was here and had demanded it. Simpson, assistant cashier, had made a pass for a gun and had been shot down by a squat bandit wearing a cowboy hat. None of the robbers had been masked, and none of them had been recognized as familiar by any of those in the bank. The whole affair had not taken five minutes. The cashier could not tell until a checkup was made how much the holdups had taken, but he admitted that it must have been considerable.

The switchboard operator passed the word down that the Chief was wanted on the phone.

"Find out who wants me," O'Sullivan snapped. "If it's not important handle it yourself, Richards."

The cashier went to the nearest receiver, listened, said "Wait a moment," and returned to the chief.

"It's Neil Cameron," he explained. "Out at the ranch, I think."

O'Sullivan hesitated. He was a busy man. Still —

"I'll take it," he said, and walked to the desk where Richards had talked.

"What do you want?" he demanded abruptly.

"I've just heard of the Valley Bank holdup," came Bucky's voice over the wire. "If there's anything I can do — any roads you want blocked —"

"How did you hear of it?" the chief interrupted. "It didn't happen more than ten minutes ago — not that long since."

"Judge Lewis called me as soon as he heard of it."

"What for?" O'Sullivan asked harshly.

"You know why, Chief. In order that I may protect myself against lies started by my enemies. That's not important now. The point is, can you use a posse of my men? If so, I'll get one on the road fast as I can."

O'Sullivan thought fast. He was not sure of Bucky. This immediate call had a suspicious aptness. The C C man was fixing his alibi. But he would want to establish that whether innocent or guilty. In any case it would do no harm to string him along, and there was always the chance that he might head off the outlaws if they were making for the Red Rock country.

"All right. Hop to it. Send your boys out. Report to me later."

"Do you know by which road the holdups left town?"

"No. I'm not even sure they have left. Soon as I learned of the robbery I sent out a broadcast to cut them off, but I haven't heard from any of my men since. Your best bet would be to patrol the road leading to the Red Rock country."

"I'll send a car out at once," Bucky promised. "I'm calling the boys back from the range. As soon as possible I'll send a posse into the hills. Do you know whether the bandits got away with much?"

"No." O'Sullivan thought of asking, "Do you?" But he decided he had better not.

Abruptly, he hung up.

CHAPTER XII

Three C C men, armed with rifles as well as revolvers, were ready to take off in a rattletrap car. Curly Teeters was in charge of them. Bucky stood with a foot on the running-board and gave last minute instructions:

"Don't take any desperate chances, boys. Run down the gunbarrel road to the willows and find cover there. What I chiefly want is to find out if any of West's gang have been in town today and are heading for home in a hurry. It is not necessary for you to arrest them unless the opportunity is too good to lose. You can't assume they are guilty, but you have authority to stop their car and search it. Unless you get the drop on them you must not try to do this. I don't want two or three of you killed or wounded. Primarily you are a scouting party."

"What about other cars?" Curly asked. "Do we search them too?"

"Yes. Stop all cars, unless the hazard is too great and those in them show fight. But be cautious, boys. Don't get gun-crazy. We're in bad enough already and can't afford any mistakes."

"We ought to get back by suppertime," Curly said. "If they're coming at all they will be through long before that."

"I won't be here," Bucky replied. "I'm going to town."

"Not alone?"

"Yes, I don't want the impression to get around that I'm holed up here because I'm afraid of the law. We're out on bond, but the bond doesn't cover the robbery of the Valley Bank."

"I'm not talking about the law," answered Curly. "It wasn't the law took those three cracks at you, Bucky. I'd call it dumb for you to go in and ask for more."

Bucky shook his head. "I've got to play this hand my own way, Curly . . . Good luck, boys."

"You'll need more of it than we will," another of the men cut in bluntly. "If you're hell bent on seeing the elephant, take Tim Murphy with you as a guard."

"Maybe I will," Bucky conceded.

He stepped back from the car and watched it go.

An hour later Murphy started with a posse of horsemen for the hills, if possible to cut off the bank robbers as they returned. Bucky had been careful not to mention to him his intention of going to Toltec. His reaction would have been the same as that of Curly but much more positive.

Bucky went upstairs and packed a suitcase. This he carried down and left in the hall. He did not want to start in time to get into town before dark.

Julia found him sitting on the porch glancing over a magazine.

"What is your suitcase doing here? Where are you going?" she asked.

"Going to run into Toltec," he said. "Want to find out if this holdup ties itself up with the one at the First National."

His voice was even and placid, but that of Julia was not.

"Oh, Bucky, Bucky — why must you do that?" she wailed.

Nancy Graham stood in the doorway. She said nothing.

"I mustn't miss any chance of getting at the truth, Julia," he explained.

"How can you get at the truth when somebody is all the time shooting at you?" she wanted to know unhappily. "You'll be — be — killed if you go."

"No. They are not worrying about me now. Too much else on their minds. When you are busy covering your tracks you don't start more trouble. I'll be perfectly safe."

Nancy went upstairs and began packing her own bag. She had decided to go to town too.

The clatter of horses' hoofs took her to the window. Three men had ridden into the yard. They swung from their horses and strode forward to the house. Something about them stirred a pulse of alarm in her throat.

A strident mocking voice said, "Thought we'd drop in and see how you was getting along from yore recent accident."

She did not wait to hear Bucky's answer but ran downstairs to the living-room. She pulled open the drawer of the desk where he worked.

Bucky knew he had been caught flatfooted. Someone in Toltec had telephoned the information to West that the C C riders were out combing the country for the bank robbers. He and his confederates had taken advantage of their absence from the ranch. Bucky was unarmed. If they meant to strike now — and it seemed to him likely they had come to do so — he was doomed.

He looked at Brad Davis coolly, no flag of terror fluttering in his eyes. What effort it cost him to drive back panic the hillmen never knew.

"I'm doing pretty well, thank you," he said. "You ought to practice shooting before you go hunting, Brad."

"That so?" the dark man jeered. "You'll prob'ly find I'm good enough right now."

The bandy-legged man in chaps spoke. "I hear you robbed another bank today."

The indolent gaze of Bucky drifted to Quinn. The devil-may-care derision in it was an achievement the C C man felt proud of later. "Where did you hear that — up in the hills *or in town?*" he asked.

"Never mind where we heard it," West broke in, a cruel leer on his malignant face. "We know where to look for bank robbers in this part of the country, so we've come to collect you. A little posse calling your own bluff. You're going to town with us."

So it was to be that way. Bucky saw their purpose written on the evil faces of the men. The intention was to arrest him, pretend to start to Toltec, and at some lonely spot kill him on the way. Their story would be that he had drawn and they had shot in self-defense. Thus neatly they would avenge the rubbing out of Dutch Dieter.

Bucky sparred for time. "I see," he said. "A personally conducted tour. You want to make sure I get there safely."

While he spoke his mind raced. If they did not know that Curly Teeters was covering the gunbarrel road there was a chance for him, providing they did not make an end of him before they reached the willows. A long shot. It was a ten to one bet they would pour lead into him as soon as they were out of sight of the house.

"You needn't bluff, fellow," Davis told him harshly. "We've got your number. You're scared as a brush rabbit that's been shot at."

"We'll run up and rope a horse for you, seeing you claim to be an invalid," West said.

Out of the house walked Nancy, slim and erect and apparently oblivious of any trouble. She carried something under a napkin. It might have been a glass of milk or a drink of medicine.

"Time to take this now, Mr. Cameron," she said quietly, standing beside her patient.

"Sure," Quinn jeered. "Take yore medicine like nurse says."

Whisking the cloth to one side, Nancy passed his revolver to Bucky. She drew a chair very close to his and sat down in it.

Bucky said "Much obliged," a jump in his voice. He was as much surprised as his enemies. Not for an instant had he guessed what she was bringing him. But as his fingers slid around the butt of the weapon his heart lifted. Abruptly the situation had changed. They had not taken the trouble to draw their weapons yet, sure they had him trapped. He had his ready.

Casually Bucky rested his hand on a knee, the barrel of the .38 pointed in the direction of the hillmen.

Quinn ripped out an astonished oath coupled with an epithet directed at the nurse.

"A lady present," Bucky reminded him. "Such language, Mr. Quinn. And by the way, we can excuse the lady now, with many thanks for the medicine."

Nancy sat tight. As long as she stayed so near Bucky, no fusillade of shots would be poured at him. "I'm going to stay here," she told him in a low voice.

"You can't get away with this, Cameron," burst out Davis angrily, his hand on his gun. "We've come here to arrest you, and we aim to take you with us. Hiding behind a woman's skirts won't do you any good."

"How about hiding behind a Colt's .38 army special?" Bucky wanted to know suavely.

"Get that girl outa the way," Quinn ordered.

"A good idea," Bucky admitted. "Nancy, beat it. You've done all you can for me. I'll play the six full you've dealt me."

"No," she cried, her calm gone, and flung her desperate challenge at the hillmen. "I won't have it. If you kill him you'd better kill me too, or I'll testify you murdered him."

Bucky rose, watching his foes steadily. "If you won't leave me I'll have to leave you. Don't push on the reins, fellows. We'll adjourn this business to the corral."

Above the clip-clop of a horse's hoofs an unmelodious voice sounded. Bucky, the three hillmen, Nancy, all listened to the song of the approaching rider, their eyes fastened on one another.

"We've lived in the saddle and ridden
    trail,
        Drink old Jordan, boys;
We'll go whooping and yelling, we'll all
    go helling!
        Drink —"

Abruptly the song died. The singer had topped the little rise and was taking in the scene. He was Bud Keller, just returning from fence-repairing, innocent of all knowledge of what had occurred during the day at Toltec.

175

He slid from the saddle and came forward, a lean, lanky, unimpressive man, with overalls climbing up the legs of his high-heeled boots. His freckled face was an amazed question-mark. That hostility was in the air he could see, but he could not understand what West and his associates were doing here. For the moment that was not important. He pushed the perplexity out of his mind and focused on one fact. He had ridden into trouble and meant to take a hand in it.

Bucky laughed, jubilantly. Things were breaking his way. "Glad to see you, Marshal Blücher," he said. "We're just starting to shoot out a little difficulty down at the corral. We'll let you in, if you like."

"I'm in," Keller said.

"Red Cowan and Dud Spiller will be here in two-three minutes," Bucky went on. "They will be sore if we don't wait for them, Bud. How about it?"

Keller rubbed his bristly chin. "Why, I dunno, Bucky. What's on the minds of these gents anyhow?"

"This is a law and order committee. They've come to arrest me for robbing the Valley Bank."

"The Valley Bank!" Bud ejaculated. "When was —?"

"An hour and a half ago. Can't give you

the exact time, since I wasn't present. Maybe the members of the committee can. I wouldn't know about that yet."

"If it's your idea to finish this now," Quinn snarled, his bowed legs wide apart, his bullet head thrust forward, "you can't come a-shooting too soon to suit me."

"I have only one idea, and that is not to leave here as your prisoner," Bucky answered. "The rest is up to you."

West did not like the way this visit was working out. It was their own fault. If they had hustled Cameron to the corral the moment they had arrived, by this time they would have been in the saddle.

"We'll let him go this time, boys," he said thickly. "We've found out he's in this business. He's scared to go to town with us."

"You're right about that last," Bucky assented. "Well, you have your hats. Don't let me hurry you, but if your business is concluded —"

"You won't hurry us," Davis interrupted angrily. "Don't think it for a minute. You never saw the day you could hurrah me."

West swung to the saddle. "Come on, Brad. We know this fellow is guilty as hell. That's enough."

He turned his horse and rode away. The others followed, reluctantly. They were spoiling for a fight. It was their opinion that West was too cautious. This insolent whippersnapper had to be bumped off some day. The sooner the better.

Nancy looked at Bucky queerly. The soft breathing color had been driven from her cheeks. She felt strangely weak.

"They meant to — kill you," she said, a quaver in her low voice.

He met her troubled blue eyes steadily. "If it hadn't been for one brave girl they would have done it. I never saw anything like the way you walked out with the revolver, as cool as could be, and handed it over to me."

Nancy felt the color beating back into her face. "'I saw them when they rode up,'" she replied, to escape the embarrassment of silence. "So I thought maybe you'd better have your gun."

"And that you had better sit down close to me so that they would hardly dare shoot at me while you were there."

"You're my patient, you know." She showed her strong beautiful teeth in a laugh. "I didn't want to have to start nursing you all over again."

Her young beauty was like spring, he thought, so fresh and tender and vivid.

"I reckon they didn't want any of your game, Bucky," said Keller admiringly to his chief.

"If you'll excuse me I'll go in and finish packing." Nancy walked toward the house.

"Packing for what?" Bucky asked. "Thought you were staying a few days more."

She flashed a glance at him over her shoulder. "I've changed my mind. I'm going in when you do."

"Girl, you'll get me a reputation as a sissy if you don't quit clucking over me like a hen with one chick."

"I'll get off the case as soon as we reach town," she promised. "But it's not my fault you're always getting into jams."

They did not start till dusk. Bucky drove fast. Near the willows Curly Teeters waved him to a halt, moving out of the blackness of the trees to find out who he was.

"Any news, Curly?" the man in the car inquired.

"Not much. Tully Arnold came along in his old flivver, with Big Bill Savage beside him. We stopped them and searched the car. Nothing doing. Tully admitted they had been in Toltec during the robbery, but he claimed he could prove an alibi. I asked him about some of the other Red Rock gents, whether they had been in town today. Said he didn't know — hadn't seen any of them."

"We had a little visit from some of them at the ranch," Bucky mentioned. "Looking for bandits, they said."

"Any trouble?" Curly asked.

"No. They thought they would take me to town, and then Miss Nancy gave me my medicine and they thought they wouldn't."

Curly knew there was some hidden meaning in the explanation, but he did not know what it was. "Maybe they figured you were too sick to travel," the C C rider said, for a lead.

"That must have been it," Bucky agreed dryly. "I was so nervous my finger twitched. Probably they noticed it. . . . No use you boys staying here any longer. Better get back to the ranch. While I'm away see that Miss Julia is never left alone. Ask Tim to sleep in the big house."

A thin crescent moon was in the sky. Later there would be stars, millions of them, to flood the desert with a silvery light, but as yet the shadows on either side of the road gave them a background vague and obscure. At times mesquite pressed close, and through the foliage a soft wind stirred.

To Nancy it seemed that anything might happen. A tremor fluttered in her breast. It was not fear. The girl's spirit courted this adventure.

She told her companion, as they traveled through the darkness, "I love it."

He said, smiling down at her, "*You* would."

"It's grand to be alive, isn't it?"

"When you are with Nancy it is," he agreed.

"I wonder if he's going to start his line," she murmured to the night.

He drew up for a moment to listen, letting the engine run. A car was coming up behind them, moving fast.

"Someone in a hurry to get to town," Bucky said. "Let's not be in their way."

He drove into the brush, winding in and out among the mesquite. Opening the door, he stepped to the ground.

"Wait here a minute," he told her, and vanished.

Nancy heard the car roar past. Presently Bucky rejoined her.

He recited, as if reading from a newspaper: "Mr. Daniel West and friends paid a short visit to town Thursday evening. The good citizens of the Red Rock district have organized themselves into a law and order committee. We understand they have volunteered to help run down the bank robbers."

"What are they going to town for?" Nancy asked.

He stepped into the car, but did not at once start the engine.

"I'm wondering that myself. Would it be for a bluff, to cover up guilt? Or just because they always have to be milling around where trouble is?"

"Or to work up public opinion against you?" she offered. "Anyhow, you'll have to be awf'ly careful. Don't let them know you are in town."

"I'll not put it in the *News*," he promised. But he knew that word of his arrival in town would reach his enemies inside of half an hour.

"Your friends would be — unhappy — if they hurt you."

"I hope so." He put an arm around the girl's waist, drawing her near, so that her face was against his.

She made no objection, unless it was to say, "I thought you were going to be an exception."

"I am an exception. I'm the only man whose life you have more or less saved twice under the fire of the enemy."

"Oh, well, that's just nonsense," she dissented. "I happened to be around and butted in."

"When a girl does that for you, what is the proper conduct?" he asked, very much aware of the fresh softness of young flesh close to his.

"Page Dorothy Dix," she suggested, mirth in her face.

He took her chin and tilted it toward him, then kissed the warm, willing lips.

She looked at him and murmured with a

smile, "No amateur."

But after a short interlude she became briskly businesslike. "Now you've paid me for more or less mixing in your war. I'm on my way to town, sir, if you please."

"I'd pay in that coin very generously," Bucky told her as he started the engine.

From the summit of a hill they looked down on the lights of Toltec. The excitement died in Nancy. In a few minutes the adventure would be over. He would leave her at her father's house and drive down into the city where danger always lay lurking for him. The muscles beneath her heart seemed to collapse and let it down. He was so foolhardy, so careless of peril, that his enemies would very likely get another chance soon. During the past days they had become good friends. They had shared a lot of jokes and spilled a lot of laughter together. Nancy was no sentimentalist but a realist. A few kisses did not mean anything. He was no more in love with her than she was with him. It would be silly to assume anything else. But when she thought of a world without Neil Cameron it brought an ache to her heart.

In front of the house she sat for a moment without leaving the car. After tonight she would pass out of his life. In nursing one made temporary friendships, but they never endured when the patient resumed his normal existence.

"I've had a swell time being bossed by you," he said.

"I've liked it too," she answered in her cool friendly manner. "I'd feel better if something didn't keep whispering to me that Miss Garside is right about you."

"About me being Toltec's Number One fool?"

"About the danger you are always walking into. It doesn't matter what I think of course. But — I wish you wouldn't."

"I won't — if I can help it."

"You've been lucky. Next time maybe you wouldn't be. They can't all be bad shots all the time . . . Good night."

She got out and walked into the house.

CHAPTER XIII

Bucky drove to the cottage where Judge Lewis lived alone, except for the old negro who looked after him and did the cooking. Before leaving the ranch Cameron had called up the lawyer and found that he expected to spend the evening at home.

Sam admitted him with his usual white-toothed smile. "Howdy, Mr. Bucky, howdy! The judge says for you to come right in."

All the curtains in the living-room had been drawn. Lewis was not inviting a shot from the darkness outside.

After his visitor was seated Lewis offered him a highball and a cigar, both of which were declined.

"Hope you have your alibi all fixed for the Valley holdup," the older man said.

"I think we have. Julia and Miss Graham and the cook all can testify I didn't leave the ranch all day. After you called me up I sent men out to check up on all the C C riders. Unless the officers take the view we're all liars and in it together we have an airtight defense."

"That's fine. This ought to help us, Neil. People are inclined to think that whoever did this robbery did the other too. Of course that doesn't in the least follow, but generally public opinion is a sheeplike business."

"Do you know who robbed the Valley? Has any evidence come out fastening it on individuals?"

"Not that I know of. None of the bandits were recognized. My opinion is that this was done by a band from outside, probably one that has held up other banks. Garside thinks so too. He reached town about an hour ago."

"Tuffy Arnold and Big Bill Savage were at Toltec during the robbery."

"I didn't know that," Lewis replied. "West and Quinn were here too, but they seem to have a perfectly good alibi."

Bucky told the lawyer about the visit they had paid the ranch.

"They are certainly on the warpath," the lawyer commented.

"Busy as bugs in a rug. By the way, they are back here again tonight. Passed me on the way in."

"Recognize you?"

"No, I drew off from the road."

"Better be careful, son."

"Yes . . . I want to see O'Sullivan at once."

"Good. Make it clear to him you're not in this. I'll walk with you to headquarters."

Bucky hesitated. "I'd let you go with me if they were better shots, Judge."

Lewis looked at him and waited for an explanation of this cryptic remark.

"They might shoot at me and hit you," Bucky explained.

"That would be unpleasant," his friend said dryly. "But maybe I need a little excitement. It has been nearly forty years since I have heard bullets whistle. The last time was when I was riding for Cameron and Cameron, just after I came out to this country as a colt. And perhaps if they are such bad shots they might miss us both."

"I've heard what a wild young buckaroo you were in those days," Bucky said, smiling at the older man. "Well, I'm not really expecting any fireworks tonight. And we can take a back street where we won't be noticed."

Just before they reached the police station, they turned into Front Street and walked down it for half a block. They spoke to several men they met.

O'Sullivan was in his office, and ordered them admitted almost at once.

He gave Bucky his stony stare. "You're always around when there's trouble, aren't you?"

"Afterward," corrected Bucky amiably.

"Prove that, can you?" the chief growled.

He was not in a good humor. The robbery at the Valley Bank had put him on the spot again. If he did not find the bandits the newspapers would ride him, ministers would preach about the rampant lawlessness in the city, and citizens would talk freely about the inefficiency of the police department.

"Yes."

"I knew you'd have a good story," O'Sullivan said offensively.

"I'm not disappointing you, then," Bucky

answered without rancor. "There's not a hole in my alibi."

He went on to tell the facts, including the visit of the Red Rock men to the ranch.

"Is it your idea that these three men came there to tackle the whole C C outfit?" the officer jeered.

"It's my idea," Bucky replied curtly, "that they knew I had sent my riders out on posses to intercept the robbers."

"How would they know that?"

Bucky met the hard gaze of the chief steadily. "A leak somewhere in Toltec. One of their spies heard you telephone to me or picked the news up later when you mentioned it. Or else got it from the girl on the wire. Or maybe from that smooth crook Jud Richman."

"Maybe I called them up and spilled it," O'Sullivan snarled. "Maybe I helped them rob the bank."

"I'm not a fool, Chief. But you talked your plans over with your men. Probably you gave information to the press. If you could put your finger on anybody who might have overheard and phoned to West —"

"I can't. And if I could, that wouldn't help me any. The fact that West tried to get the drop on you — if he did — doesn't tie him up with the robbery."

"If he had a spy keeping him in touch with

your plans, doesn't that imply a mighty strong personal interest in the bank holdup?"

"I might claim the same about you, since Judge Lewis phoned you within ten minutes of the crime."

"So you might. I want you to investigate my alibi and see whether it stands or falls."

"You can bet I will, young fellow."

The telephone bell rang. O'Sullivan spoke harshly into the transmitter. "Chief of police. Who is it?"

He listened impatiently. "He's here now — in my office . . . No . . . No . . . Let him get back to the ranch and stay there. My men are detailed on more important business." He slammed the receiver back into place, then turned and glared at Cameron. "Some woman — I didn't catch her name — wants me to give you a police guard while you hell around in town. I'll say you sure want to hog the spotlight."

"Did the name sound like Graham — or Cameron?"

"I told you I didn't catch it." The chief added bitterly: "You ought to be in the movies. You certainly are wasted here."

Bucky laughed. "I'll be at the Toltec tonight if you need me, Chief."

O'Sullivan grunted and pressed a button on his desk. As the two men went out they met a sergeant coming into the room.

"You wouldn't call the chief exactly cordial," Bucky said. "I gather that I annoy him."

"It's his busy night," the lawyer observed.

As they walked along Front Street Bucky's gaze swept back and forth. They turned the corner, to follow the same route by which they had come. Cameron's quick eye picked up a man across the street, two others on his side a little farther down. Some instinct warned him of danger. It was too late to turn back.

The roar of a gun filled the night. Bucky flung Lewis into the entrance area of the office building they were passing. Revolvers crashed. Bucky fired, and at the same moment dived into the hall. He pushed the lawyer back of the cigar stand and stood crouched near the end of it.

Brad Davis and Big Bill Savage appeared at the entrance, both armed.

"There he is!" Davis cried, and ripped out an oath.

He fired twice. A bullet shattered the glass of the cigar stand.

Bucky's finger pressed the trigger. He knew he had scored a hit. Davis clutched at his heart. The big body of the man half swung round. His knees buckled and he went down, the revolver dropping from a slack hand.

Savage turned, without firing another shot,

and bolted into the street. There was a slap of running feet, then silence.

"You all right?" Cameron asked his friend.

"Yes. And you?"

"Okay."

More feet sounded, moving cautiously toward the building.

Someone said, "They ran in there."

A policeman showed.

"It's all over," Bucky called to him. "Judge Lewis and I were attacked. I had to shoot a man."

Other men in uniform came into the lobby, their revolvers out.

Bucky and the judge moved forward. One of the officers was kneeling beside the man on the floor.

"Dead," he pronounced.

"It was self-defense," the lawyer said.

Unexpectedly another man endorsed this. "I saw it all from the drugstore. Judge Lewis is right. The other men fired at him and Mr. Cameron and followed them into this building."

Another policeman said, stooping over the dead man, "Why, it's Brad Davis."

"They were waiting for us," Bucky said. "Someone must have tipped them off we were with the chief. They would have got us if we hadn't bolted into this building. That gave me the advantage. They stood in the light, and it was darker in here."

Bucky spoke deliberately, to conceal the fact that his voice was unsteady. During the battle he had been cool and efficient, his muscles and nerves under perfect control. Now the reaction was upon him.

Guarded by the police, he and Lewis were taken back to headquarters and into the office of the chief. O'Sullivan listened to the report of his men.

"You're the luckiest daredevil alive," the chief told Bucky bluntly.

"Oh, I don't know," Bucky differed. "I have read statistics showing that in a war it takes about a half a ton of lead to extinguish one man. In four attempts I was wounded once. That's not a bad average."

"How about *your* average? One try, one man."

"I'm sorry I had to kill him. He forced it on me." Bucky added gravely: "Get me right, Chief. I didn't come back to Toltec to stir up trouble, but to protect the good name of my uncle and myself and to see that our property isn't stolen from us. I want peace, if I can get it on any decent terms."

"Looks to me as if that young woman who phoned me knew what was going to happen," O'Sullivan said. "I'll check up on where that call came from."

"My guess is that it was from Miss Graham,

who was my nurse. She was concerned about my safety."

The chief slammed the palm of his hand down on the desk in front of him. "You're either getting out of town or going to jail for safe-keeping," he announced harshly. "I've got my hands full without looking after you."

"I'll go to the Toltec tonight and leave to-morrow," agreed Bucky.

"See you do. By the way, that government man Mitchell was in to see me today."

"Did he say he was a government man?" Bucky asked, surprised.

"Yes, but he didn't want it known. Said you knew. Showed me credentials. He's here, of course, on the First National robbery. Says he'll have it cleared up before he leaves. I wish to Heaven he'd get it done soon. It's making me gray. . . . I'm sending two officers with you to the hotel. You're to stay in your room and not go out tonight."

"Yes."

"No funny business. I run a rooming-house for the city — with bars. I can put you there and know you'll stay put."

"Think I like the Toltec better. I'll not go out."

The chief called two policemen and told them to take Bucky to the Toltec and to see that Judge Lewis got home safely.

193

CHAPTER XIV

Bucky called up Mitchell on the house phone.

"I'm at the Toltec," he said. "I've promised Chief O'Sullivan not to leave my room tonight. If you're not busy, would it be too much trouble for you to step in for a little while?"

"Be up in three minutes," Mitchell replied. "What's your room number?"

Almost within the time he had set, Mitchell knocked on the door. He grinned cheerfully at his host.

"So the Valley robbery brought you back. I guessed it would. Flies to the honey. There's not much difference between an amateur and a professional detective. Both are like bloodhounds with their noses to the trail. Can't let it alone."

"That's why I came back," Bucky admitted. He looked at his visitor inquiringly. "Have you heard the latest news?"

"I can tell you that when I know what it is."

"I killed Brad Davis half an hour ago."

"Good God!" Mitchell stared at him. His eyes asked questions so urgently there was no

194

need to put them into words.

"Judge Lewis and I were leaving police headquarters when three men attacked us. At the corner of Front and Prospect. We ran into the Holden Building to escape their gunfire. Two of them followed us into the lobby. I was forced to shoot down Davis while he was firing at me."

"Do you know who the other two were?"

"One was Big Bill Savage. I didn't have time to recognize the other."

"They are determined to get you, aren't they?" Mitchell said, his eyes narrowed in thought. "Have you some evidence against them that I don't know?"

"No." Bucky added an explanation. "Perhaps I understand the psychology of these men better than you do. I was raised in constant contact with them. They don't always act on logical motives based on self-interest. To begin with, they have a constant hatred of all my family. They have stolen our stock, but we have sent several of them to the penitentiary and killed others caught rustling. My father was shot from ambush by some of them. My return filled them with resentment because they thought the Camerons were driven out for good. In my encounters with them since then I have had good luck. Once I gave them a tongue-lashing in public. They didn't like that. You must remember they are proud of their reputation as bad men. It galled them bitterly that I showed them up. Today they came to the ranch while my men were away to make an end of me, and again my luck stood up so that they had to sneak off with tails dragging. Knowing that I'm not popular now, they feel they may murder me and escape punishment for snuffing out an alleged bank robber. What I'm getting at is this: these attacks on me may not be caused by what they fear I know but by their angry hate of me."

Mitchell shook his head. "I wouldn't say so. They are in such a hurry. They can't wait. I'll tell you another thing I think. If they knew I was a detective here to clear up the First National robbery they would try to kill me too."

The telephone bell rang. Bucky answered. It was O'Sullivan talking.

"I have run down the call that came to my office while you were here," the chief said. "It was from Clem Garside's house."

Bucky said, "That's certainly a surprise."

"Miss Garside made the call. She says your friend Miss Graham told her you were in town, called her up and asked her if she could get you police protection. I gather from the way she talks that Miss Garside doesn't think a whole lot of you."

"She has mentioned that to me once or twice," Bucky replied dryly.

"I called up Miss Graham to verify the story. She says it's okay, that she was worried about you and thought Miss Garside would have more influence with us than she. So that's that."

"And Miss Garside is in the clear."

"Yes, but your friend the nurse is not. Except Judge Lewis nobody else knew you were in town. She may have tipped off to Davis or some of his crowd that you were here."

"Not in a thousand years," Bucky denied vigorously. "Nancy Graham is a fine girl, to be trusted in every way. I told you how she brought me the gun this afternoon."

"Pretty?"

"Yes. What's that got to do with it? She's absolutely dependable."

"Hmp! That's your guess. I expect you would think a girl couldn't be a double-crosser if she was pretty enough and made eyes at you. I'm having her brought in. Someone got busy mighty quick and spilled it to the Red Rock crowd that you are here."

"Sure. One of their scouts saw me on the street as I went into police headquarters, so they came swarming down from the saloon they were infesting, all hellbent for trouble."

"Might be that way."

197

"Must be. Listen, Chief. If they had been tipped off by Miss Graham, she would have told them I was heading for Judge Lewis's house and they would have picked me off from the dark as we came out. But the word came to them in the saloon where they had been drinking hard. They swarmed out like angry bees all set to sting. Couldn't wait till I had got more than a block from the city hall. You can forget Miss Graham, Chief."

"After I've had a talk with her I'll decide that."

"Suit yourself." Bucky chuckled. "You took the trouble to verify Miss Garside's story. You had in mind what I told you the other day, to dig deeper and find out who benefited most by the First National robbery."

"Nothing of the kind," O'Sullivan protested. "I still think that's all hooey. The man you're putting the finger on hadn't any more to do with it than I had."

"Yet you called up Miss Graham because you were afraid Miss Garside might have picked up some information that I was about to be attacked." Bucky's low laugh mocked the officer. "It occurred to you that maybe — by some millionth off chance — somebody in that house might be in this thing up to his neck."

The chief sputtered an angry "No" and hung up abruptly.

"Talking with O'Sullivan?" Mitchell said.

"Yes. Nothing important. About a telephone call he had."

"I'm not dumb." Mitchell smiled. "It's still in your mind that Garside is connected with these robberies."

"By Jove!"

Bucky frowned at Mitchell, struck by a new idea. He had not as yet reached a suspicion that the banker had staged the robbery of the Valley. But why not? If Garside was desperately hard up for money, if he had used funds of the bank which must be replaced to avoid discovery, why could he not have arranged this holdup to account for the cash that had disappeared? Robbing banks might have become a habit with him.

However, his view did not seem to carry much weight with either the detective or the chief of police.

He said to Mitchell: "I dare say I'm prejudiced and getting a wrong squint at this thing. If so, that's bad medicine. I want to think straight, even though I don't like Garside."

Mitchell nodded agreement. "Several times I've gone wrong on cases because I have let my feelings dominate my brain. I remember one poisoning case. The victim was a rich man. He left a young widow, lovely, pathetically helpless, stricken with grief. There was something about that woman which won all men. They wanted to protect her and take care of her. When she turned her big eyes on you they asked for kindness — and you gave it. Just the same she was a cold-blooded murderess."

"Sounds interesting. What case was it?"

"I'm awfully bad at names," Mitchell said, searching his mind. "Can't remember them. Was it Beecher? No, not just that. It will come to me in a little while."

"Doesn't matter," Bucky said carelessly. "I wondered if I had read of the case . . . To get back to a case that interests us more just now. What do you make of the Valley robbery?"

"It looks to me like the work of an experienced band. They knew just how to do the job, and they did it in minimum time, after which they made a clean getaway and left no odd ends behind. The robbery wasn't cooked up by amateurs."

"Then you don't think the Red Rock gang had anything to do with it?"

"No. It seems to me more likely that some organized gang, perhaps made up of men who don't live in the state at all, read of the first robbery and took the trouble to find when the money for the Malpais dam workers would be here. Of course one of them looked the ground over. He may have spent weeks here. I'm checking up rooming-houses to find if any suspicious strangers have been staying in town. Garages, too. Any man who has been here for some time and left today might be one of the gang we want."

"There's no connection between the two bank robberies, you think?" Bucky asked.

"If outsiders did the First National job they probably would not have taken your uncle with them but would have killed him on the ground. He did not mean anything to them. Why encumber themselves with him?"

"An outside gang did not do that job," Bucky said decisively. "I don't know about this one. You may be right. It was smooth work. Maybe professionals did it. If I knew that I wouldn't be so much interested in it."

"The name of the woman who murdered her husband was Bronson," mentioned Mitchell. "I knew it began with B and had seven letters in it."

"Was she executed?" Bucky asked.

"No. She got off. You can't convict a woman as lovely and fragile and dainty as she was. Every juryman felt she was begging him to be her champion. She made a play at each one in turn, and there wasn't one of them who wasn't thrilled by the compliment. But she was guilty as hell just the same."

"I suppose after you worked the case up it was a jolt to you to have the woman get off."

"I didn't like it," Mitchell admitted. "But that's all in the day's work. The funny thing about it was that I had been employed by her husband's brother to get evidence against the Bronson woman, and that inside of a year she had him so persuaded of her innocence, he married her."

"And they lived happily ever after?" Bucky asked.

"Far as I know. They don't send me any Christmas cards or ask me to their anniversary dinners, so I can't be sure . . . When are you leaving town?"

"Tomorrow morning. Give me a call at the ranch occasionally and let me know how you are getting along."

Mitchell promised to do that.

CHAPTER XV

Bucky read in the morning *News* over his breakfast bacon that there had been a shooting affray in front of the Holden Building on the previous evening. From the story he gathered that the combatants had belonged to different factions of lawless cattlemen from the hill country. One of those engaged in the battle had been killed by Neil Cameron, a nephew of Cliff Cameron, former president of the First National Bank, who was very much wanted by the police for questioning in connection with the robbery of that bank. On another page of the *News* there was an editorial calling upon the police to stop the reign of lawlessness that had descended upon Toltec, beginning with the murder of Buchmann and the looting of the bank with which he was connected.

Evidently Big Bill Savage had not been arrested yet. Bucky had not expected that he would be. No doubt he and his friends had been on their way to the fastnesses of the hills within five minutes of the time when he had bolted from the Holden Building.

Bucky folded the newspaper, left a tip for

the waiter, reclaimed his hat, and strolled into the street. Ten minutes later he pushed the bell at the front door of a house he had entered with less ceremony two weeks earlier. Of the Filipino who answered the ring he inquired for Mr. Garside. He learned that the banker had not come down for breakfast yet.

"Miss Garside," suggested Bucky.

The boy showed him into the living-room. Kathleen presently appeared.

"Oh, it's you," she said, her chin up.

"Yes, I came to thank you for your kind interest in me," he answered, smiling sardonically.

"Thank Miss Graham," she flashed back. "I haven't any interest in you. She asked me to telephone the chief of police, and I obliged her."

"Then I'll thank you for obliging her. Unfortunately the chief had other uses for his cops."

"So he let you walk out from his office and kill a man inside of five minutes not a block from headquarters," she flung at him.

"Yes. That annoyed him."

"*Annoyed* him!" Her voice was sharp with contempt. "It annoyed him, did it, that he was careless enough not to take precautions against murder when he had been warned?"

"Luckily it did not run to murder," Bucky mentioned.

"Didn't it? I read in the *News* that a man called Davis was killed in a street battle. Isn't that true?"

"Quite true," Bucky drawled. "He was attempting assassination and his intended victim shot him down in self-defense."

Kathleen deserted abruptly her line of attack to try another. "It's your own fault. I told you weeks ago what would happen. But you know everything so much better than anyone else. You always did, even when you were a schoolboy. If someone had dared you to jump from a roof, you would have jumped and broken your neck. It's your enormous vanity."

Bucky petted his little mustache, to irritate her. He pulled a handkerchief out of a sleeve and brushed away some imaginary dust from his coat. The fire in her dark eyes he disregarded.

"It will make Baby Face Nelson jealous to hear about Pretty Boy Cameron," she went on scornfully. "Why don't you always wear a flower in your buttonhole? And you could lisp a little."

"My best friend and most severe critic," he murmured.

A tide of angry color beat into her cheeks. Even as a small boy he had known the trick of how to make her furious. Once in school she had flung an inkwell at him and spattered the wall. His astonished innocence afterward had been accepted at face value by the teacher.

She brushed back impatiently an unruly copper curl. It was a grown-up way of stamping her foot.

"If you're quite through, don't let me detain you from taking your thanks to the proper girl," she said.

"I don't want to be ungallant after such a cordial reception, but I'd like a few words with your father too while I'm here," Bucky answered.

"Oh, that's why you came. Fernando said you wanted to see me."

"I did. I always do. Your entertainment value is immense."

"Is it? I wish you would get your amusement by absent treatment." She walked to the door, in too much of a rage to say more, and called upstairs. "Dad, Mr. Cameron is here to see you."

"Who?" boomed a heavy voice from above.

"Neil Cameron, the play actor, the movie hero."

There was a moment of silence before the banker answered. "Take him into the library."

Kathleen turned and said to the visitor, with formal politeness, "This way, Mr. Gable, if you please." She showed him to the room and left.

Garside came into the library with a chip

on his shoulder. He was always grumpy before breakfast.

"What's on your mind?" he demanded bluntly.

"I came to report progress, Mr. Garside — or rather no progress," Bucky said amiably. "You made me a little proposition. That was before you took over the receivership of the First National."

"That's not true. James Ankeny has been appointed receiver, as you know very well."

"So he has. Your man Friday. I don't know whether your offer still stands. Twenty-five thousand for the ranch and the bank — lock, stock, and barrel. Anyway, I can't deliver. I haven't been able to find Uncle Cliff. My opinion is he's dead."

"My opinion is he's in Guatemala — or Mexico — or Timbuctoo," Garside differed harshly.

"Sometimes the smartest men are the dumbest," Bucky said. "He was killed by the fellows who robbed the bank."

There was no expression but rigid arrogance in the face of the banker. "My offer is withdrawn," he told the younger man curtly. "I'll not wait any longer. You may not know it, but I have bought up the ranch mortgage. I've owned it for six months."

"I know that."

"Then perhaps you know how to clean up the back interest."

"Our beef roundup should take care of current liabilities."

Garside laughed harshly. "With rustlers running off your prime stuff?"

"How do you know that?" Bucky asked. "Have they been reporting to you?"

"Don't talk to me like that," Garside roared. "I won't have it from an impudent young squirt like you."

"Then we'll leave your rustler friends out of our conversation, if it disturbs you . . . Who robbed the Valley Bank?"

The swiftness with which Bucky flung the question startled Garside. His quick look, at once wary and suspicious, stabbed at Cameron.

"What you mean? How do I know?" His voice took on a bullying note. "Maybe you can tell me. Maybe you have important information you could give the police — if you wanted to."

"How much did the bandits get?"

"I'll tell you nothing." The banker slammed a hand down on the table. "Read the papers and find out what Chief O'Sullivan wants to give out to the public. What do you mean, coming here and bothering me with your impertinence?"

"The robbery must have been a surprise to you," Bucky commented in his soft drawl.

"What are you trying to insinuate?" stormed Garside.

"Coming so soon after that of the First National, which must have been another shock to you."

The eyes of Bucky, hard and cold as steel, fastened on those of his enemy. Was it alarm they saw filter into the stony face of the older man for just a fraction of a second before anger banished it?

"I don't know what you mean." Garside flung open the door of the library. "Get out of here, you scoundrel, or I'll throw you out. By God, any Cameron has unmitigated gall to invite himself into my house. Get out. Get out, I tell you."

"On my way," Bucky replied, still watching the face of his family foe closely. "Why get so flustered, Mr. Garside? All I said was —"

"I heard what you said, and I don't want to hear any more."

"All right with me." Bucky smiled blandly. "As Thomas Mitchell says — but no, we'll save that for another time."

This time Bucky was sure he had scored a hit. In the angry eyes he caught a flicker of dismay, instantly wiped out.

"There won't be another time. Keep out

of my way, if you know what's good for you. No killer can come here and bully me."

The banker was still shouting at Bucky as he followed him into the hall. But Cameron was no longer paying attention. He was listening to another voice, which seemed to be coming from the living-room.

"Neither you nor anyone else can treat me like a dog," it snarled. "When we meet, you'll speak to me like I was a human being or I'll —"

Kathleen's cool, contemptuous retort, with the singing sting of a whip in it, interrupted the threat: "Get out of the way and let me pass, you ruffian."

"I'll get out of the way when I'm ready. Listen, you vixen —"

Bucky whipped open the door and walked into the living-room. Backed up against a large stained-glass window with leaded panes stood Kathleen. She was facing a big-bodied, slouching man who barred the path of escape. At the sound of the door opening the man whirled. His thin-lipped ugly mouth tightened when he caught sight of Bucky. The dead slate-colored eyes narrowed. A hand started to slide under the lapel of the open coat.

"Drop your hand, West," ordered Bucky curtly.

The hand halted.

Kathleen moved to leave the room, but stopped. It had occurred to her that there was dynamite in this situation. Bucky was moving forward, evenly, his gaze on the hillman. She watched him breathlessly.

"Don't come any nearer, fellow," West warned. His fingers were not six inches from the butt of his holstered .45, and in a fraction of a second he could send a bullet crashing.

Bucky stopped, about six feet from him. "Beat it, West — *muy pronto*," he said quietly.

"You own this house?" West demanded.

"I don't like the way you talked to Miss Garside." Bucky's voice exploded suddenly like the crack of a whip. "Get going, you dirty scalawag!"

"You can't talk thataway to me," West cried venomously.

His hand jumped toward the revolver. At the same instant Bucky launched himself forward like a released spring. His shoulder caught the big man in the midriff and flung him back violently against the colored window. West went through the leaded panes as if they had been made of paper, his heavy body striking the ground below with smashing force.

Bucky ran into the conservatory and through an open French window. West lay huddled on the ground, the wind knocked out of him.

Swiftly Bucky slipped a hand under the man's coat and found the revolver in the holster. He made sure West had no other weapon.

The dull eyes of the man on the ground glared hatred at him.

"You took advantage of me when I wasn't expecting it," he said, half in a whine, half threatening.

"Get up and get out," Bucky told him.

The man rose shakily. "I'll remember this, fellow," he growled.

Bucky watched him go before he returned to the house by way of the conservatory.

"Afraid I've littered your lawn with glass," he told Kathleen. "He was reaching for a gun."

"What will he do?" the girl asked.

Bucky smiled. "Get drunk, I expect."

"I mean — isn't he dangerous?"

"So he claims." Bucky spoke carelessly. "Sorry I had to ruin the window. He didn't give me much time."

"What's it all about?" Garside demanded harshly. "Why come to my house for your rowdy fights?"

"This man West was insulting me," Kathleen told her father in a low voice.

"I don't get it," the banker snapped. "Why was he insulting you? He hasn't spoken to you four times in your life, has he?"

"No . . . I started out of the room when he came in, but he wouldn't let me go. He's . . . crazy."

"I never saw him do anything crazy," Garside said doggedly. "You must have misunderstood what he said."

"It wasn't what he said. It was the way he looked."

"He always looks as sour as curdled milk. Why pay any attention to him?"

"That's what annoyed him, Dad. He had notions I should be nice to him. Keep him out of this house after this, please. I won't have him here." The girl's level eyes challenged her father.

"What was he doing here, anyhow?" Garside asked, annoyed both at Kathleen and West.

"Said he came to see you on business. I told him you did your business at the bank."

"Would it have hurt you to be pleasant to him? Do you have to come the Queen of Sheba on him because he's a plain cowman from the hills?"

"I don't choose to have anything to do with scoundrels whose eyes insult me," she answered hotly.

"We'll talk about that later." Garside turned to Bucky. "If you're through wrecking my house, we won't detain you any longer, sir."

Kathleen said to Bucky in a stiff formal voice, her color high, "I thank you for your help."

"The pleasure was all mine," the young man told her cheerfully. "I didn't suppose I would ever get a chance to throw that fellow through a window."

"I hope you won't get into trouble on account of it."

"I won't." His smile was grim. "I'm in trouble up to the neck already. A little surplusage doesn't matter. . . . I hope you'll excuse me if I go now. This is one of my busy days. No, Mr. Garside, I really can't accept your pressing invitation to stay. I'll take a raincheck if you don't mind."

Bucky bowed himself out of the room. The ironic grin on his face might have been called impudent without injustice.

Garside glared at him angrily. The look in Kathleen's eyes was a strange one. It held hunger and wistfulness and pride.

CHAPTER XVI

Doctor Raymond met Bucky in front of the post office.

"I suppose I owe you a commission for sending me a patient," he said, manifestly amused.

"Did I recommend you to somebody?" Bucky asked. "If I did, I owe it to you for being such a swell judge of nurses."

"Miss Tingley *is* a good nurse," the doctor admitted.

"Correct, but I wasn't thinking of Miss Tingley. Who is this patient to whom I recommended you?"

"He didn't say you recommended me. You made him a patient — flung him out of a window when he wasn't looking, he says."

"Did he say he wasn't looking?" Bucky asked.

"Said he wasn't expecting it."

"That's probably true. He was reaching for a gun when I ruined a perfectly good window in the living-room of our leading citizen."

"Somebody is always reaching for a gun when you're around. Do you ever take a day off and keep out of mischief?"

215

"I'm unlucky, doctor. I wish it could be broadcasted that I am an inoffensive person who would like to be let alone."

"Why not go to the ranch and stay there?"

"They follow me there. This fellow West and two of his fellow wolves showed up at the C C yesterday to pick on me."

"And when you come to town they attack you." Raymond added, more seriously, "One of them will never attack you again."

"No," Bucky said.

"But West will. Look out for him. The man was sputtering threats while I dressed the cuts in his hands and head. Don't take this lightly, Mr. Cameron. He won't rest until you are dead, if he can bring it about. He says he always hated you. His hatred is explosive now. It is inflamed by wounded vanity. The man is gnashing his teeth, if you don't object to a cliché."

"Did he give you any hint as to how he means to get me?"

"No, except that it is going to be soon. For heaven's sake, look out, man."

"I'm going back to the ranch this morning," Bucky said. "West will have to run the gauntlet of a dozen good men before he gets to me. That won't be so easy."

"I hope not. The truth is that I could better spare a better man, Mr. Cameron. You have color. Life in Toltec would be less interesting without you."

"I'll try to stay alive on your account," Bucky promised lightly.

Thomas Mitchell came out of the post office and stopped to say good morning. Bucky introduced him to the doctor, with the added information that the newcomer was thinking of settling in Toltec.

The doctor's eyes dilated slightly as he looked at Mitchell. Then his good manners reasserted themselves. He said he hoped that Mr. Mitchell would find the town a congenial and profitable location if he decided to stay.

Bucky found Tim Murphy waiting for him at the Toltec. The foreman let out a yelp of joy at sight of him, and followed it with reproaches.

"God, Bucky, you're making me gray-haired before my time," he protested. "Why-for did you have to come to town without letting me know? You're the doggonedest idiot I ever did meet. You knew you were liable to run into trouble, like you did. Seems you go around asking to be shot."

"I haven't been shot," Bucky demurred calmly.

"Not your fault you weren't. They did their damndest. Tell me about it, boy."

"Didn't you read about it in the *News?* Judge

Lewis and I lay in wait for some honest citizens from the Red Rock district. I gather from the paper that they returned our fire."

"Oh, heck!" Tim brushed this persiflage aside. "How many of them were there? How come you to get out of the trap alive?"

"They picked the wrong place. We ducked into the Holden Building and when Davis came in after me I let him have it."

"Did he come alone?"

"Big Bill Savage was with him. There was another fellow outside, but he didn't come in with the others. I've a notion it was West. By the way, I had a little run-in with him this morning."

"Where? When?"

Bucky told the story of the adventure at the Garside place.

"I'm going to get you outa town and keep you locked up in your room, fellow," Murphy said. Not ordinarily a profane man, he let out a couple of bristling oaths. "Can't leave you alone for a minute without you hunting trouble. I never saw such a man."

"Did I invite West and his friends to the ranch?" Bucky asked defensively.

"You drove in here, knowing hell was likely to be popping. You went to Garside's house for no good reason."

"I wanted to ask Clem a question or two."

"You could have gone to the bank."

"All right." Bucky smiled. "I wanted to see his daughter too, if you will have it."

"What did West want to see Clem about?" Murphy inquired.

"He didn't tell me."

"They're in some of this deviltry together." He added, after a moment: "Maybe Garside hired his outfit to bump you off."

"Might be. After talking with Garside, I still think he was in the First National robbery. That's not all. I suspect he fixed it to have the Valley held up. He looked to me scared when I hinted at it. And that dead-pan poker face of his gave him away when I mentioned Mitchell to him. He's worried about Mitchell, or I miss my guess. Probably suspects he is a government man."

"Likely enough."

"It got to him to learn that Mitchell and I are more or less friendly."

"What's the point in going round stirring up the animals?" Tim wanted to know. "Aren't they sore enough at you already?"

"The point is that if I can get them to worrying they will make some protective move that may betray them."

"Such as filling you full of slugs."

"That would be rather an offensive move," Bucky admitted.

"Does Haskell mean to do anything about Big Bill?"

"He'll probably make a bluff. I've talked with the district attorney. He is willing to commission me an officer to arrest Savage. He is thick in the head. If we get him under lock and key he is likely to give away something when Ashley third degrees him."

"So we're going into the hills to drag out Savage?"

"I am," Bucky corrected. "It's a one-man job."

Murphy began at once to protest. His friend let him sputter until his opposition died down vocally.

"I'm standing on that proposition," Bucky said quietly. "I'll tell you why."

He did, and was not to be argued out of his purpose. Murphy offered to substitute for him, but Cameron would not have it. He intended to go get Savage, and go after him alone, he said. The man lived in a cabin a mile from his nearest neighbor. It ought to be not dangerous to arrest him and slip down out of the hills unobserved.

From that Murphy could not move him.

CHAPTER XVII

A wafer moon crescent was riding over the hills, and stars filled the sky. The slopes of the first range rose before Bucky vague and shadowy. His buckskin was an old-timer in this country, and picked the easiest way into the mountains with a certainty the rider did not attempt to improve upon by guiding. Generally the horse followed no trail, except the sketchy ones made by cows for their convenience.

In the lower foothills there was much brush. Scrub oak snatched at the stirrups. Juniper boughs whipped the legs and even the face of the man in the saddle. Bucky knew that soon he would come to a rough steep, rock-strewn, above which there would be pines marching in battalions. Travel would be easier then.

This land was as well known to Bucky as a primer is to a first-grade teacher. As a boy he had hunted over it with his father and uncle. He had ridden circle here on beef roundups. Once he and Tim Murphy, with two other men, had followed rustlers slipping away with C C stock, and after a battle had taken back the bunch of cows and one of the thieves.

But as he penetrated the cañon slashes that cut into the high hills familiar features grew more seldom. The country became rugged. He was close to the roots of splintered peaks. More than once he had to turn back and swing round to find a possible way to ascend overhanging rim rocks or to make a circuit in order to avoid impassable mountains.

Ever since he could remember, this region had been the refuge of outlaws. In the old days, not within his own memory except as wrinkled cowmen had told the stories and made them seem immediate to him, stagecoach robbers had fled for the shelter of these pockets. Killers wanted by the law had led furtive lives in the deep recesses, and always rustlers had ridden by night to collect the stock of honest settlers and transfer ownership by illegal means. Tuffy Arnold had been here for forty years, driven by an imperative urge to get away from civilization in a hurry and hide under another name from a vengeance hard at his heels. His crime had been long since forgotten and wiped off the blotter, but he had chosen not to return to his former haunts. West and Quinn and Big Bill had come in later, successors of the first reckless men who had ridden this tangle of cañons and breakneck heights. The first crop had come and gone. Many had died young, trapped at their nefarious work or cut down by the bullets of men as ruthless as they, and for the moment more lucky. Very likely, Bucky reflected, the lives of West and most of his associates would be snuffed out unless the walls of a penitentiary gave them enforced protection. Not all of these outlaws were wholly bad. Driven to the wall, they showed a flinty courage. He had seen generosity flame out unexpectedly, but it was true that in the worst of them whatever goodness may once have been had gone to seed and been blow away.

Bucky made a cold camp in a timber pocket jutting out from a small mountain park. The chill wind bit through his blankets to the bone. Once he rose and tramped a beat to get circulation back into his legs. After this he fell into troubled sleep, and woke when the first streaks of light were sifting into the sky.

He ate two beef sandwiches and drank water from the ice-cold creek. While it was still dark he saddled the buckskin and took the trail again. From a ridge he looked down into a mist-filled valley. He had seen Big Bill's place only once, but unless he had come too far to the east — as he might very easily have done — the cabin was in this park, at the edge of an aspen grove close to a rock bluff.

The buckskin dropped down the steep shale slope, picking its way at an angle which brought it to the back of the aspens. The mist was thinning. In the blur Bucky made out the vague outline of a cabin. He could see grazing horses or cattle, not clearly enough to be sure which.

Tying the buckskin, Bucky moved toward the house. As he did so he saw smoke begin to rise from the chimney. A man came out, bucket in hand, without a coat or vest, and walked to the creek. Swiftly Bucky slipped forward. He was gambling on the chance that Savage was alone. Revolver in hand, he stepped lightly through the door and swept the room with a quick glance.

Nobody was in it. Blankets had been tossed back from the bunk where Big Bill had been sleeping. A fire was crackling in the stove. Hanging on the wall was a belt, a gun in the holster. Bucky emptied the cartridges from the chamber of the .45 and dropped them in his pocket. The weapon he put back where he had found it.

Footsteps sounded. Bucky sat on a homemade bench at one side of the room and waited. Big Bill came through the door, a bucket of water in his hand.

He stopped in his stride, staring at his guest in amazement.

Bucky said, "Take it easy, Bill." The weapon in his hand was pointed toward the floor, but a twitch of the wrist would have directed it to the body of the nester.

"Where did you come from?" Savage stammered.

"Oh, I just dropped in to take you back to Toltec." The timbre of Bucky's voice was light and casual.

"I don't want to go to Toltec," the hillman said.

"Maybe I can persuade you to change your mind."

"I — I been to Toltec this week already." Savage was no fast thinker, but he knew this statement was a mistake almost before he finished making it.

"Yes, I saw you there — with Davis and West, you damned murdering wolf."

The name of West was a shot at a venture, but the big man did not make a correction.

"I came home Monday night," he said.

"Tuesday night too," Bucky added. "In a hurry. After a little difficulty in front of the Holden Building."

"No. I wasn't there."

"Not long," Bucky corrected. "You left suddenly — you and West. Brad Davis stayed."

Big Bill slid a look at the belt hanging on the wall. It might as well have been in the state museum. Before he could reach it, Cameron would have him plugged full of lead.

"Must have been someone else," he said.

"You can tell that to District Attorney Ashley."

"I don't have to go without a warrant," Savage protested sulkily.

Bucky took a paper from an inside pocket and tossed it to the man. "Strictly legal, Bill. I wouldn't want to shock your law-abiding mind. I'm a deputy empowered to bring you in."

Savage did not even look at the paper. The warrant that was going to take him to Toltec, unless he could find a way of escape, rested in Cameron's hand with its blue nose pointed downward.

"Why pick on me instead of West?" the big man growled.

"We'll get him later," Bucky promised. "Sorry to hurry you, Bill, but we won't wait for breakfast. Soon as we can rope and saddle a mount for you, we'll be off."

"Scared of something?" Big Bill jeered.

"Yes," his captor admitted. "The altitude makes me jumpy. I'll feel better when we get down to the C C."

"If I had a gun —"

"I know all about that," Bucky said. "You would certainly show me up. But you haven't one within reach. So you'll have to postpone that pleasure. Put on your coat and hat if you want them."

"How about my leaving a note telling my friends where I've gone?"

"No. They might get ideas."

Savage roped and saddled a sorrel, making slow work of it. More than once his gaze swept along the road which dipped over the hill.

"Expecting company?" Bucky asked.

"Why, no!" Big Bill slid a look at him. "What made you think that?"

"It doesn't matter. We're on our way. Climb into that saddle, and don't try any monkey tricks if you don't want to be perforated. I'd rather take you in alive than dead, but that will be up to you." Bucky dropped the loop of his rope around the neck of the prisoner and drew it tight. The other end of the rope he fastened to the horn in front of his own saddle.

"You don't have to do that," Savage said sourly. "I'd as lief go with you to Toltec as not."

"Putting a rope round your neck is a pleasure as well as a duty," Bucky answered. "I haven't forgotten you were trying to assassinate me night before last."

"No, sir. I wasn't there."

"You weren't there long — after Davis went

227

down," Bucky admitted. "You took it on the lam. Not yellow, are you, Bill?"

"You wouldn't dare say so if you didn't have the drop on me," the big man retorted angrily. "You were standing behind the cigar counter where it was dark —"

Savage stopped his justification abruptly. He was saying too much.

"Yes?" encouraged Bucky gently. "And you were in the light?"

"I didn't say any such thing," Big Bill denied.

"You just guessed I was standing in the dark by the counter."

The prisoner took refuge in sulky silence.

They were riding up the steep hillside to the lip of the saucer, zigzagging as they went. Bucky kept just behind Savage, often so close that the head of the buckskin overlapped the flank of the sorrel. As they reached the summit the rays of the sun were streaming through the needles of the lodge pole pines.

Big Bill slewed his head round for another look at the road meandering down the hill on the other side of the valley. A puff of dust billowed at the summit. In a moment riders would probably appear.

"When were they due?" Bucky asked.

"I don't know what you mean."

"Travel with your eyes in front of you. Then your bronc won't be so liable to stumble."

Savage let out a shout that was like the roar of a bull. He whirled his horse and drove it headlong at the buckskin. Cameron had no time to slip aside. He and his mount went down under the impact, but he was flung free of the saddle. Bucky landed and was on his feet in an instant. As the buckskin struggled up from the ground he caught the bridle

The frightened sorrel went sunfishing, came down on all four feet, and started to buck. The rope round the hillman's neck tightened and dragged him from the saddle. With a whistling snort his gelding bolted down the hill they had just climbed.

On the road across the valley two riders had drawn up and were looking at Bucky and his prisoner.

Bucky ordered Savage to get up. Big Bill rose, feeling his neck. It had been given a terrific jerk.

"You're traveling on foot," Bucky told him. "Understand, fellow. There isn't going to be any rescue of a live man. Get going —fast."

"My neck," Big Bill moaned.

Cameron's face was drained of all kindliness. The set of his jaw was a threat. His features were harsh and sharp.

"I've done busted something," the hillman added.

"Your choice," his captor snapped. "If you

are dead pork when I get you to the ranch, it's not my fault."

A bullet from a rifle whistled past them, not a foot from Big Bill's head.

"They're shooting at me," Savage complained.

"You asked for it."

The two riders could not recognize them at this distance. Savage began to run. A rifle cracked again. Then Bucky and the roped man dropped over the brow of the hill.

"Sharp to the right," ordered Cameron.

Big Bill did as told. He was as anxious to find cover as was Bucky. Ahead of them was a rock rim of large boulders. Into it they moved. Bucky slid from the saddle and led the buckskin back of a huge splintered quartz outcropping. He untied the end of the rope from the horn.

"Turn your back," he told Savage curtly.

The prisoner obeyed. Bucky tied him hand and foot, then gagged the man with his own bandanna.

"To keep you from committing suicide," he said grimly. "If you should work the gag loose and yell, you'll go first."

Bucky found a place for himself behind two boulders that supported each other. Between them was an opening through which he could see.

The men on horseback had reached the summit and were consulting together. One of them waved a hand toward the rocks. They turned the heads of their horses in that direction and rode forward. Bucky recognized them as West and Tuffy Arnold. About two hundred yards from the boulder field, they drew up.

West shouted a challenge. "We know you're in there. Come on out, or we'll get you."

Bucky did not answer. He saw them talk the situation over. Plainly Tuffy was of opinion that it would be foolhardy to try to dig out from the rocks anybody who might be hiding there. The other man urged him to ride forward with him and find out if the men they had seen were enemies. At last, impatiently, West moved forward alone. His rifle lay across the saddle in front of him. Continually the man's gaze swept the rimrock.

He stopped, to call out an invitation to whoever might be lying there. "If you'll come out, we'll talk this over friendly."

Still Bucky said nothing. He could have shot his enemy with no danger to himself, except for inconvenient scruples of decency.

West hesitated. He was not sure that anybody was among the rocks. The men he had seen might have disappeared into a draw and by this time be a mile away. Very likely this was the case. He had boasted to Tuffy that he meant to find out. To save face he had to ride along the rim for a bit. This might prove perilous, but he did not think so. It was his opinion the men at whom he had shot were friends, for he had afterward recognized Big Bill's horse. They were, he guessed, sore at him for firing at them without waiting to make sure of their identity, and it would please them to be able to report that he had not dared to search the rocks. He had told Tuffy that the horse they had seen running wild belonged to Big Bill, but had encouraged the idea that the men in the rocks were foes. He was making a big bluff by which he expected to gain ad-miration among his fellows. Tuffy and those in the boulder field — assuming there was any-body there — would tell how fearlessly he had advanced to rout out any enemies who might be crouched in the rimrock with their guns trained on him.

Bucky was surprised at the rashness with which the man approached. West swung from the horse and straddled the last fifty yards on foot, raffish bravado in every stride.

"Stand up, fellow, and fight if that's yore game," he called.

The man waiting for him crouched low. He was not ready yet.

West walked straight into the trap. "I'm not

scared of any damn man ever was born," he shouted. Almost he persuaded himself that he believed some of the C C riders were in the rocks.

He circled a big boulder — and pulled up sharply. All his boldness vanished. The man's jaw dropped. His dead cod eyes dilated. Stricken dumb for an instant, he gazed at Bucky Cameron. A rifle lay beside the C C man. In his hand was a revolver, and the barrel of it pointed steadily at his enemy's stomach.

"Drop that rifle and stick 'em up," Bucky ordered.

For a fraction of a second West hesitated. A wild idea of fighting it out flashed through his mind and was discarded. He would not have a chance. Cameron would drill bullets into him before he got started.

"What you doing here?" he asked, dazed. His eyes fell on Big Bill bound and prone.

"Get 'em up — quick!" warned Bucky sharply.

West dropped the gun and got his hands up. Bucky moved toward him with his jaunty catlike tread, turned the man round, and patted him to feel for weapons. He removed a revolver.

"Must be expensive to keep buying guns and have them taken away so regularly," Bucky suggested.

"What's the big idea?" snarled the hillman. He was frightened, but did not want to show it.

"I'm returning a favor. You wanted to take me to town Tuesday. Now I'm taking you there."

Bucky's voice was mild, but the timbre of it did not allay the fears of the hillman. He recalled what he had meant to do under pretense of taking Cameron to town.

"You got a lot of yore men here?" he asked unhappily.

"All I need. Just step out and bring your horse in here, West. And don't make a mistake. You'll be covered plenty. Lead the animal by the bridle, keeping in front of him every foot of the way. If you make one suspicious wiggle of a finger, you're gone. Understand?"

West said hoarsely that he did.

He went out for the horse. Tuffy called to him to ask if everything was all right. West did not answer. He was afraid that any reply might be taken the wrong way. He brought his mount back at the end of a taut bridle.

Bucky unfastened the rope and put the loop around the neck of his new prisoner. He untied Big Bill and slipped the honda end over his head. The ends of both ropes he fastened to the horn of his own saddle.

234

"Tell Tuffy to come on," Bucky commanded West. "Say everything is all right, and say it nice."

West said it nicely enough to bring the old man forward at a road gait. Tuffy was surprised at the reception he met. His fox face took on a curiously distressed look.

"Drop any guns you have," Bucky told him.

The old man let a pistol slip to the ground.

"Stay where you are," Bucky went on. "We're headed for town and you are going part of the way with us. West and Big Bill will take turns walking, and the first one who bats an eye too fast will get a load of lead in him. Fork the saddle, Bill. You get the first ride."

"We can go back and get Big Bill's horse," Tuffy suggested.

"We can, but we won't," Bucky decided. "Exercise will do your friends good. All set."

"I'm not going," West said angrily.

"Suit yourself," Bucky replied. "If your neck is tough enough to stand being dragged, it will be all right with me." He added sharply, "Take your hand off that rope."

West gave in, cursing furiously. He was in high-heeled boots, not built for walking. They threw his weight forward against the cramped toes. Before he had traveled a mile his feet burned and his heels were skinned. He was in acute torment.

For hours the little cavalcade moved toward the desert, sometimes plodding down cañons, again climbing mountain trails. When the C C ranchhouse came in sight, Bucky told Tuffy he might go home and tell the boys that crime never paid.

When Bucky and his prisoners reached the house, the hillmen were hot, dusty, and tired. Their feet were screaming with pain.

Tim Murphy looked them over derisively. "You look some played out, boys," he drawled. "Where did you collect this riffraff, Bucky?"

But the foreman's insouciance was a fraud. He had been under a heavy strain of anxiety. More than once he had come close to breaking Bucky's orders by sending a posse into the hills to assist him. Now his heart was high with triumphant relief. Not only was his friend safe. He had brought back his man, and for surplusage that other desperado Dan West. Tim was inordinately proud of the young man whom he had taught as a boy to throw his first rope and to ride his first bronco.

West said venomously, as he pulled a dusty boot from a tortured foot, "If it's the last thing in the world I ever do, I'll get you for this, Cameron."

"The same way you got my uncle?" Bucky asked. "The same way you tried to murder me night before last?"

236

"How did you get these gallows birds, Bucky?" Tim asked.

"I bumped into them," Bucky said carelessly, "and I said maybe they had better come along with me and they said they would."

"Taking them to town tonight?" the foreman inquired.

"Thought we would. From the way he's been squawking, I think maybe West wants a doctor to come to the jail to look after his feet."

"You'd think he'd get wise to it that you're poison to him," Murphy jeered. "Last time you met him it was his head and hands Doc Raymond had to fix up."

West cursed, savagely and bitterly.

"Poke the animals with a stick and hear them growl," Bud Keller said, with his usual grin.

"Take these gents to the bunkhouse, Bud, and see they are well guarded," Murphy gave orders. "Curly is down there now. He'll help you. They sure look tame as whipped curs, but don't let them get near the right end of a gun. You know how a tenderfoot can fool around with a weapon and hurt himself."

As soon as the prisoners had been led away Tim flung a question at Bucky. "How in Mexico did you pull it off?"

"Matter of surprise," his friend told him.

"Big Bill wasn't expecting me, and I got the drop on him. West bluffed he was looking for anyone who was on the prod, but it turned out he didn't mean it."

"Fine," Tim said. "Now I'll hear the story — just how it happened."

Bucky told him.

CHAPTER XVIII

Tim Murphy drove to town with Bucky when he took his prisoners in to the district attorney, but he did not stay to listen to the grilling of Big Bill by Ashley. He went to the office of the Western Union and sent a telegram for Bucky, after which he went up and down Front Street spreading the news of how his friend had gone up to the Red Rock country alone and brought back the two redoubtable bad men with ropes around their throats. In the telling Tim saw that the story lost none of its dramatic values.

It pleased him to note the change in public sentiment toward the Camerons. There had been a complete reversal of feeling. This had been brought about partly by the loyalty of family friends who held staunchly to their belief in Cliff, and partly by the attempts of Bucky's enemies to get rid of him by assassination. That young man's reckless and jaunty contempt of his foes was also a contributing factor. Mass thinking is often confused. Always eager to find a hero, it was beginning to turn admiringly toward Bucky.

Ashley had always been friendly to the Camerons, and at his invitation Bucky was present while he quizzed the big man from the hills. Inside of ten minutes the district attorney had Big Bill floundering. His confused explanations made it clear that West had been one of the three who had attacked Cameron and Lewis, in spite of his refusal to admit this.

The lawyer shifted ground so rapidly that Savage could not adjust his mind to the changes. At times he would deny guilt volubly, and again he would take refuge in sullen silence. He protested that none of the Red Rock men had tried to shoot Bucky in his room at the hospital, but he also insisted that they had not attempted to kill him at any other time. He was more convincing when he answered questions about the robbery of the Valley Bank. In support of his contention of innocence he gave the names of witnesses who would testify to being present with him and Quinn at the actual time of the holdup. Though Ashley came back to the subject more than once, Big Bill claimed he could prove he was not in town on the day or night of the First National Bank robbery. That West, Quinn, and Davis were at Toltec a few hours prior to the murder of Buchmann he had been told, but he was sure they had nothing to do with the affair. If they had been implicated he would have heard of it later. Up in the Red Rock country everybody knew all about the doing of his neighbors. He felt absolutely sure that nobody living in his vicinity was concerned in the disappearance of Cliff Cameron.

"What about the tie-up between West and Garside?" Bucky asked.

"I don't know anything about any tie-up," Savage answered sulkily.

"I happen to know that West has been at the Garside house several times lately."

"So have you," Savage flung back at him. "Maybe you and Clem are in cahoots."

Ashley laughed. "One on you, Bucky," he said.

"Have any strangers been hanging around in the Red Rocks since the Valley Bank robbery?" Cameron inquired.

"I saw one son-of-a-gun up there today," Big Bill retorted. "No others. He looked like he might be a bank robber."

"Much obliged." Bucky turned to the district attorney. "I have no more questions to ask him."

After Big Bill had been retired from circulation the two young men discussed what he had said. Both of them felt that they could tell when he was lying and when telling the truth. His expression gave him away.

"But the facts don't tie up with our impressions," Ashley admitted. "We could tell he was lying when he claimed none of his crowd ever had shot at you, but he looked as if he were on the level when he said they hadn't taken a crack at you while you were in the hospital. Maybe one of his friends did that and kept his mouth shut."

"Maybe. Or Garside may have given orders against any talking," Bucky suggested.

"Better get that maggot out of your head," the district attorney said. "I don't care for Clem. To get elected I had to bust his slate. But I'm not going to let my feelings cloud my good sense. He's a big man and wants to be a bigger one. He would not be crazy enough to get mixed in a business that could easily ruin him."

"Not unless he was financially pushed to the wall," Cameron added. "There have been a lot of stories lately about how overextended he is. He is hard as nails. If it was necessary to save himself he would go to any lengths.

The man is without any moral sense."

"Of course I've heard the stories," Ashley said. "They have been cropping up every once in a while for a year. But they are probably exaggerated. Anyone who has been making money as rapidly as Clem gets cramped for immediate funds sometimes. But his credit is good."

"Is it? I wonder about that. Warren Young says he has sunk more than a quarter of a million on that molybdenum mine at Fairview. He is up to his neck in real estate, most of it business property pretty heavily mortgaged. My guess is that he is spread out very thin and has been forced to raise every dollar he could to keep going. What would he do if he had been in a spot where he had to raise seventy-five or a hundred thousand immediately in cash?"

"I don't know. But that's a far-flung supposition."

"No, sir. He's in a jam. I'd bet heavily on it. And I'll tell you what he would do. He'd get the money any way he could. My people knew him in the old days. Clem Garside was a bold unscrupulous scoundrel then, and that's exactly what he is today."

Ashley threw up his hands. "I won't argue with you, Bucky. You are a nut on the subject of Clem. I don't blame you, since he has been

242

an enemy of you Camerons for a generation. But you don't convince me a bit."

Bucky rose. "I will before I'm through," he promised.

When Bucky met Tim Murphy at the Pioneers, the foreman had a piece of news for him.

"Mitchell left town this evening. I met him at the Toltec as he was going. He told me to tell you he thought he had a line on the Valley Bank robbers. A fellow who called himself Steve McCarthy stayed at a cheap rooming-house on Fort Street until the day of the holdup. He had been there a week, but he left just before the stick-up of the bank. Mitchell got the landlady to let him look the room over. There were two or three El Paso papers there, so Mitchell thinks he may live there. The landlady says two other fellows showed up the last day and spent a couple of hours with this McCarthy. Outside of them he never had but one visitor, a man who came to see him twice late at night. If you want to see the landlady, her address is 514 Fort Street."

"I want to see her," Bucky instantly decided out loud. "Did Mitchell say he was going to El Paso?"

"Yes. We're to keep this lead under our hats, he told me."

At 514 Fort Street, Bucky and Tim walked

up a flight of stairs and rang a bell. A somewhat frowsy blonde in the forties, wearing a gaudy kimono and bedroom slippers, shuffled out of a room and answered the bell.

Bucky mentioned why they had come.

She gave him a sharp look. "Why should I answer questions about my lodgers? How do I know who you are? What's there in it for me?"

Bucky understood that the last question was the important one. He gave her his best smile and a ten-dollar bill.

"I'm not going to get you into trouble," he promised. "All I want is to see the room and have you answer a few questions."

The blonde liked his smile. Most women did. She liked even better the steel engraving of Alexander Hamilton. Her amiable smile met his.

"I know you now," she said. "You're Mr. Bucky Cameron. Well, I'm a decent woman, and I don't hold with crooks. If these men were bank robbers, and you are trying to get them, I'll help you all I can. This way, gentlemen."

She led the way down the hall and with a skeleton key unlocked a door.

"This was McCarthy's room?" Bucky asked.

"Yes, sir. He was here eight days. I never

did like his looks — or his ways, for that matter. Though I will say he didn't make any trouble."

"Did he get any mail while he was here?"

"Not addressed to the place here. If he got any it must have come general delivery."

"That's how it would come. You didn't see any letters lying around?"

"No."

"Then you couldn't have noticed postmarks. Perhaps you know whether he wrote any letters in his room."

"Yes. At least I saw him carrying out a letter to mail."

"Never mentioned where he came from or said anything about what his business is?"

"No. But he had plenty of money. When he paid for his room he flashed a roll that would choke a horse."

"Do you know where he hung out in town?" Bucky asked.

The woman said she did not. The description she gave of her lodger fitted very well that of the man who had driven the car the day of the robbery. He was heavy-set, with veins showing in his gross beefy face. A scar ran across his forehead to the corner of the right eye.

Bucky was more interested in the appearance of the man who had visited McCarthy twice at night. Unfortunately she could tell him very little. He was a big man with a husky voice. His face was wrapped up in a muffler because he had neuralgia and did not want to catch a cold.

"He said that, did he?" Cameron inquired.

"Yes. I didn't notice him particular. There's only one light in the hall on account of expense, and he wasn't standing close to it. So I didn't get a good look at him."

"Would you know him again?"

"I might, but I dunno as I would."

"About what would he weigh?"

"Well," she hesitated, "say two hundred."

"Didn't remind you of anybody you know by sight?"

"No-o. Fact is, I had a gentleman friend visiting me and was kinda anxious to get back to my apartment. I pointed out McCarthy's room and beat it."

"How about the second time he called?"

"I just happened to see him coming into this room. He looked like the same man, but I couldn't be sure of that, for I was at the other end of the hall and saw him only a moment."

Bucky looked round the room. One could see a thousand like it in cheap lodging-houses. The carpet was old, the wallpaper peeling in spots. Iron bedstead, table, and chairs could have been duplicated from a second-hand store for ten dollars. In spite of Mr. Mc-Carthy's roll of bills that would choke a horse he had manifestly wanted to stay in an inconspicuous place. It was a fair guess that the last thing he wished was publicity.

No doubt Mitchell had gone over the room with a fine-tooth comb. If its latest occupant had left anything that told a story his keen eye would have picked it up. But as a matter of form Bucky made an examination.

"No use," the landlady said, shaking her blonde head. "He didn't leave a thing except the El Paso papers, and anyhow the maid has cleaned up since."

On the wall, where a man might have written it while lying on the bed, Bucky found a telephone number scrawled. It was Main 2747. The figures vaguely rang a bell in his mind.

"Do you know how long that has been written there, Mrs. Michins?" he asked.

"Never noticed it before," she said.

There was no telephone in the room, but Bucky recalled having seen a pay one in the hall. Evidently somebody had written the number in order to remember it.

Bucky had a swift brain-flash, born either of intuition or a fugitive memory. "Would you mind getting me a telephone book?" he asked the landlady.

She brought him one. He looked up the Valley Bank. The number Main 2747 stared at him. Somebody who occupied this room had wanted to have handy the bank number. He had written it to save himself the trouble of taking the book to the hall light and looking it up again.

Excitement raced through the veins of the young man. If Mrs. Michins's lodger was one of the bandits and if he had penciled the number on the wall — two suppositions about which Bucky had very little doubt — a possible, even a probable connection between the outlaws and Clem Garside was established. McCarthy had come to Toltec to rob the Valley Bank, but the telephone number was not necessary for that purpose — *unless the job was an inside one and he had wanted to get in touch with his confederate.*

"How much do you get for this room by the week, Mrs. Michins?" he asked.

"Four dollars," she told him.

"I'll take it for two weeks," he answered. "Cash on the barrel head. Leave it exactly as it is. Don't change anything — not even to dust up. I want left even the pencil number on the wall — as a sample of the man's handwriting. Probably I won't live here, but I'll take a key."

He gave her eight dollars.

"I'll see nobody else gets into the room," she promised.

Bucky and Tim walked back to the Toltec.

"I don't get it about the telephone number," Tim said. "Are you figuring on identifying this bird by his handwriting? I would say he didn't leave enough of it to do you any good."

"Probably you are right, Tim," agreed Bucky. "I tossed that in about his handwriting to get Mrs. Michins's mind on the wrong track. It was the number itself interested me. If you were to call up Main 2747, you would get the Valley Bank."

Tim's eyes had been startled into sudden interest. "What you driving at, boy?"

"McCarthy wrote the number because he wanted to call up the bank. What for?"

"How would I know?"

"Because he knew somebody in the bank — somebody who was going to give him a tip-off that the Malpais dam payroll had arrived, somebody who could tell him when and how best to pull off the job they had in mind. McCarthy calls up this man and makes an appointment to meet him that night in his room. The man comes, taking care not to be recognized. No harm in calling on an old friend, but Mr. X — that's a more mysterious name than Garside — plays a hand close to his belly.

There's a chance McCarthy may be caught or shot down, so he must not leave any loose threads that lead to him."

Tim took his time before he answered. "There's no law against guessing, Bucky. I'll not say Mr. X is not Clem. Plenty of people would tell us we're crazy in figuring our leading banker a partner of criminals. But we know Garside. He was a crook when he was a young gambler trying to make a four-flush stand up. Any old-timer can tell you he'd go through hell and high water to win out. Still, he's riding high and handsome now. He would have to be driven pretty hard before he would go into a thing like this."

"The bank examiner dropped into town today to look over the Valley's books. Let's say Clem knew he was coming and knew he would find a shortage of funds. This deficiency had to be covered up before the inspector checked up. So Clem fakes a bank robbery. His story is that the robbers got the money. Would anybody suspect it wasn't true?"

"You mean the bank wasn't really robbed?"

"It was robbed all right. The bandits got the Malpais payroll — maybe a little more. But I'm riding a hunch the bank had already been looted. That was what had to be covered up."

"That's all it is — a hunch."

"Not if Clem is Mr. X."

"No, but that's a big 'if.' " Tim added, as they turned into Front Street, "No way of proving it, anyhow."

"How do you know there isn't? If Mitchell drags McCarthy back the fellow may squeal to save his own hide."

"You're loaded to the guards with 'ifs.' "

"So is life," Bucky answered with a defensive grin. "We'll reach the Toltec in a couple of minutes if a building doesn't fall on us or if we're not run over by a car."

"Or shot down by some of the gents who spend their time gunning for you."

"Right, Tim," his friend agreed blithely. "In the midst of life we are in 'ifs.' "

They reached the Toltec, registered, and went to their room. Next day they drove out to the ranch.

CHAPTER XIX

Bucky picked up the telephone receiver and heard the voice of Mitchell.

"When did you get back?" young Cameron asked.

"Not half an hour ago," the answer came.

"Any luck?"

"Some. When can we talk?"

"The sooner the better. I'll send a man into town with a car for you. Come out to the ranch and have dinner. Pack a bag and stay all night. Or if you prefer I'll send you back this evening. We can talk more comfortably here than at the hotel."

Mitchell said he would be glad to come. Two hours later he arrived. Bucky took him into the room that used to be his uncle's office. Before asking any questions about what was on his mind Bucky prepared Scotch-and-sodas for himself and guest. He pushed a box of cigars across the desk.

The rites of hospitality performed, he leaned back in a swivel chair and said, "Did you find McCarthy?"

"Yes, I found him," Mitchell replied, lighting a cigar. "Only his name isn't McCarthy at El Paso. It's McCall."

"Is he one of the bank robbers?"

"I think so, but I can't be sure yet. He was away from El Paso about ten days before and just after the robbery. Got back there the next day. He is being shadowed."

"Why not bring him back and see if somebody can't identify him as the driver of the bandit car?" Bucky questioned.

"Because we don't know yet who are the other men in it with him. If they are in El

Paso they will get together soon. We want to bag the whole caboodle."

"Of course," Bucky nodded. "I hadn't thought of that. Did you tie this McCall up with the crime in any way?"

"We searched his room while he was out," Mitchell said. "There was an automobile road-map of this state, one that had been used a good deal. And in an old coat there was an envelope postmarked Toltec. No letter in it. The date was twelve days before the Valley Bank holdup. McCall must have come here just after getting the letter."

"Was the address typewritten?"

"Yes. Typed by an amateur and not by a stenographer, and by someone who doesn't use a machine much. There was no space in the El Paso between the l and the P."

"Someone who is used to dictating his letters," Bucky hazarded. "But who did not want to dictate this one."

Mitchell smiled, a little grimly. "I'll have a talk with your friend Garside. Not that I think there is a thing in your idea. But he can give me a line on his employees."

"Ask him for a line on McCall."

"I will." Bucky caught, as he had done once before, the flash of deadly hatred in the eyes of Mitchell. A moment later he almost doubted what he had seen. The mask was on again.

"I'll just mention McCall to him."

"You might mention that McCall wrote the bank telephone number in his room here and see how he takes that."

"I saw that number," Mitchell said. "And I'll agree that someone in the bank may have been tipping off McCall."

"When will you talk with Garside?" asked Bucky carelessly.

"Sometime tomorrow."

"Like to know how he reacts to what you tell him. I'll get in touch with you later . . . Didn't find anything else in McCall's room?"

"Nothing bearing on the case. You didn't expect him to leave there a signed confession, did you?"

Bucky grinned. "I think you did pretty well. I'll make a prophecy that if you talk with Garside and tell him what you know McCall will be warned by air mail at once. Make sure the fellow is shadowed closely."

"Maybe I had better leave McCall out of my talk with Garside," Mitchell said reflectively. "No need of broadcasting that McCall is under suspicion."

"Unless you want to find out whether McCall would take it on the lam."

Julia came to the door and announced that dinner was ready.

"Another spot of Scotch before you go?"

Bucky asked his guest. "You can take it to the table with you."

Mitchell shook his head. "One is enough."

Bucky locked the door of the office after him. "I don't want any of our riders slipping in and drinking up my liquor," he explained. "They are good boys, but there are one or two rum-hounds among them."

His cousin looked at him, a little surprised. She did not offer any comment.

During dinner Mitchell proved himself an entertaining guest. Julia had just seen *Top Hat* on the screen. It appeared that the detective knew a good many of the Hollywood stars. Recently he had been employed on a case to recover the stolen diamonds of one of the reigning queens of the cinema, one whose name he could not divulge. But he told lively gossip about several of the others. His employer had introduced him as a friend at two or three parties and he had met Astaire, Gable, Will Rogers, and half a dozen other luminaries of the first magnitude. Julia plied him with questions, which he answered with animated interest. He was, they gathered, a moving picture fan.

Shortly after dinner he excused himself on a plea of business and returned to town.

"He's very interesting," Julia said to her cousin. "Let's have him again."

Bucky nodded. "Yes, I'd say he had been places. He seemed to enjoy himself here. I expect he gets tired of hotel food. We might have him any time."

He returned to the office to take care of some business he had left unfinished.

CHAPTER XX

Bucky said to Tim, "We're going to town."

"What for?" Tim wanted to know.

"To hole up at 514 Fort Street."

The foreman stared at his friend. "I don't get the point."

"No use paying rent on a place you don't use," Bucky said airily.

"You've got some crazy idea in yore nut," Murphy told him. "What is it?"

"I'm not sure whether it is crazy or not," Bucky admitted, "but at least I'm betting on a long shot."

"You mostly do. What is it?"

"Just so you won't laugh at me I'll wait and tell you later — if I pull it off."

"Mysterious, aren't you?"

"Put a toothbrush in your suitcase. We'll be there all night, maybe."

Dusk was giving way to darkness before they reached town. Just outside of Toltec, Bucky took a side road that brought them into the city through the suburbs in such a way as to miss most of the lighted business section. He parked the car on Fort Street, a block distant from the number he wanted. At a drugstore he telephoned to Judge Lewis and invited him to join them. Fifteen minutes later the lawyer arrived.

"What's it all about?" he asked.

"I'll tell you later," Bucky said, and he led the way to the rooming-house at 514.

He produced a key and let his friends into the room he had rented.

"Make yourselves comfortable," he told them. "I'll be back in a minute."

Bucky knocked on the door of the rooms occupied by the landlady.

"Nobody has approached you since I telephoned?" he asked.

"No, sir."

"Good." He slipped the woman a five-dollar bill. "There will be another if this works out as I hope. All you have to do is to bring him to the door, unlock it, and leave him alone with us."

"There isn't going be any . . . violence?" she asked.

His smile was reassuring. "I'm not looking

for anything like that."

"All right. I'll bring him if he comes."

"Of course you're not to tell him we are in the room."

"I understand that."

Bucky returned to the room where he had left his companions. He locked the door and turned out the light.

"What's this play-acting for, Bucky?" inquired Lewis, amused.

"I'm expecting a visitor sometime this evening."

"Didn't he say when he would be here?" Tim asked.

"No. He didn't mention that." Bucky added information. "He doesn't know I'm expecting him."

"Why the darkness?" the lawyer questioned.

"I don't want to frighten him off."

"How will he get in with the door locked?"

"Mrs. Michins will let him in with her key."

"Sometime between now and midnight, I suppose."

"Or after," Bucky amended. "If he comes at all."

"So he may not come?"

"Quite likely he won't." Bucky laughed. "If he doesn't I'll feel like a fool keeping you here."

A moon shone through the window. They could see one another, but not in sharp outline.

"Has the mysterious Mr. Cameron any objection to us smoking?" asked Lewis.

"None in the world." Bucky opened a window, found a chair, and lit a cigarette.

From his case Lewis offered a cigar to Murphy and snipped the end of another for himself. Tim threw a leg over the arm of his chair. He struck a match, held it poised, and put a question.

"Conversation barred?"

"No. If we stop talking whenever we hear footsteps in the hall."

"You're not looking for that fellow McCarthy to come back?" Tim quizzed.

"He would surprise me if he did."

Lewis shifted uneasily his heavy body in the chair. "Last time I went places with you, Bucky, three anxious gentlemen flung bullets at me. Nothing like that tonight, I hope. If so, let me mention in time that I am not armed and anyhow am out of practice."

"I don't think our visitor will start that kind of trouble," Bucky answered.

"Hmp! I'd like you to be quite sure about it."

Bucky said, "I'll give you a written guarantee, good unless it turns out I'm wrong."

"That will be valuable," the lawyer told him dryly.

"This adventure isn't going to run to bullets, gentlemen." Bucky added a promise: "If our caller isn't here inside of an hour, I'll tell you all about it. I'm a little shy about confiding in you, because I don't want to be laughed out of court."

More than once they heard footsteps in the passage outside, and on each occasion their talk died away instantly. But none of the passers stopped. They were going to or from other rooms.

The hour was almost up when the waiting men came to rigid attention at the sound of a voice drawing closer. Bucky recognized it as that of Mrs. Michins. She was making talk, in a high note born of excitement.

Bucky moved to a place back of the door, on swift noiseless feet. A key fumbled at the lock. The door opened. A man's voice said curtly, "You needn't stop, madam."

The visitor waited until Mrs. Michins turned away before his hand groped for the light switch. Simultaneously the room leaped to light and Bucky slammed the door shut.

For a fraction of a second a startled face stared wildly at those in the room. Then a quick hand threw off the switch and the room was plunged into darkness.

Bucky charged instantly, to prevent a gun from getting into action. His arms closed on a thick body and pinned two wrists beneath them. He tried to lift from the ground the feet of the man he had attacked, in order to throw him down. But his opponent showed great strength. He braced his feet apart and broke the grip about his waist. Again Bucky's arms found a hold. A fist beat into his face furiously. He lowered his head and clung tightly to his foe.

They tossed about the room, a chair crashing beneath them as they went down. A strong hand gripped at Bucky's throat.

"Let go, Tim!" he shouted, struggling to escape.

Light filled the room again. Lewis had found the switch.

Tim released Bucky and fastened on the visitor. The foreman was a man of very great physical power. He dragged his victim up and pinned him against the wall.

"Let me go, you scoundrel!" a voice raged.

"Clem Garside!" cried Murphy, astonished.

From a holster beneath the banker's armpit Bucky removed a revolver.

"Let the gentleman go, Tim," said Bucky reproachfully. "I'm surprised at you, being so rough with a guest."

Garside glared at one and another. His eyes

fastened on the lawyer.

"What does this mean?" he demanded.

Lewis was shocked. "I don't know, Clem. It's as much a surprise to me as to you." He turned upon Bucky severely. "Will you tell me, young man, what you mean by this attack on Mr. Garside?"

Bucky straightened his twisted necktie, a smile on his battered bleeding mouth. "I'll tell you all about it, gentlemen," he said, his back to the door. "It will take a little time. What say we all sit down comfortably and talk it over."

"Get away from that door or I'll fling you out of the window," Garside threatened angrily. "I'll not stay here a moment. Never in my life have I seen such damn fool impudence. You'll pay for this, every one of you."

"You can go whenever you like, Garside," said Bucky quietly, his cool gaze holding fast to the banker. "But don't make a mistake. If you go now, the story will be in the papers tomorrow morning."

"What story?" stormed Garside. "That you and your ruffians assaulted me for no cause, intending to murder me?"

"I expect a reporter would discount that," Cameron replied. "There wouldn't have been any assault if you hadn't turned the light out and reached for a gun. The story would be

262

a lot more interesting than the fairy tale you are suggesting. Maybe you would like to hear it."

"No!" the banker shouted. "Get out of my way."

"Certainly." Bucky moved aside. "But don't forget to read the paper. You'll find the story in the place of honor on the front page. Probably there will be a photograph of this room, where one of the Valley Bank robbers lived ten days and where you visited him twice secretly."

The words stopped Garside as effectively as a blow in the solar plexus. He stared at Bucky from a gray stunned face. The shock had gone heavily home to him.

"It's a lie," he said dully, in a thick voice that lacked indignant defiance.

"There will probably be a photograph of your bank telephone number taken from the place where it is scribbled on the wall," Bucky went on. "And the account of how you sneaked back to the room to erase the evidence — and got caught before you could do it."

"Lies. All lies." Garside flung the words out more boldly. He was still groping for a defense, but the native hardihood of the man rallied to his aid.

"In that case you can sue me for libel after I have printed the account of it," answered Bucky.

Lewis had been watching them both, his shrewd eyes first on one and then on the other. "This is a very serious charge, Cameron," he said. "Unless you can back it with absolute proof, I would advise you to be very careful not to make it outside of this room."

Bucky showed his fine teeth in a satiric smile. "Perhaps Mr. Garside can explain why he came to this room tonight," he said.

"I can, but I won't," his enemy retorted harshly. "I'll explain nothing to you. Nothing. You came of a rotten tribe, and you're the worst of the lot. I've stood between you and the men who wanted to kill you, but I'll do it no longer." With a violent gesture he seemed to sweep Bucky aside.

"Maybe you can teach them to shoot straighter than they have been doing," Bucky said.

His words reminded Garside of his transferred property. "I'll take my gun," he said bluntly.

Cameron removed the cartridges from the chamber and handed the weapon to its owner. "You may need it," he replied with an acid grin, "if you are not going to stand between me and the men who want me killed."

"You'll go the way your father and your uncle went," Garside prophesied with fury.

"How did my uncle go?" Bucky flashed

back. "I've been trying to find that out."

Garside corrected his slip. "He went out of the country a hunted murderer with fifty thousand dollars he had stolen from those who trusted him. But you'll have no such luck. You've gone too far, but not far enough until you go to hell on a shutter."

"You're more honorable than your friends," Bucky taunted. "You give warning of your intentions."

"I've stood enough from you. All I intend to put up with."

Cameron nodded, his eyes narrowed. "I think I won't take the story to the newspapers yet but keep it in my safe-deposit box to be given the press in the event of my sudden death. In the box with it there will be a copy of a photograph of the telephone number on the wall, one taken with a powerful lens and quite clear." He added, with cheerful mockery: "I'm sure we have both enjoyed this little reunion, but I feel I ought not to detain you any longer."

Garside strode out of the room and down the passage to the stairs.

Tim Murphy was the first to speak. "Plenty mad — and scared."

"How did you know Clem was coming here tonight, Bucky?" asked Lewis.

"I didn't know it. Maybe I had better start

at the beginning. Mitchell discovered that Mc-Carthy, alias McCall, who was probably one of the bank robbers, had lived here while in town prior to the holdup of the Valley." Bucky showed the lawyer the penciled telephone number. "He also noticed this scrawled on the wall and took a photograph of it, as I did later. Last night he told me he was going to have a talk with Clem today. I checked up and found that he did."

"How did you check up?" asked Tim. "You didn't leave the ranch till late in the afternoon."

"I used a telephone and put a detective on the job. He is a man who has been doing quite a bit of work for me since my return to town after the First National robbery. Now Mitchell hates Garside. Do your own guessing as to the reason. Clem has done dirt to a lot of men in his time. Maybe this young fellow is one of them. I knew that if Mitchell got into a talk with friend Clem he couldn't keep from telling him how he had the whip hand. At least I hoped he couldn't. It turned out I was right. He told Garside what he knew and suspected. They had a quarrel. My man heard this from one of the bank employees. I put myself in Clem's place. What would he do?"

"Come to this room and destroy the evidence connecting the robbers with somebody inside the bank," suggested Lewis.

"I figured he would, soon after it got dark. If he came, it would be because he was frightened. So I thought it a good idea to be here, with witnesses, to see if he came."

"Was it wise to let him know the evidence against him before you have nearly enough to convict?" the lawyer asked. "For instance, can you prove he visited McCarthy here?"

"No. That is one of the weak joints in our thin case against him. If I had had plenty of evidence I wouldn't have told him anything until after his arrest. But we are a long way from having enough against him to go into court. My thought was to scare him into action. He will have to communicate with Mc-Carthy or some of the robbers. McCarthy is under constant observation. How will Garside try to reach him with a warning? By a wire or by phone? All calls and messages will be checked. By going personally to El Paso where McCarthy is now staying? Risky, wouldn't you say? By air mail? The government men are watching all letters that go to McCarthy. He can't move without danger, and he has to move."

"At least he thinks he has," Lewis said thoughtfully. "Since he doesn't know you were bluffing when you said you could prove he visited McCarthy. Yes, he has to get McCarthy and the others to disappear — if they were the bandits."

"I'll bet he's already feeling like a hunted man," Tim commented. "And he won't love Mitchell much better than he does you, Bucky."

"No. He'll think Mitchell and I are working together against him."

"As you are."

"As we are," Bucky assented briefly.

"We had better get out of here," Lewis said sharply. "Someone may have heard the row and reported it to the police."

"Or Clem's gun-minded friends may arrange a reception for us," hazarded Tim. "Next time they do, you and Bucky may not be as lucky as you were the other night. I'd get a guard for a few days, Judge, until we have this business cleaned up."

The lawyer flushed. "I'll do no such thing," he said doggedly. "I can't believe Clem would stoop to assassination. We've never been friends, but we haven't been as bitter enemies as that."

"He'll probably concentrate on Tim and me, but I would watch my step if I were you, Judge." The eyes of Cameron were agate-hard. "He's as guilty as the devil, and I don't think he would stop at anything. But he does not need to bother you. His story about to-night will likely be that he was decoyed here by a message that information would be given him as to the Valley Bank robbery. You can't prove that isn't true. So why should he worry about you?"

None the less the two men from the ranch drove Lewis to his home and saw him safely behind a locked door, after which they went to the Toltec and called up Mitchell on the house telephone. Five minutes later the amateur and the professional detective were in the room of the latter comparing notes.

"We really came to warn you," Bucky explained presently. "Garside will think you and I laid a trap to draw him to the rooming-house. He is going to have to move fast, and he is likely to strike at you as well as at me. Look out for yourself."

The lines of Mitchell's mouth tightened. "Don't worry. I'll take care of myself." He added, with a flare of cold fury, "I'd like to see that whited sepulchre with a rope around his neck on the gallows."

"You may have your wish some day," Tim said grimly.

Bucky made no comment. There jumped to his mind a vision of a girl, her golden head lifted gallantly, courage in all her untamed vivid personality. Much as he hated Clem Garside, he could not desire to see the spirit of Kathleen forever crushed, her pride trampled down beyond all possible recovery.

CHAPTER XXI

From two sources next morning Bucky heard that he had lured Clem Garside into a trap on the previous evening and tried to murder him.

"I wouldn't stand for it," Tim advised. "I'd shoot the works to the newspapers."

Bucky shook his head. "Not yet. I have a hunch things are going to move fast from now on. The best way to defend ourselves against libels is to prove who the guilty parties are in these crimes that have occurred."

Through one of the maids in the house a rumor of the story came to Kathleen just before dinner. She went straight to her father's room and said, "May I come in?"

Garside was shaving. He had to attend a dinner given by the Toltec Development Club in honor of the Secretary of the Interior.

"You might fix the studs in that shirt for me," he said, screwing up his face to give the razor a plane surface free of wrinkles.

Kathleen began to put the studs and cuff links into the shirt.

"Hope you have a good time at the dinner," she said.

"Did anyone ever have a good time at one of those damned stiff public banquets?"

"Then why do they have them?"

"I don't know. By the way, I had a little talk with that fellow Dan West today. He had just been released from jail on bond. You are probably right about him. He mentioned your name in a way I didn't like and when it wasn't necessary. I told him to keep his eyes and tongue off of you. The fellow took it badly. I had to lay the law down. He has a violent temper and went off in a rage. I'm mentioning it because if he ever annoys you, I want you to let me know and I'll take care of him."

"I don't suppose he'll annoy me," Kathleen answered. "He's not worth thinking about."

"This man is a bad lot. I don't look for any trouble, but there might be. You can't dispose of a mad dog by saying not to think of it."

The girl's mind was on something else. She had been trying to find an easy approach, but could not think of one. So she went directly to the point.

"What's this crazy story about Neil Cameron trying to murder you?" she demanded.

He turned on her, the safety razor poised. "What have you heard?" he asked sharply.

"I've heard he enticed you by some false message into the lower part of town and set on you with his gang, that he shot at you several times."

"That's not true — all of it," he snapped. "Where did you hear it?"

"From Delia. The grocery delivery boy told her. I knew it couldn't be true."

"How did you know that?" he flung at her belligerently.

"Because I know Neil Cameron. He may be a foolhardy publicity hound, but he isn't a murderer." Kathleen put the shirt on the bed, and said, "I'll fix your tie when you are ready."

"All right. I'll be through shaving in a minute. . . . You know practically everything, don't you?"

He soaped his face again with the lather.

"How much of it is true?" she asked, excitement strumming in her veins.

Before answering, he finished scraping his chin. This gave him time to choose words carefully.

"I received a note during the day through the mail that if I wanted to get a clue to the robbers of the Valley I was to call at a certain rooming-house on Fort Street. Knowing it might be a decoy message, I took a gun with me. In the room to which I had been directed I found Cameron and two of his men. When I turned to go they assaulted me. From what I can gather it appears, if they were telling the truth, that one of the Valley robbers stayed in this room while he was in town. The trap was to draw me down there in order to make it seem that I had known him and perhaps even that I had visited him there prior to the robbery."

"But why?" she asked, frowning in bewilderment. "Why would you do that? It's absurd."

"Of course it's absurd. I suppose it was an association of ideas. That young devil Cameron thought that since his uncle robbed his bank he could persuade the public that I had robbed mine."

"Oh, no!" she cried. "He wouldn't do that."

"I thought you knew the Camerons, how they've been trying to down me ever since I came into this country nearly forty years ago," he told her harshly. "No trick was too vile for them to try on me because I wouldn't bow down and accept them as the big moguls of this district. He's like the rest of his clan, a slick, smooth talker who gets away with it until people get on to him. He's got nerve. I'll grant him that. All the Camerons had. And that's all. Don't let him fool you."

"How do you know he wrote the note?"

"Why would he be waiting there in the room, in the darkness, if he hadn't been expecting me?"

Chill gripped the heart of the girl. Neil Cameron was her enemy. A hundred times she had told herself so. She could not remember the time when they had not been in antagonism. But a deep emotion in her clamored for belief in him. Often she had told herself that she could hate without despising him. Of course he hated her too. But in spite of the mockery with which he always met her she believed that he respected her, and sometimes there surged up in her a queer certainty that he liked her as much as . . . as she liked him.

"Do you have the note?" Kathleen asked. "The handwriting might show something."

"They took it away from me. The letter said I was to come alone, or no information would be given me. I thought it worth taking a chance."

"Did you know the men with Bucky Cameron?"

"There were only two. One was his foreman, Murphy. The other was Judge Lewis."

"Judge Lewis." A tune strummed in Kathleen's veins. "Then there is a mistake somewhere. Judge Lewis is one of the finest men

274

I ever knew. I have met him at the home of Mary Lewis, often. She is his niece, you know. I felt there must be a catch. Much as I detest Bucky Cameron's show-off ways, I was sure he wouldn't do anything like that."

"The answer is that he did," the banker said heavily.

"Maybe they just wanted to meet you and have a talk. Very likely that was it. They didn't want any publicity, as there would have been if they had seen you at some other place and time, so they just —"

"— knocked me down, took my gun from me, and threatened to broadcast lies against my good repute if I wouldn't let them dictate terms," he finished for her. "I'm not going to argue this with you, as I have done forty-eleven other times. This fellow is a scoundrel. So are those tied up with him. That's all there is to it. I won't listen to any defense of them."

Garside's voice rose as he talked. He ended in angry excitement.

Kathleen knew that on the subject of the Camerons her father was prejudiced. In part no doubt he was right. They were a stiff-necked rampant family. Bucky was filled with cocksure devil-may-care effrontery.

"They were trying to get the best of you some way," she admitted soothingly. "That is sure. I expect they attacked you because you resisted." Anger grew in her at the affront paid her father. "I never heard of anything so — so outrageous. I'd have them all arrested. Even though they didn't mean to kill you —"

"How do you know they didn't?" Garside challenged. "They were waiting in the dark, as I said. My idea is that when I managed to switch the light on they lost their nerve and daren't kill me while I was looking at them."

His daughter did not think so, but already the ruddy color in her father's face had deepened almost to purple from anger. It was always so when she suggested the Camerons were not such complete villains as he thought them. There was no use annoying him further now. If she did, he would be a roaring bull.

She handed him his dress shirt. "Your studs are old-fashioned, Dad. I'll get you a new set, cuff links and all, for your birthday."

"These suit me all right," he growled. "It's all foolishness anyhow putting on these doo-dads to go eat. I'm an old cattleman, not a society Johnny."

"But you do look swell when you are dressed up," his daughter comforted. "There won't be anybody as handsome as you at the dinner."

"Hmp!" he snorted. "You needn't soft-soap me."

She adjusted his black tie and kissed him. "Don't get tight, Clem."

"Did you ever see me tight?" he asked.

"Never. But you must have been sometimes in your rip-roaring days before you became a model citizen."

"I hope you take your own advice."

"I do, thank you. One cocktail for Kathie, two on a big day."

"How often do you have a big day?"

"Not often. I'll have one when my dad is elected United States senator."

"Which will be never."

"Which will be very soon."

She kissed him again. He pinched her cheek.

"What are you trying to get out of me, young lady?" inquired Garside suspiciously.

"Nothing at all. Take care of yourself, and don't answer any decoy notes in the hope that they were written by a beautiful young woman."

"Not ever again," he assured her. "By the way, I'm expecting a man at the house to talk over some business with me. He will probably be late. Tell Fernando he needn't wait up. I'll let him in myself."

Kathleen went into the living-room and sat down at the piano. She played absently, her mind occupied with the perverseness of life. You knew a hundred men, grave, gay, handsome, homely, rich, poor; and only one of them stirred your pulses. He had to be the most unavailable of the lot, one whom it was your duty to hate and with whom you had fought all your life.

Abruptly she rose. She was falling into this kind of mood too frequently of late. Anyhow, she had to dress for a dinner-dance at the Country Club.

CHAPTER XXII

Fernando opened the door of the living-room and walked in. It was his duty each morning to make the downstairs presentable before the family appeared. He drew back a window curtain, turned, and let out a strangled gasp. Swiftly he bolted out of the room, calling for help as he ran.

Out of the kitchen came the cook and a maid. Kathleen showed at the head of the stairs, in a dressing-gown. She joined the others in the hall.

"What's the matter, Fernando?" she asked.

He goggled at her, wild-eyed, and pointed to the living-room. "He — he — dead!"

Kathleen stared at him, fear flooding her

bosom. She pushed past the servants into the living-room, a prescience of disaster in her heart. She stopped, gaze fixed on the bulky figure huddled in the big chair. With a cry she ran forward.

"Father! Father!"

When she put a hand on the nearest shoulder, the inert head and torso slumped heavily against her. Terror swirled through the girl, rose to her throat, and choked her. She swayed, caught at the chair, steadied herself.

"Get a doctor — quick!" she managed to cry.

But she knew no doctor could ever bring a flicker of life into that still heart. Her father was dead. There was a small hole in the forehead, and below it a little stream of dried blood. Probably he had been sitting in that chair, slack and lifeless, when she had passed through the hall to her room on the way back from the dinner-dance early this morning.

Kathleen gently eased the body to the floor. She took a moment to subdue the wild panic within. The maid was screaming hysterically.

"Stop that noise, Maud, and call the police," her mistress ordered sharply. "Fernando, help me lift Father to the couch."

To Kathleen it seemed that the doctor would never come. She was in a fever of anxious despair, though she knew his coming would do no good. Yet it could have been only a few minutes until he arrived on the heels of Chief O'Sullivan. The most casual examination was enough to show the banker was dead.

"Who found Clem?" the chief asked, looking round. "And where?"

"Fernando found him," Kathleen answered, her lips ashen pale, "sitting on that chair. When I touched him he . . . fell."

O'Sullivan turned to the Filipino. "How long ago?"

"A quarter of an hour — maybe," the house boy guessed hesitantly.

"How long has he been dead?" This question was fired at Doctor Raymond.

"I should think about eight or nine hours."

"That means between ten and twelve last night."

"Probably an hour outside that time, one way or another."

Mitchell walked into the room. O'Sullivan nodded to him. "Thought you might be of use, so I sent for you."

The detective glanced down at the body on the lounge. "Good God, Garside!" he cried.

"When was your father last seen alive, as far as you know?" the chief asked Kathleen, the harshness gone out of his voice.

"I don't know. He went to the Development Club dinner. At least I suppose he went. I

. . . I didn't . . . see him again after he left the house. When I came home from the Country Club dance, it must have been half-past two." The face of the girl was colorless. Manifestly she was fighting down any display of emotion.

O'Sullivan gave orders that the servants were to be taken into another room and detained there until he was ready to question them.

"Do you want me to stay here?" Kathleen asked in a low voice.

"If you don't mind answering a few questions, Miss Garside. I don't want to distress you, but it is best not to lose any time."

"I understand," the girl answered. "Please ask me anything you want to know."

Mitchell moved forward a chair for her, putting it in such a position that she did not have to look at the body of her father. She dropped into it. A wave of sickness was sweeping through her.

"Have you any reason to suspect anybody in the house?" the chief asked.

"None whatever."

"Assuming that the crime occurred in this room, it is necessary for us to find out how the assassin made an entry. Were any of the doors found open or any of the windows unlatched when the servants came down this morning?"

"I don't know. I haven't had time to talk with them." The eyes of the girl dilated. "My father may have let him in himself. He told me he expected a visitor after he got back from the dinner. I was to tell Fernando he needn't wait up."

"Did you tell him?"

"Yes."

Mitchell asked a question. "Did your father say who the expected visitor was?"

"No."

"Perhaps some of the servants may have been up and admitted him," the detective suggested.

"I don't know about that. The man may not have come."

A policeman spoke. "Here's a gun in the drawer of this table, Chief."

"Don't touch it," O'Sullivan ordered. "Don't touch anything. We'll have the room dusted for fingerprints."

The table was close to the chair in which the body of Garside had been found, and the drawer was open about six inches.

"Was this open when you came into the room this morning, Miss Garside?"

"I think so. I'm sure it has not been touched since."

"Do you know whether this is your father's gun?"

Kathleen walked to the table and looked at the weapon. "It is his gun," she said, a queer contraction at her heart. "I know it by the handle. You don't think —"

Doctor Raymond answered her unfinished question. "No. It would have been almost impossible for him to have inflicted such a wound on himself."

"Have you any reason to suspect anybody of this, Miss Garside?" the chief asked. "I mean, any enemy your father may have spoken of lately?"

"He told me last night about a man called Dan West with whom he had quarreled during the day."

"Did he say what about?"

"Yes." There was a perceptible pause. When Kathleen continued, it was in a low voice. "Father thought his manner toward me was insulting and told him so. The man left him in a violent rage." Inside, the girl was a river of woe. She was asking herself despairingly if she had been the cause of her father's death.

"Do you know this man West well?"

"Scarcely at all."

"Have you ever had any trouble with him?"

"Once."

"Will you tell me what took place then?"

Kathleen told how Neil Cameron had flung

West through the window and taken his gun from him.

The mention of Bucky's name brought O'Sullivan to another suspect.

"Did your father say anything about some recent trouble with Cameron?"

Dismay swept through her. She had not thought of Bucky in connection with the death of his enemy. Instantly she repudiated the misgiving. Not Bucky. Anybody but him, she cried to herself.

"Can't I go now?" she begged. "Until some other time, please. I'm feeling faint."

"I'm sorry," O'Sullivan apologized. "I ought to have known."

He jumped to his feet and offered to support her as she left the room. Kathleen declined. "I'll be all right," she said.

After she had gone, the chief got busy on the telephone. He gave orders for the rounding up of West, Cameron, and Murphy for questioning. Also, he told the desk sergeant to send the fingerprint experts to the scene at once.

With Mitchell he made a careful examination of the room. The windows were all latched. There was no evidence of forcible entry. In the ash tray on the table beside where Garside had been sitting were the stub and débris of a cigar, but there were no ashes in any of the other trays. If Clem had had a visitor the man either had not smoked or had removed the signs of it.

O'Sullivan left the fingerprint men to do their work in the living-room while he examined the servants. None of the staff had been up when their master returned home the preceding evening, it appeared. They had heard no sound of quarreling and no shot. All the doors of the house had been properly fastened when they came down this morning; nor had any of them heard Garside say who was the visitor expected so late at night. The chief brought out that Fernando had heard words between Neil Cameron and the banker a few days earlier on the occasion of the C C man's visit to the house. Garside had told the other to leave his house and never come back.

Within two hours West and Cameron were brought into the office of the chief. Both of them had alibis, which O'Sullivan viewed with scowling suspicion. That of West depended upon the testimony of some of his Red Rock friends, with whom he claimed to have been playing poker in the rear of an unsavory saloon.

Bucky's witness was Nancy Graham. His story, corroborated by her, was that after a picture show he had taken her for a long drive up Buckhorn Cañon and back to town by way of the Ledge road.

"Meet anybody?" the chief asked, shifting a skeptical gaze from Bucky to Nancy and back again.

"Met several cars," Bucky answered. "But with the headlights on, it was impossible for any of the people in them to have recognized us."

"What time did you leave the picture show?"

"About a quarter to ten. That right, Nancy?"

"Yes. I looked at my wrist watch to decide if we had time to run up Buckhorn."

"And you got back when?"

"At one." Bucky asked for no confirmation of this.

"Exactly?"

"Yes. The clock in the Johnson Building struck as we passed."

"Obliging of the clock," the chief said, with obvious sarcasm. "Will you explain this, Miss Graham? You looked at your watch to find out whether you had time to make the run up Buckhorn. I can do the cañon and back by the Ledge road in an hour and a half, and it took you over three hours. If you were pressed for time —"

"We weren't going to a fire," Nancy explained. "Sometimes a girl makes excuses about doing something she knows she means to do. I didn't really care how late we were."

"There was a swell moon, Chief," added Bucky with a grin.

"Got any witnesses as to the exact time you got back?"

"One of my brothers got home just before I did," Nancy said. "We went to the icebox and made a sandwich."

"Cameron have a sandwich too?"

"No. He didn't go into the house."

"So your brother didn't see him and can't prove you two were together till one o'clock."

"No." Nancy gave the chief a confident smile. "Mr. Cameron proves that by me."

"You two engaged?" O'Sullivan blurted.

"Not to each other, if that's what you mean." Nancy's voice held an ironic little sting. "I don't know about Mr. Cameron, but I am quite free. If this is a proposal —"

"Don't get gay with me, young woman," O'Sullivan advised, his face red.

"I don't mean to be, but I can't see why you are concerned about my private matrimonial prospects unless it is of personal interest to you."

Bucky chuckled. "That's a fair hit, Chief. A handsome widower like you can't go around asking young ladies whether they are engaged without having them think you mean something by it."

"I'm not satisfied with your alibi, Cameron," the officer said bluntly.

"Well, it's the only one I have," Bucky said amiably. "You'll have to take it or leave it."

"Did you have an engagement to meet Clem at his home late last night?"

"No. The last time I was in his house he eased me out with adjectives. I gathered he would be pleased never to see me there again."

"Any of your men have a date with him? Tim Murphy, say?"

"Not as far as I know. You may count them out, Chief."

"I'll count out who I please without any help from you."

"I was trying to save you from wasting time," Bucky said mildly.

O'Sullivan's poker face lost its dead-pan look. This young man's coolness, so bland in its occasional effrontery, got under the chief's hide, as he himself expressed it.

"If you're so anxious to save me from wasting time, come clean with all you know," he said, exasperated. "For instance, what about that business down at the Fort Street rooming-house? Why did you and Lewis lay a trap for Clem? The story is you tried to kill him then, but he flashed the light on and you hadn't the nerve to go through with it."

"That's a story you don't believe, Chief. I took Judge Lewis with me because he stands so high in the community nobody could fall for any such nonsense. I'll tell you all about it. We've nothing to conceal."

"Nobody has," the officer countered bitterly. "Three men have been killed and two wounded in this town since the robbers walked into the First National Bank that night. But nobody is to blame. Everybody is as innocent as Shirley Temple. You killed a man not more than a block from here, but you've turned so damned righteous, butter wouldn't melt in your mouth. Maybe you've forgotten what a wild rip-roaring hellion you used to be, but, by Moses, I haven't. I'll listen to what you've got to say about this lodging-house row, and if I don't like it I'll throw you behind the bars. I may have been a friend of Cliff Cameron once, but you can't go around making a monkey of me."

Bucky told the story of the Fort Street episode. The chief was inclined to believe it true, but the implications of it angered him.

"What the hell right have you to pull off a stunt like that?" he demanded. "I'm the head of the law enforcement department of this town. If you had anything on Clem or anybody else you should have come to me with your information. But no. You're one of these smart guys. You have to run the show yourself. By God, I won't have it." O'Sullivan's heavy fist smashed down on the desk in front of him. "I'll have you know I'm chief of police. Pull anything like this again, and you'll go to jail and like it."

Bucky knew the man's official vanity was touched. "That's right. I should have thought of that. I'll certainly come to you next time." The young man's manner was remorseful. "I'm honestly trying to help you, Chief, and if I get anywhere you'll get all the credit. I'll see to that."

O'Sullivan dismissed them gruffly. "You may go. But stick around, Cameron, where I can reach you easily by phone. I'll probably want you later."

Bucky lingered to ask a question. "Anybody hear the shot, Chief?"

"If so, he's holding out on me. Why?"

"I was thinking about the gentleman with the silencer," Bucky drawled.

O'Sullivan stared at him. "All right. Find him for me."

"I will," Bucky promised. "Soon."

The eye of the chief was cynical. "Everybody knows a cop's business better than a cop. I'll bet you fifty dollars you don't find him."

"Too easy," Bucky said, shaking his head. "I'll give you a better wager than that. Fifty even I turn over to you the First National Bank murderers. Fifty more I put my finger on the man who killed Garside."

"When are you going to do all that?" scoffed O'Sullivan.

"Within a week. On one condition. If I want any assistance from your department, you are to give it and ask no questions."

"What sort of assistance?"

"Access to any documentary evidence I would like to see."

"You're on. I'll take both bets, and I certainly hope you win, though I know you won't. It will be worth a lot more to me than a hundred iron men to get my hands on those fellows. Understand, you've got to give me evidence enough to convict. I'll not be satisfied with one of your crazy hunches."

"Neither shall I." Bucky was briskly business-like. "First, Chief, I would like to make an appointment with your fingerprint expert for this afternoon. Second, I want an order to look over some papers at the First National which I think bear on the crime. You can send an officer with me to make sure I don't steal, deface, or destroy anything of value."

"I don't know what you are driving at, but since I've started, I'll go through."

"You won't regret it, Chief. I'm hot on the trail. If this works out as I think it will, I'll see you get the credit for it in the papers."

"It won't work out," O'Sullivan said with

harsh skepticism. "All I'll get out of it is a hundred dollars. You've got a hell of a nerve thinking you know more than the whole police department. Now scram. I'm busy."

Outside, Nancy turned a doubtful glance on Bucky. "Is it all a bluff? Or do you really know all you claim you do?"

"It's a bluff," he admitted cheerfully, "but if I'm lucky enough, I'll make it good."

"And if you are not lucky you will be out a hundred dollars."

"I'm paying that for O'Sullivan's co-operation."

"I suppose it's a secret — what you have in mind?"

"Yes, but I think Mitchell is moving toward the answer too. He's going to beat me to it if I don't hurry."

"Professional jealousy," Nancy mentioned, grinning at him. "You're afraid he'll get the glory."

"Well, I came back here to solve this case," he said. "I don't want to take a back seat for somebody else. You know I'm supposed to have a lot of vanity that likes to bask in the limelight. I think I'm a couple of jumps ahead of O'Sullivan. But Mitchell is a born detective and he is as close to a solution as I am."

"You told the chief he could have the credit."

"So he can, in the newspapers, but among my friends I want it known I was the fair-haired lad who did the job."

The girl slanted a quizzical look at him. "Miss Garside says you are wasted because you are not in the movies."

"She has had my number ever since we were in the third grade together," he said ruefully. "Neil Cameron, poseur."

"Only it doesn't happen to be true," Nancy said carelessly.

"Much obliged, young fellow. Sometimes I'm not sure she isn't right."

They had reached a corner. Nancy stopped. "I must go back to the hospital. I'm on a case."

"Be seeing you soon. It really was a swell moon, Nancy."

"I thought so too," the girl laughed.

"Since you are so fancy-free we might give it another chance."

"I don't guarantee statements I make to the police under pressure," she told him. "A fortune-teller hinted at a dark young man in the offing."

"Not really dark," he amended.

Bucky watched her walk down the street with that light-limbed grace which seemed an expression of joy in life bubbling within her.

CHAPTER XXIII

Kathleen found it as difficult to answer Bucky's note of condolence as it had been for him to write it. She wasted a good many sheets of paper trying to convey the exact shade of reserved and formal thanks demanded. It was important to her, and had been to him, that no trace of hypocrisy or sentimentality should appear. He had asked her if he could not meet her in person to clear up certain points. At first she had been ready to send an indignant refusal. He had assaulted her father the day before his death. If he thought she was prepared to forgive such an affront he was mistaken. All her loyalty was engaged in defense of the dead man's memory.

But life goes on. Her father was dead and buried. If Bucky had any justification for his conduct she wanted to know what it was. There was an imperative urge in her to think well of this man who occupied her mind so much of the time.

The letter she at last decided upon made no reference to his sympathy. It addressed him as *Dear Sir*, and consisted of one short sentence:

I shall be at home tomorrow afternoon at five o'clock.

Beneath this was her signature.

For hours before his arrival she was in a fever of restlessness. She fortified herself with a cocktail but had no intention of offering him one. Though this was to be an hour of truce, no amenities were required. He and his family had always been enemies of her father. They had fought a long war bitterly. Yet she was tired — just now desperately so — of the destruction this feud had brought. It had destroyed her father and his, perhaps too his uncle. How true was the old prophecy that they who take the sword shall perish by the sword. Still, there could be no friendship between this man and her. The effects of hatred cannot be snuffed out like a lighted candle.

When Kathleen rose to meet Bucky in the living-room he could see no sign of the agitation which filled her being. She was pale and withdrawn. Never, he thought, had he seen her so lovely, perhaps because of the grief that tempered her sharpness. Sad shadows darkened the eyes. The girl was strong as steel, but she looked exhausted. Her father had been the only close relative. His loss had been a blow. It had shaken the security that had been at the foundation of her pride. Bucky felt a wave of deep sympathy. She had suffered, and must suffer more, perhaps. For to prove the Camerons innocent of crime might be to shift the guilt to Clem Garside.

Her visitor bowed, not offering to shake hands. She did not ask him to sit down, nor did she sit herself.

Without any preamble Bucky told her why he had wished to see her. "I don't know what you have been told or what you think," he said. "All sorts of wild rumors are current, but if you have any doubt in your mind, any thought that I am connected with this last crime —"

"If I had believed this, do you think I would be meeting you here?" she asked in a low voice.

"No, but I couldn't know you were entirely sure of this. I had to find out. . . . I'm the same boy who went to school with you, grown up now. I'm not an assassin. You are certain of this, aren't you?"

"Will you explain why you laid a trap and assaulted him the night before . . . before his death?" she asked.

"I didn't lay a trap for him and I didn't assault him," he answered after a moment of hesitation.

"He told me you did."

Bucky chose his words carefully. He must say nothing she could consider an attack on her dead father.

"I can see how he might think so. There is a story that I tricked him with a note to bring him down to the rooming-house. That is not true."

The dark eyes looking straight at him were hostile. He felt anger stir in her voice. "Someone else sent him the note, and you just happened to be sitting there in the dark with your friends."

"I thought he might come, but I did nothing to bring him there. When he saw us he switched out the light. Perhaps he thought we intended to injure him. I closed with him for fear he might use a weapon. There was no time for explanations. I was careful not to hurt him."

"You have not told me why you expected him."

"I can't go into that, Kathleen." The name slipped out without volition. He had not called her by it since they had been children in school. "We were not friends. You know that. There was a state of warfare between us. I shall not try to defend all my actions. The reason I came back to Toltec was to clear the name of my uncle. This brought me into conflict with your father."

"He stood between you and the ruffians who wanted to kill you," she said, defense sharp in her voice.

"Yes, I think he did that." He spoke quietly, gravely. "We can't agree on the right and the wrong of all the things the Garsides and the Camerons have done. Must we take them all up and thresh them out? Can't we let them be water under the bridge?"

"If we only could." The words were a sigh, scarcely audible. She was heart sick of violence, of bitterness, of associations with evil men to bolster partisan positions. Emotion ran through her like a flame and broke into words. "Oh, Neil, I'm so tired of it! What has it got us? Your father and mine murdered, your life in constant danger, mine so unhappy. Have we all gone mad? Isn't there peace for us anywhere, at any price?"

"It rests with us," he said gently. "There can't be war between us if neither of us will fight."

"No," she agreed. "But we've fought all our lives, you and I."

He smiled. "I was a pest, if ever a boy was. And all the time I thought you the swellest girl I knew."

Tears brimmed her eyes. "I liked you too — and never spoke a decent word to you."

"I never gave you a chance. Always I was

the smart aleck trying to get the best of you."

"And you did usually, because I am red-headed and lost my temper," she admitted.

"I suppose I liked to see the fireworks," he confessed, his fine teeth flashing in a smile. "From now on I'm a reformed character."

"I wonder if you are," she said. "I wonder if I am. Just at present I'm different because of father. But that won't last. Pretty soon I'll be the same old Kathleen, acting as if I was one of God's anointed and could be a law to myself."

"And I'll be understudying Clark Gable," he suggested.

"I'll try to remember you're not really showing off, if you'll remember that sometimes I'm just a girl not very sure of herself putting on a Greta Garbo act in self-defense."

"It's a bargain," he said, and offered a hand to seal the truce.

Fingers clasped, they looked at each other. Their eyes held, and a tumult of blood began to pound in her. He was aware of it. The flame leaped from her veins to his. Without volition, drawn by irresistible urge, she was in his arms clinging tightly to him, her lips fast to his.

The bell of warning rang first in her. She drew back, frightened at the intensity of her emotion. They looked at each other with startled eyes, a common thought in their minds.

It wouldn't do. Too much violence — too many graves — lay between them. Too many years of family bitterness. Too many fixed opinions that would have to be padlocked as long as life lasted.

We have torn it now, Bucky told himself. Why had he let go because of a moment's hot-blooded desire?

Kathleen read his mind, since it was her own, and would not let him take the blame. "My fault, not yours," she said. "I've been nervous and unstrung, so I made a fool of myself. Please go now at once — without saying anything."

Bucky hesitated, then turned sharply on his heel and left.

All the way to town he reproached himself. This was not just a case of kissing a girl who was ready to meet him halfway. Kathleen had always been a child of wild impulse, her feelings passionately keen. Why did a man have to be a scut because a girl's heart was tender with sorrow and filled with remorse? Why take advantage of her grief at a time when she was swept by waves of regret for the pain she had sometimes made her father suffer? The only excuse he could offer was that he had been moved by deep sympathy, and that was one which explained nothing.

CHAPTER XXIV

O'Sullivan introduced Bucky to Sergeant Swensen, the fingerprint expert of the department, with instructions to the officer to help him in any way he could.

"We've met each other," Swensen said with a grin. "Once I arrested him for stealing a taxicab. Must have been six or seven years ago, when I was on a beat. No hard feelings?"

"Not any," Bucky agreed. "I needed that taxi for half an hour, but I didn't know it was going to cost me two nights in jail and fifty dollars, plus a thumping headache from that crack you gave me. We shook hands on it later, didn't we?"

"Yes, you were a good sport. Sorry I had to land on you, but I got sore when you called me a big Swede . . . Jimmy Dyer said you were in here getting him to do a little job for you the other day."

Dyer was the assistant of Swensen. The chief looked at Bucky sharply. "What kind of a job?" he asked.

"I'll tell you about that, Chief, when I collect the hundred dollars from you," Bucky said, with friendly malice.

"Hmp! This fellow is the world's greatest detective, Sergeant," O'Sullivan said, heavy sarcasm in his voice. "He has Sherlock Holmes and all these other book sharks backed off the map. You may not know it, but he practically has these bank cases and recent murders solved. He looked at the butt of a cigarette, saw it was a Camel, and the whole thing was clear to him instantly."

Bucky laughed. "The chief isn't sure I didn't do the jobs myself. You'd better finger-print me now you have me here."

"That's an idea, too," O'Sullivan snapped. "Do that, Swensen, and compare his prints with the ones found on the table of the Garside living-room."

The chief left the other two alone. He had business in the office demanding his attention.

"About the fingerprints in the living-room of the Garsides," Bucky suggested. "Did you find any?"

"Plenty. Some of Clem, several of his daughter, more of the Filipino boy who cleans the room."

"The chief mentioned some on the table."

"One print of a hand." Swensen found a photograph in a drawer and tossed it across the desk to his visitor. "I'll do some guessing. Left by a gent in a hell of a hurry, but who found time to wipe out any other prints he had left on the arms of his chair, on the light switch he snapped off, and on the knob of the door through which he walked into the hall."

"Why did he leave that one?"

"I'll have to guess again. Say he was nervous while he was sitting in the chair by the table and got to fooling with a magazine which he drew over the print he had made. When Clem reached for the gun close to him, this bird let him have it between the eyes with a lead pill. He forgot his hand had been lying on the table under the magazine. Natural enough, under the circumstances."

"How do you know the print wasn't made by somebody else's hand two or three days earlier?" Bucky wanted to know.

"The Filipino boy is absolutely sure he dusted the table and polished it with a cloth the day before the murder. During the day nobody but the family and the servants were in the room. In the evening a man called on Clem by appointment. It looks as if he left his calling card on the table, doesn't it?"

Bucky nodded. An extraordinary excitement filled him. This photograph might prove or disprove the whole theory upon which he was working. From his pocket he drew a second photograph, also one of a set of fingerprints.

"Compare these, Sergeant," he said. "With those I've just seen!"

Swensen examined them with a microscope, first one and then the other. He studied carefully the whorls, the characteristic lineation marking the inside of the first joints. When he looked up at Bucky, his eyes were shining.

"Is this the photo Jim Dyer took for you?" he asked.

"Yes. Are these fingerprints of the same man?"

"Absolutely. Beyond any doubt. God, man, we've got him. Who is he?"

"Not quite so fast, Sergeant. There are one or two little links I have to tie up first. It won't take long. As soon as I have done that, I'll talk with O'Sullivan and let him have the credit of the arrest."

"But the chief won't stand for that — not for a minute. He isn't going to let you keep vital evidence from him. He would be crazy to do that. You'll have to tell him what you know."

Bucky's jaw set. "I have made a bargain with the chief. He'll live up to it. I haven't finished my work yet. As soon as I have done that I'll turn over all the evidence I have to him. And not a minute before that time."

"But, great guns, man! Suppose something happened to you. What if you got shot? You can't let us run a risk like that."

"I'll go straight from here to Judge Lewis's office. There I'll type the story and put it in my safety-deposit box with instructions for the chief to have access to it in case I am killed. There's no use getting excited, Sergeant. It's going to be that way."

"You'll have to settle that with the chief," Swensen said curtly. "I won't take the responsibility of letting you go without telling us."

"All right. We'll see the chief."

O'Sullivan exploded. He would not put up with such a thing for a moment. Bucky had got to come clean with everything he knew. Who did he think he was that he could conceal the identity of a murderer wanted by the police? It was a penitentiary offense to do what he was doing.

Bucky leaned back in his chair with a bland smile and listened. He waited until the fireworks were over, then asked a question.

"Do you want only the man who killed Garside? Or would you like the bank robberies cleared up too?"

"You know damned well I want the whole business settled."

"So do I. We're not ready for an arrest yet. Give me twenty-four hours to let me finish my job. Do that, and you'll have the biggest cleanup in your life. You'll be so solid in your job that no politician could possibly pry you loose."

"I could fling you in a cell and have the district attorney indict you," O'Sullivan stormed.

But Bucky knew he was weakening, that he was making a play to save face. "You could," agreed Buck calmly, "but you have too much sense to do that. I'm not standing in the way of justice. All I want is to do a thorough job."

"Would it keep you from doing a thorough job to tell me what you know? The trouble with you is you're so conceited that you want to play a lone hand. After it's over you want to thump yourself on the chest and call to everybody, 'What a big boy am I?' That's what is eating you."

"I promised that you could have the newspaper credit," Bucky mentioned.

"What's the big idea? Are you afraid to trust me? Don't you think I want to catch these fellows as much as you do?"

"If I told you what I knew, Chief, you would have to begin taking precautions to see the guilty men don't escape. There's a very clever brain at the back of this. You couldn't tail any suspects without its being found out. The men we want would be alarmed. That is just what we don't want."

"How do you know they won't skip out as it is? Maybe they know how close you are on their heels."

"In that case they will try to bump me off. In which sad event — assuming they succeed — I would advise you to go *muy pronto* to my safety-deposit box, read the story you will find there, and make any arrests that seem justified."

"Yeah," jeered O'Sullivan. "It's too bad they got Clem Garside. If they hadn't, you would have had his name at the top of your list of guilty men. Shows what a swell detective you are . . . By the way, Swensen, did you get Cameron's fingerprints?"

"Not yet."

"Take them. And compare them with those left on the table of the Garside living-room. This smart young man wants to be thorough. All right. We'll be thorough too."

"Good . . . And if you're not going to arrest me right way, how about letting Sergeant Swensen go with me to the First National and look over the records I want to see?"

"All right. I've arranged with Ankeny, the receiver for the bank, to let you see whatever papers you want to examine." The chief spoke angrily, with evident reluctance. He would have liked to put this young upstart in his place. But that would have to be done later.

Cameron would have to be humored as long as he seemed to have inside information. "Are you trying to hook this thing on Ferrill? If so, you don't have to be so damned secret. He's under arrest already."

"Under arrest?" Bucky repeated in surprise. "For robbing the First National?"

"Yes," O'Sullivan replied grimly. "Ought I to have waited to ask you before I arrested him?"

"You must have a lot of evidence I don't know anything about," Bucky observed.

"I probably have. Is it your notion the rest of us have all been asleep?"

"So you think Ferrill killed Buchmann?"

"I didn't say so. I said he robbed the bank."

"You know that?"

"You bet I do." The chief gloated triumphantly. "He stole several thousand from the bank. We don't know how much yet. He was short in his accounts — had fixed the books to cover the defalcation."

"Ankeny has discovered this?"

"Yes, after I told him he had better check back."

Bucky looked properly impressed. He thought it as well not to mention that he had given O'Sullivan the original tip-off to investigate Ferrill.

"Do you think this steal had anything to

308

do with the robbery of the First National later?" he asked.

"Why not? Buchmann was an expert at accounts. Maybe he discovered the shortage. Say Ferrill killed him when he found the game was up, then went ahead and robbed the bank. Isn't that reasonable?"

"Might be," Bucky admitted.

His assent was not enthusiastic enough for the officer. "You hate to admit a plain cop could be on the right trail, don't you?" the chief jeered. "Answer me one question. Why did the robbers burn the bank?"

"To conceal evidence. There couldn't have been any other reason."

"Go to the head of the class, bright boy," O'Sullivan said, with sarcastic admiration. "Now tell me what evidence."

Bucky waited to be informed. It was not his turn to talk. The chief wanted to be the instructor.

"They could not have wanted to hide the fact that there had been a robbery. That was bound to come out in the morning. By setting fire to the bank they only hurried the discovery. What they wanted to do was to burn up the books so that Ferrill's steal would never be found out. The evidence against him would be destroyed."

O'Sullivan glared at Bucky, as if challenging

him to deny anything so obvious.

Bucky's comment, if it could be considered critical at all, was only mildly so. "Looks like a promising lead," he said. "One thing sticks in my mind. The fellows who did this were ruthless. Young Ferrill is the playboy type. Has he it in him to be so thorough?"

"Ruthless, hell! He got caught in a jam and bumped Buchmann off because he was scared."

"To account for the disappearance of Uncle Cliff we have to assume that Ferrill was working with the Red Rock gang or some other criminals."

"Might have been that way. I haven't tied him up with anyone else yet. It's not proved he wasn't a confederate of Cliff himself." The eyes of the chief were hard as obsidian, his mouth a straight thin line. "But when I've got through with that young man he will have told me everything."

Bucky thought it likely. A third degree at the hands of O'Sullivan was no joke.

"I'll be interested to know how much it is," he said.

The chief snorted. "Hmp! You've got the nerve of a rhino. You want to be told everything and to tell nothing."

"Pretty soon I'll tell you all I know," Bucky promised, "and if it turns out to be worth anything you'll get some swell headlines . . . Now how about letting me have Sergeant Swensen for an hour or two while I do some checking up at the First National?"

The chief hesitated. "Look here, young fellow. Ferrill is my baby. I know you are going to check up on him. That's all right, but you are to come to me with anything more you find out. I'll do the talking to the newspapers. Understand?"

Bucky said he did. Once more he assured O'Sullivan that all the public glory would be his.

With Swensen striding beside him he walked to the bank building. Mitchell came down the street as they knocked on the side door. Bucky explained to him about Ferrill, that he was short in his accounts and was under arrest. He added that O'Sullivan believed he was connected with the big robbery later.

"What do you think?" Mitchell asked.

"I think it's worth checking up. He might be. If Buchmann found out about the defalcation Ferrill may have murdered him on the theory that dead men tell no tales. From the killing it would be only a step to the robbery. Might as well be hanged for a sheep as a lamb, you know."

"You've come to get dope on him? Mind if I go in with you?"

"Not at all, if Sergeant Swensen doesn't care."

It turned out that Swensen did not. But the investigation had to be postponed. Receiver Ankeny and his staff had knocked off work for the day and had departed.

CHAPTER XXV

It was an hour later that O'Sullivan telephoned Mitchell.

"I have that fellow McCarthy or McCall or Butch Millikan, whichever you want to call him, over here in my city hotel. He has just been brought in from El Paso. Seeing that you helped get him, I thought maybe you'd like to be present when I put him over the hurdles."

Mitchell said he would, and was advised to get to police headquarters as fast as he could. He was so prompt that the chief was not quite ready to start the quiz. The district attorney, it appeared, would like to be at the examination, and he would reach O'Sullivan's office in a few minutes.

After Mitchell had taken a proffered chair, he offered the chief a cigar and lit one himself.

"Quick work," he told the officer. "Have you a line on his accomplices?"

"We think we have the men spotted, but they haven't been found yet. Red Grogan is one, and another is probably Mike Soretti. The dragnet is out after them."

"Good . . . I just met young Cameron and Sergeant Swensen at the First National. Bucky says you have discovered Ferrill is a defaulter and have arrested him."

"Yes. Looks like he is in the first robbery anyhow." The chief's eyes gleamed savagely. "When we get through with this business, I'm going to tell Bucky Cameron a few things in damned plain English."

"What's he been up to now?" Mitchell asked.

"You and he are thick as thieves. That's all right. I'd just as soon tell him as you. Trouble with him is he's a wise guy. He knows so much, and he goes around being mysterious about it. I won't deny he has brains, but he has been mighty lucky too."

"Sounds interesting."

"I don't know where in time he got it, but he has a photograph of fingerprints that match those Clem Garside's visitor left on the living-room table."

Mitchell leaned forward, the eyes between his narrowed lids pinpoints of interest. "That so? Then he has been holding out on me. We're supposed to be working together, but the fact is we've both been a little slow in telling each other what we suspect. He wants to get credit for solving this case, just as much as I do. I don't care about the local end of it. All the glory here goes to you, Chief, if we get anywhere. But I'd like through it to get a boost with my boss at Washington."

"He has been holding out on me, too, a hell of a lot," O'Sullivan complained.

"You think he has spotted the man who killed Garside?"

"Yes, if the man who called on Clem that night did the killing. Fingerprints don't lie. Swensen and I have compared pictures under a microscope. They are prints of the same hand. No question of it."

"And you don't know whose hand?"

"No. The young devil wouldn't tell me. Said he still had some loose ends to draw together. I had half a mind to throw him in a cell and keep him there. I'm certainly fed up with the young squirt."

"What more is he waiting for? What else does he expect to prove?"

"Wants to tie up this fellow who killed Clem with the gang who robbed the First National. Says in twenty-four hours he'll be ready to talk. His story is that he is afraid to tell me for fear I would tail the guy and scare him off. And I've been a cop for twenty-five years."

Mitchell took his time to answer. "Bucky is a good fellow, Chief, even if he is so all-fired wise. He is probably fed up with detective stories, and like a lot of amateurs would like to beat us professionals at our own game. Personally I'm not convinced that the man who left his fingerprints on the Garside table is the one who killed Clem. A dozen of us were milling around there for an hour. Any one of us might have put a hand on the table."

"No. I warned the boys to be careful."

Ashley, the district attorney, walked into the room, nodded to Mitchell, and said to the chief, "Sorry I'm late."

O'Sullivan ordered the prisoner to be brought in for examination.

Defiantly McCall walked into the room and looked round at the little group of men facing him. He was a heavy-set, tough-looking specimen with small shifty eyes set in a beefy veined face.

The chief looked at him stonily. "You go by the name of Steve McCarthy and Bob McCall and Butch Millikan," he said harshly. "You were in the Colorado state penitentiary at Cañon City four years for killing a policeman while escaping after robbing a bank. Six months after you got out you helped hold up a bank at Goldfield and another at Crown Hill, both in Oklahoma. You served a term at Leavenworth for passing counterfeit. You did three years at San Quentin for another bank robbery."

McCall looked at his inquisitor with an impudent and sullen sneer. He said nothing.

"Well, what have you to say?" O'Sullivan snapped.

"Not a thing. You know so much I wouldn't interrupt."

"Don't get hard with me," the chief warned. "You'll find it doesn't pay."

The prisoner matched looks with him doggedly, in silence.

"When did you last see Red Grogan?" the officer demanded.

"I don't remember."

"Where is he now?"

"I wouldn't know."

"Mike Soretti?"

"Haven't seen him for a year."

"That's a lie."

"If you know better than I do, why ask me?"

"Get heavy and you'll have a sweet time as my guest, McCall." O'Sullivan glared at him and tried again. "Just before you came to Toltec to rob the Valley Bank you got a letter from this town. Who wrote it?"

"I didn't get any such letter, and I didn't come here to rob the bank."

"What were you doing here?"

"Looking for a job."

"When you were arrested in El Paso twelve thousand dollars was found under the carpet in your room. Where did you get that money?"

McCall shook his head. "I don't have to answer that."

"Two men identified you an hour ago as the driver of the bandit car, picked you out of a dozen men."

"They picked the wrong fellow. Probably you coached them."

"Why did you write the telephone number of the Valley Bank on the wall of your room?"

"I didn't."

"Who was the man that visited you twice at night in your room before the robbery?"

"I don't remember any such man."

"Was it Clem Garside?"

"No."

"Jud Richman?"

"Never heard of him."

"Bucky Cameron — Dan West — a bank clerk named Ferrill?" Between each name O'Sullivan paused for an answer.

"I told you nobody visited me, far as I know."

"When you reached El Paso you were alone. Where did Grogan and Soretti and the other man leave you?"

"Sticking to your story, ain't you?" jeered McCall.

"Did they take a train for Minneapolis?"

"You're barking up the wrong tree. I haven't seen them. I don't know where they are."

O'Sullivan cajoled, stormed, threatened. The prisoner stuck to his tale. He had not robbed the bank. He did not know who had done it. He had been brought back to be framed on account of his record.

The chief sent him back to his cell.

"He's a tough nut and will take a good deal of cracking," the district attorney suggested.

"Yes, but I'll soften him," O'Sullivan said grimly. "We've got him and we'll have his pals in a few days. What I'd like to do is tie them up with their local friends, if any. I'm not worrying. Before it comes to trial, one of those birds will squawk."

The district attorney agreed that it was likely.

CHAPTER XXVI

A car roared up alongside of the one Kathleen was driving and crowded her to the side of the road. It leaped ahead of the coupe and edged the girl toward the ditch. She was pocketed. When the heavier car slackened and stopped, she was forced to do the same.

Two men jumped from the sedan and came toward her.

"What's the matter?" she asked. "What do you want?"

Already a bell of alarm was ringing in her. She did not like the way she had been halted. She did not like the appearance of these men. Both of them were hard-looking customers.

"We want to talk with you, Miss," one of them said. He was a man of medium size, dressed in a suit of loud checks and a derby hat. His eyes were light blue, cold and cruel and shallow.

The other grinned, a thin-lipped, crooked smile which held malice and not mirth. Smaller than his companion, he was more furtive and more deadly. "Don't you worry, lady," he soothed, and the word slid out of the corner of the most vicious mouth the girl had ever seen. "This isn't a holdup and it isn't a snatch — not if you play ball with us."

Kathleen found nothing to allay her alarm in what the little man told her. Even while it was occupied with concern for her own safety, the mind of the young woman noted that he was an Italian, probably born in this country, since he had no trace of accent. Both men were criminals. Of that she was sure.

"Get your car from there and let me go," she ordered, and knew that in spite of her firm voice the fear in her betrayed itself.

"You're the Garside girl, aren't you?" the first man asked sharply.

"Yes."

"All right. We'll give the orders, Miss, not you. We're going to have a talk with you. Savvy? You'll jump through a hoop if we snap our fingers."

"I don't understand. If it isn't a holdup —"

"We're just pals of yours, like we were of your old man," the smaller scoundrel jeered.

She looked at him, and sickened at the sight. A slimy gangster, she guessed, one of the kind that bolstered courage with dope. Never had she seen anyone like him before. Phrases from her reading flashed to mind . . . being put on the spot . . . taken for a ride. But it was inconceivable that anything like this should happen to her.

"I don't know what you mean," she faltered.

"Sure you don't," the larger man said. "Don't be scared of Mike. He wouldn't hurt a baby, not unless he was drove to it. We got to have a nice long talk, but not here on the main road."

"There's nothing I can talk about with you," she cried desperately. "If it's some business you had with my father, he's — dead."

"That's it," the one called Mike nodded. "Business with your father, and, seeing he has been rubbed out, with his daughter."

"You had better see his lawyer, Mr. Gardiner. I haven't had time to find out much about his business. But Mr. Gardiner —"

"We'll tell you all about this particular business you need to know. Gardiner ain't it, or any other lawyer of his kind. It's between you and us. Ain't that so, Pete?"

"Yep," the blue-eyed man answered. "I'll drive back to town with you in your car. Mike will follow in ours. You can sit behind the wheel, but you'll go straight to your house. There we'll fix things up. No tricks, missy, if you know what's good for you. We won't do you a mite of harm if you don't get smart with us."

Kathleen drove back to Toltec and stopped

in the driveway of her own home. She led the way into the living-room. Mike parked his car in the road by the curb, where it would be ready for a quick getaway if necessary. The door of the house had been left ajar, and he followed the others inside.

Pete suggested that before they got down to cases a drink would be in order.

"Sure," agreed Mike. "And don't make any mistake. If you tip off your servant with even a look, we'll put the blast on you. Act like we're friends who have dropped in for a visit."

Fernando answered the bell and was told by his mistress to bring Scotch-and-soda. Each man poured his own drink. Their unwilling hostess did not join them.

After the Filipino boy had gone, Pete explained what they wanted. "We've got a friend in stir here and we've got to spring him. Since all three of us were mixed up in a deal with your father, we figured you would be glad to help us."

The heart of the girl died within her. What did they mean by claiming her father was mixed up in one of their nefarious schemes? She did not believe it. Not for a moment. And yet she knew he had queer acquaintances. For instance, Dan West, who very likely had murdered him.

"If you would speak plainer, please," she

said. "I don't know what you mean by somebody being in a stir-up of some kind or what
springing him is."

"He's in stir — in jail — and we've got
to get him out."

"But how could I get him out, even if I
wanted to do it?"

"Maybe you better give her some of the
lowdown, Pete," the small man said, out of
the twisted corner of his vicious mouth. "Tell
her how her old man comes into this."

"I'll do the talking, Mike," the other answered, and slanted a warning look from his
cold washed-out eyes. "No need going into
details, Miss. The less you know the better
for you. A man named McCall has just been
brought here from El Paso and flung into the
cooler. He was a friend of your father, so naturally you'd want to help him get out."

Kathleen turned on him a startled gaze. "He's
the man arrested for the robbery of the Valley
Bank, isn't he? I saw his name in the paper."

Pete nodded. "Sure. Same guy. And like I
said, seeing he was a pal of your father —"

"He never was," she cried indignantly.

"You'll find out whether he was or not, if
Butch ever comes to trial. Unless you want
all your friends to know you're the daughter
of a man who fixed it to have his own bank
stuck up —"

"It's not true," Kathleen interrupted. "I don't believe a word of it."

"You'll start believing it right this minute, for it's the God's truth. We got no time for monkey business. From right damn now you begin helping us. See?"

Kathleen came to another discovery. "You're two of the other men who were in the robbery."

"No, we're just pals of theirs," Pete denied. "You can forget that. But don't forget for a minute that if you act stubborn, your father's name will be broadcast all over this country as a crook."

"You're lying to me," she flung at him. "My father was a decent man. You can't tell me anything different."

"Stick to your story if you like, Miss," the man said, with a thin, cruel smile. "That's okay with us. But you're going to help us just the same."

"I won't lift a hand for you."

Mike folded his arms on the table and looked across at her with his crooked, evil grin. "You don't quite get us," he said gently. "We're telling you, not asking you." Apparently without relevance, he added a sinister question: "Which chair was it Garside was sitting in when he got his?"

The girl stared at him, her face like chalk.

Her lips framed three whispered words. "You — killed him?"

"Why, no," he sneered, his lip lifted. "Didn't I tell you he was our pal? I just happened to wonder about it."

She had been standing. Now she sat down suddenly, the hinges of her knees weak. Aloud, she said to herself, "God, what shall I do?"

"Don't worry about God," Mike mocked. "We'll tell you what to do."

"We don't aim to get you into any trouble, Miss," Pete said, trying amiable reassurance. "If your father had been alive, he would have fixed this for us, but since he isn't, you've got to do it. First off, do you know any shyster lawyer who wants to earn five hundred dollars easy?"

"One who'll keep his trap shut," the dark little man added.

Kathleen shook her head. "No, I don't."

She felt faint, oppressed by a stifling sensation of having been transported into a world of unreality that existed only in the pages of the newspapers and the moving pictures, one punctuated by the rat-tat-tat of machine guns.

"Think, Miss," urged Pete. "A guy that won't squeal and has plenty of guts."

To Kathleen's mind there jumped the picture of a cool and debonair young man, who had been an enemy all her life and was now a friend. At the next words of the smaller gangster, she pushed the thought from her.

"He'd better not throw us down, unless he wants his gullet slit."

No, not Bucky, she decided. To drag him into new peril would be dreadful. These rats would destroy him without compunction.

"I don't know anybody like that," she said.

"Some fixer who does political dirty work," suggested Pete. "We'll run to a grand if necessary. All he has to do is to take a message to Butch."

"And slip him a little package," his companion contributed. "If he's a wise guy, nobody can hang it on him."

Kathleen could never tell, when she thought it over later, why Mitchell came to her mind. Her father had told her the man was a detective, a government man. She knew, rather vaguely, that he had been working with O'Sullivan and with Bucky. He had been here with the chief the morning after her father had been killed and had been paid considerable deference. It was in his line of work to handle men of this stripe. Probably he was clever enough not to give himself away when he found what they wanted with him.

"There's a man who might do," she said slowly, building up the lie as she went. "I don't know him very well, but they say he is out to make every dollar he can without caring how he does it. He's some sort of a go-between, I've been told. Mitchell is his name."

"You want to be sure of him," Mike said, and the words slid out significantly. "For his sake and for yours too, Miss."

"Couldn't you talk with him, without telling him too much at first, and sort of size him up? I think maybe he is the man you want."

"Maybe isn't good enough," the man called Pete told her bluntly.

"What do you expect?" Kathleen asked, exasperation in her voice. "I haven't spent my life among — among crooks. This man has some influence with the police, my father told me. I suppose he passes money to them from the underworld, but I don't know about that. If he won't do for you, find someone who will. He is not a lawyer, though. I can give you plenty of lawyers' names, but they are all reputable men."

"What does this Mitchell do for a living?" Pete demanded.

"I don't know. He's in a lot of illegal traffic, they say. But for all I know, that's just talk."

"How can we get in touch with him? He sounds like the kind of bird we want."

"I think he lives at the Toltec House, but I'm not sure."

The two men held a whispered consultation.

"All right, Miss," Pete said. "We'll talk with this Mitchell. If you're lying to us, you'll sure be out of luck. Get him on the phone and ask him to come to see you here at once. Say it's important. Nothing but that. Understand? Just make one break, and another Garside will be bumped off."

Already Kathleen was prepared to doubt her judgment. If Mitchell did not understand the situation — and she did not see how he could possibly appreciate it — he might betray himself as soon as he met these ruffians. It was not fair to bring him here. Still . . .

Her hand shook when she picked up the receiver and called the number of the Toltec House, nor was her voice steady when she asked for Mitchell. She was thoroughly frightened. Two evil faces were thrust close to hers when she made contact with the man she wanted.

"No mistakes, Miss," Pete growled hoarsely.

She made her message as brief as she could. Mitchell seemed to hesitate, asked a question or two which she evaded, and promised to give her a few minutes. He intimated that he was very busy.

Kathleen hung up the receiver. "He's coming," she said tremulously. "I do hope it will be all right. If you don't make a bargain with him, I can't help it."

"We'll do the talking," Mike said brusquely. "Mum's the word for you."

Mitchell came in a taxicab. Fernando ushered him into the room.

"I don't know the names of these men, Mr. Mitchell," she said. "I'm afraid they will have to introduce themselves."

Her latest guest looked at the other men and back at his hostess in surprise. She was very pale and nervous.

"Doesn't matter about our names," Pete said bluntly. "This young lady here thinks you might be interested in making a grand, Mr. Mitchell. How about it?"

Mitchell said dryly that he did not know many men who would not like to make a thousand dollars if it could be done easily enough.

"This way is easy, if you've got the savvy and the guts and can keep yore mouth shut," Mike told him.

"I'll listen," Mitchell told them.

He saw that Kathleen was standing rigidly, her big eyes fixed on him. The message in them he understood. She was afraid, and she begged him without words to help her. What she wanted him to do he did not yet know.

Pete talked. A friend of theirs was under arrest in the city jail. Through a go-between they wanted to communicate with him. The messenger would have to be somebody who had influence enough to see the prisoner alone.

"Have you got pull enough for that?" demanded Mike.

"Maybe. I think so, if I have a reasonable excuse."

"Say, what are you, Mister? A stool-pigeon?"

"If I take your money, I'll deliver the goods," Mitchell replied curtly. "Who is the man you want me to see?"

"Wait a minute," Pete answered. "We're coming to that, when we're satisfied you'll be on the level with us. What's yore business?"

"I do little jobs for people — get them out of jams — grease the wheels of the law."

The outlaws asked more questions. More than once a snarling threat crept into the manner of the Italian.

Mitchell looked at him, level-eyed. "Listen," he said. "Hire me or not, just as you please, providing the job suits me. But don't pull any Black Hand stuff on me. I'll say one thing. The man that pays me gets a loyal service from me."

"He's all right," Pete said abruptly to his companion.

Mike nodded sulkily. "Shoot the works," he growled.

"A man called McCall is the one we want you to see. They claim he is connected with the Valley Bank robbery. Would it be possible to get him out on bond?"

"Not a chance," Mitchell said, without hesitation.

Pete leaned forward. "Well, we've got a sort of plan," he murmured, "and we want to wise Butch up so he can —"

"Wait a minute," Mitchell cut in sharply. "The fewer who know this the better. Why discuss it before the young lady?"

"That's right," Pete agreed. He looked at Kathleen doubtfully. The trouble was that they dared not let her out of their sight for fear she'd telephone the police. "She knows too much already. Might as well let her hear the rest."

"No," decided Mitchell. He spoke to the girl. "Miss Garside, you sent for me to help you out of a hole. I'll do that. But you've got to trust me. Leave this in my hands completely. No phoning the police or talking with friends. I can't have any interference. You see why. My life is at stake. I must be sure you don't lose your head and gum the works. If I am to take care of this, let me do it my own way. That's fair, isn't it?"

"Yes," she assented.

"I want your word of honor not to tell a soul in the world about this. Unless you give it to me, I can't move."

She knew he was telling her, without saying it in so many words, that he was on her side.

"I promise," she said. "Word of honor."

"Good. Will you go to the piano, Miss Garside, and play us a good lively piece of music? I want to talk with these men, and I don't want you to hear. This may be a lawless business, and I would rather not have you involved."

Kathleen nodded, gifts in her grateful eyes. She walked to the piano and began to play "Alla en el Rancho Grande." Out of the corner of her eye she saw the three heads close together in whispered consultation. They talked, a long time. It seemed to her that she played hours, shifting from one piece to another.

Once the telephone bell rang.

"If it's for you, say you're busy," the Italian ordered.

Fernando came into the room to say that Miss Betty Filson wanted to talk with her.

"Take the message if you can," Kathleen told him. "If you can't, tell her I'll call later."

The talk and the piano recital were renewed. Kathleen thought of Bucky. This was one danger in which he had not become involved. Had she done right in bringing Mitchell into it? She did not know, but there was a cold self-reliance about him that made her feel he could take care of himself. Her mind must have been on Bucky a good deal, because during a momentary lull at the end of a piece she thought she heard his murmured name. That was imagination, she decided, and she plunged into another popular song.

She became aware that the conference was over, that they had reached an understanding of some sort. The men had risen. One of them passed to Mitchell a small parcel.

"You'll be back soon as you can," he said.

"I'll be back before dark."

"See you do." The thin, broken-toothed grin of the Italian slid across to the girl. The menace in it was unmistakable. She was a hostage.

"They won't hurt you," Mitchell promised Kathleen. "Not if you keep your pledge. It all depends on that."

He was very serious about it. She could see he felt this was vital.

"I'll not talk with anybody about this," she said.

The other men spent most of their time drinking while Mitchell was gone, but though they emptied the bottle of Scotch, neither of them showed any sign of intoxication except in a certain relaxing of wariness. They talked of themselves more freely. Practically they admitted that they were implicated in the robbery of the Valley. They boasted about the courage which had brought them back to manage a jail-break for McCall.

"By morning we'll be out of here and won't bother you any more," one said. "If it works out right."

Kathleen hoped desperately that it would.

CHAPTER XXVII

Bucky walked out of the Toltec House with Tim Murphy and got into his car. The foreman put his foot on the running board.

"There isn't going to be any kickback on this job, is there?" he asked.

"You're in the clear," Bucky answered. "Judge Lewis arranged for the permit. He will be with you. The Mexicans who do the work won't have the slightest idea what it's all about. Sorry I can't be along, but there is just a chance I might be tailed and that wouldn't do."

"A fat lot you're sorry," Murphy snorted. "It's a nice cheerful party you hate to shift on me. I know you, young fellow . . . And if you think there's a chance you are going to be followed, what's the idea in chasing up the hills with a girl? You'd better stay here in the hotel."

"I know you would like to tuck me up in my bed," Bucky replied, with a grin. "But not tonight, old-timer. You see, I'm not going with *a* girl but with *the* girl. Shall I tell her the misogynist sends his love?"

"You go to blazes, boy. I'm still able to do my own talking."

"All right. I'll tell her you will bring it yourself. We ought to be back by midnight. Drop into my room and see me later."

"Okay. You think you'll be ready for the big blowoff tomorrow?"

"Then or never. I'll know by noon whether I'm a dumbbell or a Sherlock Holmes."

Tim still kept his foot on the running-board, regardless of the fact that his friend had started the engine. "I hate to turn you loose alone tonight. You're such a doggoned idiot."

"I won't be alone," Bucky told him blithely. "I'll be with Miss Nancy Graham." His gaze followed a man on the sidewalk who was passing the car, an evil-looking furtive specimen whose eyes had taken a long, narrowed interest in Cameron. "Do you know that rat, Tim?" he inquired, nodding toward the fellow.

Murphy's regard took in the sloping shoulders and the slouching gait. "Didn't see his face. Why?"

"Not important . . . well, good luck."

"I oughtn't to let you go," the foreman said

reluctantly. "I'd ought to stay beside you until you've shot off yore fireworks. Anything might happen to you because you're such a crazy galoot."

"Like getting engaged?" Bucky asked innocently.

"Like getting pumped full of lead. If these fellows guess you've got it on them —"

"How can anyone guess? Outside of you and Judge Lewis, the only person I have given even a hint to is O'Sullivan, and he doesn't know enough about my game to queer it — even if he wanted to, which he doesn't."

"You're smart as a newly painted wagon, Bucky. Maybe you are too smart. It doesn't pay to underestimate the other fellow. He has some brains too, likely."

Bucky admitted it. "Sure. Plenty . . . Be seeing you." He shifted the clutch and started.

Nancy was waiting for him in a trim tan sport suit and a close-fitting little hat set jauntily on one side of her curly corn-colored hair.

"Sweet of you to take a poor working girl to dinner," she said.

"I'm giving myself this party, not you," he explained. "Haven't you discovered yet I'm no altruist?"

She flashed white teeth at him, laughter bubbling in her face. "You do say the nicest things. I suppose you'll drop me somewhere up the cañon if I'm not entertaining."

"Always the little gentleman," he promised.

"I didn't know that was a necessary part of the tired business man's equipment when he is out with complaisant pulchritude."

"So many of my finer qualities you haven't discovered yet," he mentioned reproachfully. "But you'll have a long life to find and appreciate them."

"Shall I?" she asked, and shot a quick look at him.

"Yes. You're healthy, aren't you?"

"I'm healthy enough, but if other people aren't I'll be too busy to spend all my time admiring you . . . Where are we going to dinner? I warn you I'm ravenous."

"Crest Inn. I'll see you get second helpings."

He headed toward the foothills behind which the sun was sinking in a splash of gaudy, brilliant coloring. They climbed steadily, first on a paved road running between irrigated fields and later on one of disintegrated granite which marched up and down over the spurs projecting from the front range. This turned abruptly and plunged into a cañon, crawling along a high ledge protected at the curves by iron chains set in cement posts. Presently the highway dipped down to the stream winding tortuously toward the plains. When the gulch widened they could see banners of sunshine still streaming across the summits of the mountains, but as they got deeper into the hills the last flickers of it vanished from the peaks.

There was a good deal of travel, for the mining camp of Silverplume lay in the second range far up toward the Continental Divide. Moreover, Bear Gulch was one of the favorite drives of Toltec. At the summit there were mountain parks covered with pine, owned and cared for by the city, to which poured hundreds of picnickers. Even on a week day, during the summer and autumn, there were plenty of pleasure-seekers coming and going.

Bucky parked at Crest Inn. They did not go inside at once but walked over to the rock rim from which they could look down into the valley below where pinpricks of light marked ranchhouses. The ground fell away from their feet in a sharp precipice. Half a dozen trails wound down among the rocks, worn by the feet of thousands of young people through the years.

"I wonder how many lovers have exchanged eternal vows on those paths," Bucky said.

"And how many forgot them inside of three months," she said lightly. "Did you bring me here to feed me, or to listen to a poem?"

"There's no romance in your soul," he said

with a stage sigh. "You think only of calories and charts, and you have a hot-water bottle for a heart."

They had their cocktails in a bar called the Santa Fe Room, a cozy den decorated with Navajo rugs, strings of peppers and painted gourds, and two paintings done by Taos artists.

In spite of what Nancy had said of her appetite she was not too hungry to join Bucky on the floor after the fruit cup. The music was good, and they danced together beautifully. Nancy was light on her feet, and the girl's slender body yielded with easy grace to his guidance. He sensed her great pleasure. The warmth in her eyes, the little sigh with which she relaxed to his embrace, were more assurance than words.

"Happy?" he asked.

She nodded.

The feminine perfume of her rose to his nostrils like heady wine. His pulses quickened to the rhythm of their movements, to the slight occasional pressure of her figure against his as they swayed to the music. This golden girl both suited and excited him.

They had a grand time at dinner, each storing up memories of what the other said and did not say. Back of the laughter and the gaiety were unvoiced significances.

It was while the waiter was serving them with broccoli that Bucky caught in her eyes a break in the harmony. She was staring out of the window, her gaze startled and alert.

"What is it?" her friend asked.

"A man's face," she said. "A horrible face."

Instantly Bucky rose and drew the curtain. "Someone you know?" he inquired.

Nancy shook her head. "No. I don't think so. He was looking at you."

Bucky thought: "I've been a damned fool. I shouldn't have brought Nancy or come myself." He said, "Probably some tramp."

"Yes," she agreed, and was not at all convinced.

"We'll dance," he announced.

Nancy rose at once. A pulse of excitement was beating in her throat. She heard Bucky give low-voiced instructions to the waiter.

In leading, Bucky kept away from the doors, near the center of the floor, close to other couples. When the music stopped, he led the way to an alcove, to which their table had been transferred.

"It's a progressive dinner," he explained. "We move from one place to another."

"Fine," she approved, playing up to him. "As long as the food moves with us."

The window curtains had been drawn. From where Bucky sat now he faced all the entrances to the dining-room.

"Is there anything I can do?" Nancy asked as soon as the waiter had gone.

"Not yet. I dare say I'm overcautious. We'll sit tight awhile. I'm trying to make up my mind whether to call up Chief O'Sullivan."

"That's just what I'm going to do," the girl replied, with swift decision, rising to her feet.

"Wait a minute," he suggested. "Let me send someone to scout around the house first. We don't want to be foolish about this. A face at the window isn't enough to go on."

"I saw the face. You didn't. It was . . . awful. I'm going to ask for help, no matter who thinks I'm a 'fraid-cat."

Ignoring his protest, Nancy walked quickly across the room. She stopped to ask the head waiter where she could find a telephone. He directed her down a passage to a small room.

She asked for long distance.

A voice came back to her presently. "Long distance."

"I want the chief of police at Toltec," she said.

A husky voice growled, "Police headquarters."

"This is Nancy Graham. I'm with Bucky Cameron at —"

The transmitter was snatched from her hand and slammed back on the hook. Into the small of her back something hard pressed painfully.

"Yelp, and I'll let you have it," she was warned.

The girl's heart died inside her. She knew that the enemies of Bucky had cut him off from help.

"Wh-what do you want?" she quavered.

The man tucked his arm under hers, an automatic resting close to her ribs. "Go along with me. Act like we're friends stepping outside for some air. Make a break, and hell will break loose."

Nancy walked beside him out of the back door at the end of the passage.

CHAPTER XXVIII

Bucky waited what seemed to him a reasonable time for the return of Nancy, then decided to join her at the telephone. There was no occasion for alarm. Nothing could have happened to her. When he did not find her at the phone, he concluded she had stepped into the ladies' room to freshen up.

The bell in front of him began to buzz. He could never tell later why he decided to pick up the receiver.

A voice asked, "Crest Inn?"

"Yes," Bucky answered.

"Police headquarters, Toltec. Someone just called the chief — gave her name as Nancy Graham — said she was with Bucky Cameron. Before she gave her message she hung up. We traced the call. Nothing wrong up there?"

"This is Bucky Cameron," the owner of the name said. "Miss Graham thinks we have been followed here. She wanted to tell the chief so. I don't know why she didn't finish what she had to say, unless —"

He broke off abruptly, snatched into sudden fear. "She must have been stopped by someone out to get me. Tell the chief to get help to us as soon as he can. Miss Graham was seized while she was phoning."

Bucky turned from the telephone and walked into the corridor. He met a woman coming out of the ladies' room.

"A girl in a tan sports suit isn't in the ladies' room?" he asked.

"No. She went out the back door with a man — about three minutes ago."

Dread flooded through Bucky. His enemies had taken her, to prevent her from telephoning. If she got in their way, if it was necessary to wipe her out because of what she had seen, they would not hesitate to destroy her.

Bucky did not follow them out of the door.

A straight line is not always the shortest distance between two points, especially when guns are waiting to stab at one trying to cover the distance. He dragged a waiter away from the table nearest the corridor and handed him five dollars.

"I want to get out of here without being seen. What is the best way?"

"How about this back door here?"

"No. Some other way."

"There's a servants' entrance. This way, Mister."

The waiter led him through a narrow hall, across a court, and to a narrow gate. "Slip outa here and you'll be okay," he said.

Bucky lifted the latch very gingerly and opened the gate a few inches. It was dark outside, and he could see no sign of life. He listened intently, heard nothing, and slid through the gate.

From its holster under the left armpit he drew a revolver. He was under no delusions. There was going to be trouble, and it was much better to surprise than to be caught unprepared. Within a minute or two his enemies would know he was missing from the hotel. Then, a search for him, and — fireworks. That would be the program, unless he anticipated it.

The situation was complicated by the capture of Nancy. He could not attack nor could he answer gunfire until he knew she was not in the fighting zone.

In front of him there was an immense cottonwood, its foliage vague and shadowy in the darkness. On his tiptoes he moved across to it, half expecting to hear a blast of guns shatter the stillness. None came. Inside the inn music started. Soon he heard the shuffling of feet and saw the figures of dancers gliding past the windows.

His car was parked to the right with a row of others. There were a dozen or more of them, all facing the rim of the great hill scarp which looked down into the valley. All of them but one. Bucky knew he would find one car with its radiator toward the road. The killers would want to get away in a hurry after they had done their job. Very likely Nancy was in the back seat of that automobile under guard of one of the ruffians.

From the shadows of the cottonwood he crept across the open space between him and the cars. A moon was riding a sky of scudding clouds. Inside the dining-room the orchestra was playing "A Little Bit Independent."

Bucky had almost reached the nearest car when a voice snapped an order. "Stop right there, fellow, till I look you over."

Obedience did not seem wise. Bucky kept

going. The call came from the left, so he swung sharply to the right. Behind him a gun crashed. He ducked between two automobiles, ran forward to the rimrock, and collided with a heavy-set fellow traveling fast. Bucky's arm lashed up and down. The barrel of his .38 struck the rim of his opponent's hat and sent him reeling against a radiator.

The mind of the hunted man worked in swift flashes. He could hear the thudding feet of a third man coming up from the right. The gunman who had challenged him had his retreat cut off. In front was the low stone wall built to keep cars from going over the precipice.

Bucky took the wall in his stride, struck the steep slope, and plunged down on his shoulder. He rolled over and over, was stopped by a large outcropping rock.

From above a gun roared. Instantly Bucky got to his feet. He was on one of the trails leading down to the scrub oak below. Recklessly, with no regard for safe footing, he raced along the path. Two weapons were in action now, but fortunately the moon was momentarily under a cloud. A bullet zipped against a boulder. Another cut through the leaves of the bushes below him. He dodged around a corner formed by a huddle of rocks tossed together.

The revolver was still in his hand. He had clung to it as he hurtled down the hill. That he was going to need it he did not doubt. The way of escape was open. He could keep moving down the trail into the jungle of brush and find excellent cover there. If they tried to comb him out of it, all the advantage would be his. But he had to consider Nancy. They might decide pursuit was too dangerous and let him go. That would not do. He could not run away and leave her in the hands of these villains. He must keep them busy until O'Sullivan's men arrived. That the chief would answer his call for help he had no doubt, but the police car would not come roaring up to the inn for nearly half an hour.

They would be down after him presently. It was time to be moving. He fired a shot into the air, to tell them where he was, and before the echo of it had died away he was stepping lightly along the path toward a little field of rocks lower on the cliff. Cautiously they would storm the position he had just left, only to find it deserted. Very likely he would have to waste another shot, though perhaps if he shouted to them it would be enough. He had to keep bullets enough for actual defense.

The moon came out from behind a cloud. He could see, vaguely bulked, the figures of men among the rocks above. A plan of action came to him, worked out even to detail. In front of him lay a loose boulder about the size of his head. He sent it crashing down the hills, as if by accident.

Again the blast of guns sounded. Bucky ran along the path to the point where it worked back to a lower level. Flying clouds obscured the moon once more. Unseen in the darkness, he took the lower arm of the angle elbow. It could not have been more than forty yards from here that another trail ran into the one he had been following. It led upward. As silently as he could Bucky moved along it.

He heard the sound of a breaking twig. Frustrated, he stopped. One of his foes was blocking the trail. Out of the darkness a figure came.

Bucky said: "You're covered. Don't make a sound. Reach for the sky."

The panicky voice of a girl cried, "Oh, Bucky — Bucky."

A great relief lifted him. He caught Nancy by the hand and swept her into his arms.

"How did you get away?" he whispered.

"The man who was watching me left when the firing began. I knew you were down in the rocks on the hill side, so I took the first trail I saw."

"You crazy girl," he said, his voice low and

rough. "You might have been killed."

He felt her trembling. "When I heard all the shooting, I thought — I was afraid —"

The voice of Nancy died away. She clung to him, desperately, her lover who had come back to her out of the valley of the shadow.

Even in that moment when danger still pressed close to them he exulted in her confession. She had come down that perilous path to save him if she could. A woman does that for only one man in the world. He would remember that later. Now he brought himself back to earth.

"How many of them?" he asked.

"I don't know. One of them is —"

A voice, too near for comfort, cut in with rasping irritation. "He must be right around here somewhere."

Bucky said, in Nancy's ear, "We'll drift."

"Yes," she said, and tried to fight down the fear rising to her throat. If they found him they would kill him.

Gun in hand, Bucky followed along the path. They came to an intersection. Another trail cut across the one they trod.

He caught an elbow of the girl. "Down," he ordered.

Without question she turned toward the valley.

Circumstances had changed his plan. With

her beside him, he did not need to get back to the inn. He could hear the snorting of cars above. Frightened at the shots, guests of the hotel were heading for Toltec. There must be a great deal of confusion up there, but even so there might be a man watching for him. It would be better to work down into the valley through the scrub oak. If they could escape unnoticed and reach a ranchhouse their troubles would be over. The worries of his enemies would be just beginning, unless they got out before O'Sullivan's riot squad arrived.

A figure appeared on the leg of the path above them. In the shadow of a bush Bucky dragged Nancy down beside him. It was possible they might be seen. He did not know. His arm was round the girl, his hand over her fast-beating heart. The gunman moved along the trail and came to the intersection. Would he go up or come down? Bucky counted eternity in seconds before the fellow made up his mind and turned his back on them. Noiselessly, her crisp fair hair brushing his cheek, Bucky held Nancy down, the two crouched together on the rubble.

"Now," he murmured at last.

Another man might appear on the path above, but they had to take a chance. He led the way swiftly, and she followed at heel across a long open stretch which brought them to a thick tangle of scrub oaks.

Again the wind had swept the clouds from the face of the moon. Her slim pale beauty touched him. He understood that from the moment she had seen the face at the window she had drawn in fear at every breath and that most of her terror had been for him. She was still shaken and fearfilled.

He said, lightly, "Three loud whispered cheers."

"Are we — do you think —?"

"They'll never find us in the scrub," he promised.

"We'd better keep going," she urged.

Bucky was of that opinion himself. "All right," he said. "There was something else in my mind, but I'll take a raincheck on that."

A quarter of an hour later he pointed to a light. "There the owner of the Bar B L sits reading the *News,* unaware that he is about to entertain angels. We'll take it easy the rest of the way. This isn't an Olympic Marathon."

"Listen," Nancy cried.

From above there came to them the far, faint popping of crackers.

"Enter the riot squad," Bucky cheered. "Our friends the enemy are having plenty trouble with the minions of the law. We'll let them do the worrying now, young fellow."

She laughed, tremulously. "It turned out to

be the most exciting dance I ever attended. Of course it was only your daily quota."

"Some dance," he agreed. "With a swell ending. They lived happily ever afterward. By the way, were you ever engaged before?"

"Sort of," she admitted, before she caught the implication of the last word he had used. "Didn't you say you wanted to telephone Chief O'Sullivan?"

"Yes, but that can wait. I want to tell him how right his guess was once about me and a girl. That sort-of engagement of yours could not have been as thrilling as this one. It wasn't celebrated with so many fireworks, was it?" He took her in his arms, a gay excitement racing through him. "Now don't make it an anticlimax by saying we're not engaged, sweetheart."

In the way that lovers have he convinced her that they were.

From the ranchhouse Bucky talked with O'Sullivan at Toltec.

"It turned out you were a prophet, Chief, when you guessed I was engaged to a certain young lady," he said. "You may congratulate me."

The chief had a good deal to say, and he said it with sputtering, explosive vehemence. He had never known such an infernal nuisance as Cameron. Every time he heard from him it meant trouble. He had worries of his own without taking care of those of crazy idiots who didn't have sense enough to come out of the rain. Specifically, he was sore tonight because that fellow McCall had pulled off a jail-break by holding up a guard.

"He's up here at Crest Inn," Bucky told the officer. "At least I think it was he. I met him only once, the time you introduced us in his cell. It is a little dark tonight, not light enough for accurate shooting, so I don't want to swear it's the same man. If it's any comfort to you, the riot squad have made contact with him and his friends. We heard a lot of shooting a while ago."

"Where are you — at the inn?" snapped O'Sullivan.

"We're at the Bar B L Ranch, as far from the danger zone as we could get . . . Listen, Chief. I've been promising you a break for quite some time. Here it is. You've been hot as pepper to make an arrest, but you didn't feel sure about who you ought to put in your jug. Are you there?"

"Of course I'm here," roared the chief. "Where the hell did you think I was — in Kalamazoo?"

"Then go out and get busy," Bucky said, and gave him names.

CHAPTER XXIX

From the hour the bandits left the house, just before dark, Kathleen did not have an easy moment until morning. She had expected them to return, but they did not appear. Nor did Mitchell. He did not even telephone. Had they murdered him? She thought it very likely.

Anxiously she paced the floor, uncertain what she ought to do. Mitchell had warned her, definitely, again and again, that his life depended upon her silence. She had urgent impulses to call up the chief of police, but that was one of the things she had been especially told not to do.

She was at the door to get the morning paper from the carrier. What she read in the headlines splashed across the page was amazing. Bucky had been brought into it after all. In spite of her effort to keep him out of more trouble, he had walked into the thick of it and spent a half-hour dodging bullets. Nancy Graham had been with him. There was a picture of her in her nurse's uniform, taken at graduation, a gay and smiling portrait of a girl very much alive. Beneath it was a caption mentioning that she was engaged to Bucky.

Kathleen looked at it a long time. She knew in her heart that Nancy was the girl for him. Even if it had been possible to tear down permanently the barrier of the family feud, Kathleen felt that she and Bucky were not temperamentally fitted for each other. It was not enough to feel a wild longing for a man. There had to be back of it all the gay and cheerful understanding that made the life of a man and a woman together desirable. Before she put away the paper she had made up her mind to root out of her being this crazy passion for him. To begin with, she would go to Europe and spend six months in travel.

She called Chief O'Sullivan up and asked for an appointment. There was something important that she wanted to tell him, just as soon as it was possible. She was afraid for Mitchell. The newspaper story said that Mike Soretti had been killed by the police and his two companions captured. The name of Mitchell was not mentioned. What had these villains done with him? Had they killed him in the cañon and flung his body over a cliff? Nothing seemed to her more likely. If so, she was responsible for it. She had invited him to his death and had kept silent instead of going to the police. The desk sergeant told her to be at headquarters in half an hour.

O'Sullivan listened to her story grimly. He slammed a fist down on the table. "What a life!" he exclaimed bitterly. "I'm supposed to be in charge of the police in this city and nobody ever tells me anything. If you had phoned to me, I could have protected Mitchell. It's only by the grace of God that young Cameron and his girl weren't rubbed out. These scoundrels knew he had helped catch McCall and they were out to get him. Now you go home and leave this to me, and if you ever get in such a jam again, try telling the cops what you know, Miss."

"I ought to have told you," she admitted miserably. "But Mr. Mitchell said —"

"It didn't matter what he said," interrupted the chief. "The fact is he was scared stiff, and he figured he would play it the safe way. Well, he didn't." O'Sullivan relented a little at the girl's colorless face. "But don't blame yourself too much. He brought it on himself. You were probably sick with fear and so did what he told you to do."

As Kathleen was leaving Chief O'Sullivan's office she met Bucky coming into the room. The sight of him, so fit and jaunty and debonair, was a shock to her. It brought to mind how closely he had missed death, because of her silence.

She shook hands shakily. "I almost killed you," she said.

Astounded, he stared at her. "What do you mean?"

"Ask Chief O'Sullivan. He will tell you. My bad judgment may have killed another man. I'm not sure yet."

"It doesn't make sense to me, Kathleen," he said.

"Wait till you hear." She stood up like a drum major and said her little piece on another subject. "I want to congratulate you, Bucky. Nancy Graham is one of the very nicest girls I know. You're doing awf'ly well for yourself."

Bucky thanked her and said he thought he was.

"I've just been through a dreadful experience," she went on. "Chief O'Sullivan knows about it. I can't stand any more — not just now. I'm going to Europe for a year to study music."

The heart of the young man went out to her. Never before had he seen in her spirited face the look of the defeated. He knew that the increasing rumors of her father's wrongdoing were distressing her greatly, and he guessed another cause for her despair. Kathleen's unhappiness was temporary. He knew that. She was too vitally resilient to be broken.

None the less he was glad she was going. There would be more talk about her father as the days passed. It was much better she should be far away.

"It's the best thing you can do," he said. "When are you leaving?"

"Tonight. I'll be in New York a week or two." She smiled. "Long enough to buy you a wedding present if the happy event is to be at once."

"We haven't had time to talk of that. But I think it will be soon . . . Happy hunting, Kathleen."

They shook hands and Kathleen went on her way briskly.

CHAPTER XXX

The office of the chief was filling up. Sheriff Haskell was there and the district attorney and the editors of both the papers, as well as Bucky and Tim Murphy and Judge Lewis. Mitchell walked in beside Sergeant Swensen. Two or three other leading citizens were among those present.

O'Sullivan looked at his watch. "Might as well begin," he said. "I want to tell you gentlemen we have this whole business cleared up."

"You mean the bank robberies too?" asked the district attorney.

"Yes, sir. We've solved this thing from start to finish."

"Then you've done wonders," Ashley said.

"I've had help," the chief admitted. "Bucky Cameron has been invaluable, so has Mr. Mitchell. I have learned a lot from both of them as we ran the clues down. I may say that in a way we all worked together to solve the problem, though I didn't get full co-operation from either of the gentlemen."

Bucky grinned and looked across at Mitchell.

"Each of them was playing his own hand," O'Sullivan continued. "He was willing to help me just as far as it suited him. Now, I'm no talker. Bucky is a swell orator. He can make you think black is white, and after he has persuaded you he'll show you what a fool you were for believing him. So I'm going to let you listen to Bucky while he tells this story from his angle. A good deal of what he says will be cockeyed, but that doesn't matter so long as he helped me to the right solution." The chief lit a cigar and waved a hand at Bucky. "Shoot the works, young fellow."

Bucky began by paying the proper compliment to O'Sullivan. "It is nice of the chief to hand out bouquets to me and Mr. Mitchell, but of course we all know he was the man had this job in charge. I butted in to clear my uncle's name. That is why I came back to Toltec. I knew he didn't rob that bank any more than —" he looked around the group and picked one of them — "any more than Judge Lewis did."

Lewis nodded thanks. "Much obliged for exonerating me."

"The chief didn't believe Uncle Cliff looted the First National any more than I did, but I annoyed him a lot by sticking around and getting shot at. He had enough on his hands without having another killing to work out. Some of my theories he scoffed at, but I still think there was a good deal in them.

"From time to time I had various different suspects in my mind. There were our friends from the Red Rock country, always ready to do anything against the Camerons. Tim thought they were guilty, but this did not look to me like their kind of a job, unless someone with brains put them up to it."

His gaze rested for a moment on Richman.

"Having anyone particular in mind?" asked Richman, his professional smile still working.

"Yes, I did have someone in mind," Bucky drawled. "In fact two or three of them. One of them is dead now, and I won't go into that, except to say that I was looking for the man who gained most by the robbing of the bank. He might not be the guilty person, but then again he might."

"I don't get you, Bucky," Haskell said. "The fellow that got the dough must have gained most."

"Must he?" Bucky looked at the politician steadily. "Think that over again, Sheriff."

"Just one of Bucky's cockeyed ideas," O'Sullivan interposed.

"You thought so then, Chief, but you don't now," Bucky rapped back. "One of our first problems was to find out what had become of Uncle Cliff, assuming that he had not robbed his own bank and decamped. That we have just found out. I'll come back to that point later."

"You have found the body of Cliff Cameron?" asked Mitchell, his eyes gleaming with excitement.

"That isn't what I said," Bucky replied, smiling at him. "I said we know what became of him. There's a difference, isn't there?"

"Have you had a letter from him?" the other man insisted.

"Let me tell this my own way, Mitchell," suggested Bucky. "You'll have a chance later to chip in with questions and answers. . . . A few days ago Chief O'Sullivan learned that young Ferrill, a teller of the First National, had been short in his accounts at the time of Buchmann's death. This opened a new field for speculation. Was it possible that Buchmann had discovered the defalcation and that Ferrill killed him in order to keep him quiet, robbing the bank again afterward? The objection to this theory was that Uncle Cliff was missing. What had become of him? Had Ferrill murdered him too? If so, what had he done with the body? The chief grilled Ferrill and became convinced that the teller knew nothing whatever about the murder. He was simply a young man living beyond his means who had yielded to the temptation of taking the bank funds and falsifying his books."

"Why don't you tell us who did it?" Haskell asked, with a touch of irritation. "No use all this beating around the bush if you really know."

"I'll tell you first who didn't do it, Sheriff," Bucky answered. "You didn't, though it has never been explained how you and Richman happened to be around the bank at half-past one in the morning just in time to discover the fire."

Haskell bristled. "If you claim I had anything to do with this bank robbery —"

"I just told you that you didn't. Keep your shirt on, Sheriff. If you are in such a hurry, you can take your hat and go."

"Cut out this quarreling," O'Sullivan ordered curtly. "Go on with your story, Bucky, and don't say things you can't back."

"I suspected a lot of people at one time or another," Bucky continued. "Good citizens like Jud Richman, because he has always fronted for the Red Rock rustlers and because he is the agent for renting the empty house from which someone tried to assassinate me. I even suspected Mitchell, for no reason at all except that he was on the ground so soon after I had been shot at in the hospital and said he had seen at the corner of Wilson and Fifth Streets a man hurrying away from the scene of the shooting."

"You have nothing on me," Mitchell said coolly. "I suspected you, even after I pretended that I didn't. But I don't quite get that about the corner of Wilson and Fifth. What had that to do with it?"

"It seemed odd that you would know the names of those two streets, out in the suburbs, when you were a stranger in town stopping at a hotel in a business section."

Mitchell shrugged his shoulders. "A detective is trained to observe. When I see a suspicious character hurrying away I check up on the location. I would be a fine sleuth if I didn't."

"I suppose so," Bucky admitted. "But it was a little too pat, I thought. If you had taken that shot at me and were afraid you might have been seen making your getaway, it would take the sting out of my suspicion to come to me with a story of having seen near the spot a man who had already tried to kill me."

"All right. Why would I want to shoot at you?"

"Just what I asked myself," Bucky said, smiling at him. "Of course I knew you hated Garside. The first time I saw you together, that was plain to me. You had just come out of the Valley Bank after having had a row with him."

"Another of your brainstorms," Mitchell answered impatiently. "I hadn't a thing against Garside. It isn't reasonable that I would hate a man I had never seen until I came to Toltec."

"You mean the first time you came to Toltec?" Bucky asked suavely.

A curious change came over the face of Mitchell. One can sometimes see the same look in the eyes of a fighter in the ring who has just been shocked into the knowledge that he is going to be defeated.

"I don't know what you mean," he said. "I've never been here before."

"I was sure you and Garside knew each

other some time in the past, and I made up my mind to know where and when." The voice of Bucky was even, almost gentle, but his eyes were hard and cold as jade. "So I made inquiries, sent telegrams. You let me think you a G-man. I found out you weren't."

"I never claimed to be one," Mitchell denied. "You jumped to that conclusion."

"You showed Chief O'Sullivan faked credentials stating you were a G-man. Then you told me you had worked on the Bronson poisoning case. The authorities had never heard of you in connection with it. I found out you had been a motion-picture character actor for some time. About two years ago you dropped out of Hollywood and vanished. Nobody seemed to know what had become of you."

"What's all this about?" snapped Henning, of the *News*. "You don't claim Mr. Mitchell is implicated in these crimes, do you?"

Bucky paid not the slightest attention to him. His gaze did not lift from Mitchell. "Something about you puzzled several people here," he continued steadily. "Both Doctor Raymond and my nurse Miss Graham were reminded of somebody when they saw you, but they could not think who it was. Maybe they had seen you in motion pictures, or maybe they had seen you here in Toltec when you were here before."

"I told you this is the first time I was ever here." Mitchell rose, with a manner of blustering anger. "I'm not going to stay here and listen to this tommyrot."

Sergeant Swensen had risen with him, but it was Chief O'Sullivan who spoke. "Sit down, Mitchell," he ordered curtly. "Let Bucky tell this his own way."

Mitchell hesitated, sat down reluctantly. "I did not come here to be insulted," he said. "What has this got to do with these crimes?"

"Only this." The chief leaned forward, his face as harsh as the Day of Judgment. "I'm arresting you for the robbery of the First National Bank and the murder of Clifford Cameron, and for the later murder of Clement Garside."

Leaping to his feet again, Mitchell dashed for the door. Swensen and Tim Murphy closed with him. He fought desperately, trying to drag a weapon from his pocket. But he had not a chance. Either of the two men could have handled him easily without aid. In a minute they had him disarmed and handcuffed. His fury collapsed. He stood, white and defiant, facing his accusers.

The chief waved to Cameron. "Get on with your story," he said. "And make it snappy."

Bucky nodded. "When Chief O'Sullivan said Mitchell had helped him, he meant that his suspicious actions and his mistakes made it possible to fasten the crimes on him. For instance, he twisted the facts to try to make me believe that my Red Rock enemies had taken my uncle away with them the night of the bank robbery, though he knew Uncle Cliff was dead before the hillmen left town and that they could not possibly have carried his body with them."

"Lies, all lies!" Mitchell spat at him.

"It was quite clear to me and to the chief that Dan West and his friends had not done this job," Cameron said. "Not up their alley. They had not brains for it. The fellow who planned it was someone who wanted to pull off the perfect crime. The gun that killed Uncle Cliff probably had a silencer. So had the one from which a bullet was fired at me while I was in my room at the hospital. The criminal was beginning to feel I had found out too much or at least was on my way to a discovery. He thought it safer to get me out of the way."

"You haven't said a single thing that ties me up with these crimes," the accused man cried angrily. "Nothing but crazy suspicions."

"You'll get plenty of facts," retorted Bucky, his hard eyes boring into those of the prisoner. "The first is that you called yourself Max Buchmann when you were at Toltec before."

Blank astonishment was written on the faces of most of those present. The district attorney was the first to speak.

"But that's impossible. Buchmann was killed."

"No," corrected Cameron sharply. "Uncle Cliff was killed — by Buchmann. His face was disfigured and his body burned, to prevent identification. Since the dead man was in Buchmann's clothes and wore his thick-soled shoe, since he was bald-headed and the bookkeeper's glasses lay broken beside him, the natural assumption was that the murdered man was Buchmann. Last night the body was exhumed. On the head was hair that had grown after the burial. It was identified by an old bullet wound and a tooth filling as that of Clifford Cameron."

"But this man Mitchell doesn't look in the least like Buchmann," objected Ashley. "He is young — not over thirty — and Buchmann was forty-five if he was a day. The bookkeeper was bald, lame, fattish. He was a German with thick-lensed glasses. In his mouth there was a very prominent gold incisor. No, Bucky, that won't do."

"Why won't it?" O'Sullivan demanded. "The fellow came here disguised. He was a character actor, and he knew how to make up. He wore a wig, and everybody knew he was bald as a billiard ball. But I'll bet ten dollars nobody saw him take off that wig the last six months he was here. As for being lame, nothing to that but a thick-soled shoe. The gold tooth was a false sheath. His clothes were padded to make him look fat. So were his cheeks, to an extent that completely altered the contour of his face. Nobody ever saw him without the glasses. The bristly mustache was dyed red, and the clothes he wore were badly made hand-me-downs."

"That's not convincing," the district attorney said.

"I have evidence that is. Cliff had the whole staff of the bank fingerprinted. Mitchell's fingerprints are the same as those of Buchmann."

"You know that?" Ashley asked. "You're not guessing?"

"Yes, I know it," O'Sullivan flung back. "Bucky got Mitchell's prints on a highball glass one day at the ranch and we developed them. What's more, this fellow here left his prints on the table of the Garside living-room the night he killed Clem. He left them on the gun we found outside Crest Inn, where he had gone with the Valley Bank bandits to kill Bucky."

"Was he in the Valley robbery too?" asked the sheriff.

"No. He was tied up with the outlaws yesterday by a queer fluke. They wanted someone to help them spring McCall from jail and they got in touch with him. He made a deal with the bandits to help their friend break out, and they were to join him in rubbing Bucky from the slate. By a smooth trick McCall got out — and I'll say right here that two jailors lose their jobs on account of it. The four of them followed Bucky to Crest Inn. They almost got him, but not quite. My men trapped the gangsters, killed Mike Soretti, and captured the other two. Mitchell escaped. About an hour ago we picked him up trying to leave town. I did not have him arrested, since we did not have a report yet on the identity of the exhumed body, but I had him covered every minute of the time and he knew it. He did not come to this meeting with any joy, but he daren't try to stay away. So he came, hoping we hadn't proof enough against him."

The face of Mitchell had lost its ruddy color, but he faced the chief boldly enough. "You haven't," he sneered. "Say, for the sake of argument, I am Buchmann. That doesn't prove I robbed the bank or killed Cameron. The fingerprints on the table of the Garside living-room prove nothing. I probably made them during the investigation after the murder."

"No, you didn't. I took pains to see none of the furniture was touched. You made them the night before. We are going to prove Clem was killed by a bullet fired from your gun. We have the bullet and the gun, the one you dropped when you were escaping at Crest Inn."

"It's absurd. I had no motive for killing him. Another point. If I was guilty of robbery and murder, why would I come back to Toltec and run the risk of getting caught?"

O'Sullivan leaned forward, on his hard face the look of a hunter ready for the kill. "You came back to get your share of the loot from the robbery. The fellow who put you up to the job double-crossed you. He was in a financial jam, and he spent your share of the stolen money as well as his own. The two of you quarreled about it after your return. He wouldn't or couldn't disgorge. Then he robbed another bank, and you caught him with the goods. My guess is he tried to get rid of you and that you beat him to the draw. That's how and why you killed your pal — Clem Garside."

A stir passed through the room, as plain to be seen as a summer wind rippling over a field of wheat.

"Careful, Chief," advised Lewis. "Mustn't malign a dead man unless you are sure."

"There's no doubt at all that Clem was a bad egg," O'Sullivan retorted brusquely. "He arranged for the robbery of his own bank because he was in a hole financially. The bandits did not get one fourth as much as he claimed from the insurance company. One of the two men we caught last night has confessed. I can't prove Garside was in the First National robbery, but there's plenty of inferential evidence that he was. He cleaned up an urgent debt of forty thousand dollars two days later. The only plausible ground for a quarrel between him and Mitchell is that he had double-crossed this guy. He hated Cameron and wanted to put him out of business. Buchmann, or Mitchell, whatever his name is, no doubt did the actual killing, but Clem was a silent partner. It was his idea for Buchmann to light out, leaving the dough with him for a later divvy. When the showdown came, he threw down his partner and wouldn't pay."

Apparently O'Sullivan had finished his story.

"It doesn't matter about Clem, since he is dead," the district attorney said. "What is important is that we have Mitchell and the gangsters."

"You didn't mention, Chief, that we found a silencer in Mitchell's room at the hotel," Swensen added.

"That's right," O'Sullivan agreed. "Well, that's my case, gentlemen. Unless I'm away off, it's good enough to send Buchmann to the gallows and these gangsters to prison for a long term."

Ashley agreed with him. "You've done a fine job, Chief, with Bucky's help. Toltec isn't likely to forget it for a long time."

The district attorney gave the signal for the breakup of the meeting by rising and shaking hands warmly with the head of the police force. Most of the others present joined in congratulating O'Sullivan as they filed from the room.

Mitchell stopped in front of Bucky while Swensen was leading him out. His face was dark with fury.

"I knew all the time I ought to kill you," he spat out of a mouth distorted to a savage, malignant rage.

"Don't blame yourself," Bucky told him coldly. "You did your best. Not your fault it wasn't good enough."

"I hope to God the Red Rock rustlers get you," the prisoner cried, and added a fervent curse.

"They won't," Cameron answered. "Friend West and his gang are done. Either they leave the country or go to the penitentiary."

Swensen urged Mitchell forward out of the

room. Bucky lingered, for a word alone with the chief.

"What about that hundred-dollar bet?" he asked, tilting a smile at the officer. "Do I win it? Or don't I?"

"You win it," O'Sullivan answered, grinning at him. "And I'm mighty glad to pay it. You're a high-heeled, impudent son-of-a-gun, Bucky. I've cussed you plenty. I thought you a confounded nuisance. But there's something about you I liked all the time."

He sat down and wrote a check while Bucky waited, one leg flung over the edge of the desk.

The chief flipped it to him. "You can buy a wedding present with it for the young lady who went through hell and high water with you," he said sardonically.

"I'm on my way to meet her now," Bucky responded. "I'll tell her it comes with your compliments."

From a window O'Sullivan watched him moving jauntily down the street, a carefree young man finished with one high adventure and ready to begin another.

"The lucky scamp," he murmured enviously.

THORNDIKE PRESS hopes you have enjoyed this Large Print book. All our Large Print titles are designed for easy reading, and all our books are made to last. Other Thorndike Large Print books are available at your library, through selected bookstores, or directly from the publisher. For more information about current and upcoming titles, please call or mail your name and address to:

THORNDIKE PRESS
PO Box 159
Thorndike, Maine 04986
800/223-6121
207/948-2962